A Stolen
COMPROMISE

A Stolen COMPROMISE

Bari Marla

ARCHWAY
PUBLISHING

Copyright © 2019 Bari Marla.

All rights reserved. No part of this book may be used or reproduced by any means, graphic, electronic, or mechanical, including photocopying, recording, taping or by any information storage retrieval system without the written permission of the author except in the case of brief quotations embodied in critical articles and reviews.

Archway Publishing books may be ordered through booksellers or by contacting:

Archway Publishing
1663 Liberty Drive
Bloomington, IN 47403
www.archwaypublishing.com
1 (888) 242-5904

Because of the dynamic nature of the Internet, any web addresses or links contained in this book may have changed since publication and may no longer be valid. The views expressed in this work are solely those of the author and do not necessarily reflect the views of the publisher, and the publisher hereby disclaims any responsibility for them.

Any people depicted in stock imagery provided by Getty Images are models, and such images are being used for illustrative purposes only. Certain stock imagery © Getty Images.

This is a work of fiction. All of the characters, names, incidents, organizations, and dialogue in this novel are either the products of the author's imagination or are used fictitiously.

ISBN: 978-1-4808-7530-2 (sc)
ISBN: 978-1-4808-7531-9 (hc)
ISBN: 978-1-4808-7529-6 (e)

Library of Congress Control Number: 2019902830

Print information available on the last page.

Archway Publishing rev. date: 03/28/2019

In loving memory of my mother and father, and
to my family for their endless support.

"Man is the only animal that laughs and weeps; for he is the only animal that is struck with the difference between what things are, and what they ought to be."

- William Hazlitt

One

"Rachel, what time is it?"

Rubbing the sleep from her eyes, Dora Landau rolled over and turned to face her daughter. The cancer had numbed her senses; she no longer knew the difference between night and day.

"It's a little after four o'clock, Mom."

"Four in the morning?"

"Yes, Mom, four o'clock in the morning. Try to get some sleep."

"There is plenty of time for that. Not so many moments to look at you."

"Stop talking this way. You're a true fighter and you're not going anywhere."

"Honesty is what you need to have, my precious girl. It's hard to believe that my youngest baby is all grown up. Always remember that you have given me great pleasure — you're a highly respected attorney in the state of New York. You are in a profession that helps people and promotes justice."

Rachel looked intensely at her mother's frail body, now riddled with cancer. Thinking of stories her mother had told about those terrible days she had endured at Auschwitz and reflecting back to her childhood, the middle-aged attorney longed for the mother she remembered — a woman who had a tenacious zest for life; not the skeleton of the weak human being lying before her.

"Mom, Michael will be back in Scarsdale in a few hours. I spoke with him last night. He and the children are taking the redeye from London. David will pick them up at the airport and everyone will be with you."

David was Rachel's only child, and she adored him.

"Your brother never stops working. The building he is constructing over there made the papers. 'Famous American Architect Takes UK by Storm,'" she said with pride, pointing to the front page.

With the name *Michael Landau* inscribed on any edifice, a company was placed on a pedestal among the most powerful organizations across the globe.

Michael was divorced from Kayla Miley, a former *Vogue* model who turned out to be a gold-digging opportunist. She was a neglectful, selfish mother and unfaithful wife. Michael was swept away by her long blonde hair and model-like shape and charm, until he learned about infidelities she committed. She had always pretended to be a caring and devoted parent, but she had other intentions. Although at first blinded by love, he now knew deep down in his heart that Kayla was not as she appeared. Michael came to the tragic, but necessary decision that the marriage was over.

As exemplified during his marriage, he was a caring and loving father who always displayed patience and warmth. Scott was seven and Lisa was only three when single parenthood became his way of life. When the divorce was finalized, they moved to London and his architectural work became renowned across the pond.

"I remember when we were kids; he told me that one day fame and fortune would find him," Rachel said.

Michael certainly kept his word, and she enjoyed boasting about how her brother had outdone himself in England. His down-to-earth nature and nurturing demeanor made people feel safe, making him wildly successful.

"I wish all my children could be with me now," Dora said.

"We will be, Mom. I just told you that David went to the airport to pick up Michael, Scott, and Lisa. Everyone is going to be here soon."

"Not everyone, Rachel. There is another. I know there is."

Rachel placed her hand gently on her mother's shoulder and remained silent.

Rachel stepped away from her mother's side and glanced out the window just in time to see the car pull into the driveway.

"Mom, they're here!"

Dora's eyes opened wide. She smiled warmly, adjusting her position to sit up in bed and greet her children. Rachel hadn't seen her mother look hopeful and happy in a long time.

Michael, a striking, athletic man who towered at six feet and one inch tall, entered his mother's room and was shocked to see the vivacious woman he once knew lying listless in bed. As a young girl, Dora, who was now 79, had loved riding horses, but never boasted about her talents, despite earning many trophies for her equestrienne pursuits and contests — she was a humble and gracious woman who, although raised as a debutante from her early years, was unpretentious and down-to-earth.

Witnessing what this person of stature and poise had been reduced to, tears fell from his amber-brown eyes. He tried to keep his composure, but she could read him nonetheless.

"Is it that bad?"

"That bad what? You're still the prettiest girl I know," Michael said.

"Remember when you were little and wanted to marry me? You asked your father if he minded looking for a new wife."

The two laughed. Dora smiled, gripping Michael's hand.

"What's this? No hug for your mother? I promise I won't break."

Michael leaned over and clung to her.

"I love you, Mom."

She clutched her hands around his pale face.

"I love you too, my handsome son."

After helping the kids with their bags, Rachel ran to her brother. She hugged and kissed him warmly.

"Hey, sis. What's up?"

"I'm really glad to see you."

Michael smiled and grabbed his sister's hand.

"Where are my gorgeous grandchildren?" Dora said, glancing around the room.

Lisa and Scott appeared at her bedside. Scott looked at his father then smiled, leaned over, and hugged her.

"Hey, Grams. Any of Lila's famous chocolate chip cookies?"

"As a matter of fact, she made some yesterday and promised me you wouldn't be disappointed," Dora said, smirking at her grandson.

"Hi, Grandma. I missed you," Lisa said, grabbing Dora's hand.

"Not as much as I missed you, my little sunshine," Dora said. "Children, go to the kitchen. Lila has prepared a feast. All she's been saying is, 'Michael likes this. Scott and Lisa like that.' So don't disappoint her. Say that you're starving and can't wait to have all the yummy treats. Rachel, go with them. You haven't eaten anything today. You're going to look like Twiggy soon."

"Thanks, Mom."

"I'm serious. *Gay essen*, my *kinda*. When you're done, Michael, I want you to tell me all the latest gossip on the royal family," Dora said, using the Yiddish phrase to instruct her children to eat.

"Ah, so you want the scoop? I'll be happy to fill you in. And don't you worry. Shelly will eat."

He always called Rachel by her nickname, "Shelly." *Rachel* had been too hard to pronounce when he was three years old. He thought it sounded like *Royshel*. His parents tried correcting him, but in his frustration, he told them, "She's my Shelly."

"Is that my Lila?" Michael said, his booming voice filling up the kitchen as he entered.

Lila was a stocky, five-foot-one, African-American woman with a heart of gold. She cooked incredible meals and made silver shine brighter than the sun. She'd left Alabama at the age of eighteen and had been married to Clive Jessep, an abusive alcoholic whom she ran away from.

It had been over forty years since Dora opened the door to their Upper East Side brownstone to pick up the milk delivery outside. She looked down toward the lower apartment area and saw a woman huddled in a corner, trying to keep warm. The sight reminded Dora of her own past and how she had struggled to survive. The Landaus welcomed Lila into their home and made her part of their family. She loved the children as though they had been her own.

"Mikey, is that you? Come here and give Lila some sugar."

The two embraced.

"Lord, don't they feed you in that foreign place?" Lila said. "I could break you in half with one hand."

"Now, Lila, my weight is perfect."

"No, you are too skinny. As a boy, you were much more round."

"Round? I was fat from your incredible cooking. No one makes a meal like you in the UK, and I miss your food every day. How are you, sweet lady?"

"Well, child, I have my good days and my bad ones," Lila said. "It's hard seeing your mama suffering this way. Miss Dora acts brave when she thinks no one is looking, but I see the pain in her eyes. It isn't fair."

Lila sighed and reached up to take out a plate from the cabinet.

"Now you sit down and let me put some meat back on those bones of yours."

Michael smiled at her, eagerly awaiting her famous chicken and dumplings. He looked toward his sister.

"How are you holding up, Shell?"

"The nights are endless. Mom has trouble sleeping, and then when she doses off I get scared that I won't see her beautiful blue eyes open again."

Dora had deep blue eyes that sparkled with a zest for life. She was a striking woman before the cancer prevailed. Her frame was tall and slender, with hair of auburn and a pale complexion, which she passed on to her children. When Dora Landau walked into a room, heads turned. Her blue eyes could hypnotize and charm anyone. Neither Michael nor Rachel had inherited their mother's eye color; they resembled their father, Nathan, who had amber-brown eyes.

Nathan Landau's family was in the fur business in Berlin prior to Hitler's rise to power. He married then- 22-year-old Dora Stern after they had completed their studies at the University of Berlin. She came from a family of diamond merchants who were native to Germany. Both were raised in a society with affluent means; they were well-cultured and educated individuals. They were given all the advantages money could offer; her equestrienne pursuits and his appreciation of Baroque art were enabled by their wealth. The two had dated for six years and were wed in 1939. Together they were happy.

Nathan lived until 1991, then passed away at 74, five years before Dora fell ill. Her once gleaming and entrancing eyes had faded, and would continue to grow dimmer. Their love endured unusual sorrow and hardship spanning from their youth in Germany through the Holocaust. It haunted them throughout their lives.

In December of 1941, life for Jews in Berlin became surreal and demoralizing. They were forced to wear armbands with yellow stars to signify their Jewish heritage. They were mocked, humiliated and made to be a spectacle as if they were animals. Living under a madman created devastating times, it was clear that leaving Germany was the only viable option.

Fortunately, having the financial means would make it easier to escape Hitler's tyranny. Dora, then 24, was eight months pregnant. The practical choice would be to send Nathan, his father, Arthur, and Dora's brother, Aaron, to New York City to put down roots for the families. Dora's parents, Morris and Rose, stayed behind with her in Germany. They planned to follow once the baby was born. Nathan was reluctant to leave, but she insisted it was imperative to establish a new home for the baby, who would be his mother's namesake. Bertha Landau passed away shortly before Dora and Nathan had wed. The child would become a beacon of hope for the future.

The following month she gave birth in Berlin at the Hospital of the Jewish Community, *Krankenhaus der Judishen Gemeinder,* on Heinz-Galinski Straße. Dora had been in labor for almost two days and was mentally and physically exhausted. Trying to avoid any complications and additional stress, the doctor decided to perform a cesarean section. An anesthetic had been administered to numb the excruciating pain, placing her in a semi-conscious state. Finally, the infant was taken from her womb.

According to the doctor he was stillborn, but until this day, she swore she heard the infant cry and the doctor saying, "It's a boy."

"My Benjamin," Dora said, smiling.

When she professed that her son was alive and heard him clearly, Dr. Edmund Fried responded that it was simply a hallucination based on her arduous ordeal. In reality, enduring 36 hours of labor could affect any woman. She was haunted by her disbelief, which embedded itself within her. There was no doubt in her mind that she had heard her baby's cry.

During the following weeks, the recovery process had been emotionally and physically brutal. The vivacious young woman had lost her enthusiasm and fell into a deep depression. The family tried to snap Dora out of her downward spiral of hopelessness, but their efforts fell short. Weeks went by, and though her mind and will to live were fading, she was well enough to leave Germany.

Dora was living in the Brandenburg home where she grew up. Her father went into the city to finalize their travel arrangements while the women were rigorously preparing for the journey to join their families. Suddenly, they heard a rapid loud pounding at the door and voices screaming *"Mach schnell, mach schnell!"* The Nazis used the German phrase for "make it quick."

They trembled. Finally, Rose opened the entryway and tried to present a calm demeanor. Three Nazis entered, roughly pushing past her.

"Jew, what took you so long to open the fuckin' door?" the Commandant said, glaring at her.

Mrs. Stern, mortified by the words, was still trying to keep her composure.

"Forgive me, gentlemen, I was upstairs in the attic and didn't hear the knocking at the door."

"Then you must be a deaf old cunt."

She remained still and pretended to appear unaffected by the vulgarity.

"How can I help you?"

He pushed a paper in front of her face.

"Gestapo headquarters has taken occupancy of this house," the Commandant said, staring contemptibly at the woman. "Pack and do it fast; you have twenty minutes. And when you're done, go outside and wait. You've all been assigned to a relocation work camp."

He glanced at the other two men with a great big satisfying smile.

"*Geh zur arbeit* — a new phrase for these rich Jew whores," the Commandant said, using the German phrase for "go to work" to command them.

The women looked at one another after the officers left.

"Where is Papa?" Dora asked. Her voice was filled with fright.

"He should have been back by now."

"This is my fault; if you both left with the others, everyone would be safe," she said, weeping. "Forgive me, Mama."

"My place is and was with you. No tears; God will protect us," Mrs. Stern said, placing her hands on Dora's face.

They collected their belongings and did as they were told. Outside, they hoped to find Morris in the crowd. The streets were covered with the most affluent Jews in the area, standing about in a hysterical panic to see where they would be taken.

On the sidewalk, the Commandant blew a whistle and motioned his hands in a forward gesture.

"*Mach schnell*, you worthless swine!" he said.

"Where are you taking us?" an older woman cried out.

He pulled out a pistol, pointed it at her head, and the blood-curdling sound of the shot was deafening. The Nazi leader placed the revolver back in his holster, looked at the crowd and smiled.

"Any other questions, vermin?"

Silence fell upon the hordes of people as they marched at a rapid pace toward the railroad station. At the location, Rose saw Isaac Baum, a neighbor, standing with his family. He was heading into the city around the same time Morris had earlier that day. She ran toward him.

"Have you seen Morris?" she said.

He remained silent.

"Please, if you know something, I beg you to tell me," she said.

Isaac looked into her desperate eyes.

"We were waiting for the train this morning and an SS soldier was there. He had a cigarette in his mouth and I heard him say to Morris, 'Jew, do you have a light?' His reply was 'No officer, I'm sorry, I don't.' The bastard pulled out a gun and shot him."

Rose began to shake. Dora held her as their irrepressible tears fell.

The commanding officer began to speak into a bullhorn.

"Form ten lines quickly," he said, his voice echoing among the crowd.

They were thrust like cattle into the freight cars. The smell of mildew permeated the cars, and the lack of space created little room for movement and breathing. Many of the elderly were unable to endure the wretched conditions, and their deaths simply resembled a deep sleep. The survivors of the trip rode for several hours, numb and silent, unsure of whether or not they would meet an even more treacherous demise on the other side.

When arriving at their final destination, violinists played Wagner as they walked into the camp. A sign across the top of the entrance at Auschwitz read **Arbeit Macht Frei** — *Work makes one free.*

The music and words that were meant to calm and soothe made it difficult to imagine what torture and terror would unknowingly lie ahead.

People were divided; male and female prisoners existed separately.

Each sector was placed into groups — younger and older. After they were forced to get undressed, everyone would need a shower to be deloused and their hair was shaved off. Elderly people were taken to a different location for cleansing.

"The concept behind the division is because older individuals are frail and need to be cared for in a delicate manner," Frau Ada Müller, a guard, said. "We want to make your stay here enjoyable and comfortable."

"I'll see you soon, *shayna velt*," Dora's mother said, calling her by the Yiddish term of endearment meaning "my pretty world."

She grabbed her hand. In this moment, neither of them knew it would be the last time they would ever touch.

Senior citizens were justifiably extinguishable, fragile, and had no value to the Reich. If they were unable to work for the Nazis, then why let them live? Throughout the years, Dora spoke about what happened and compared it to a horror movie.

She would say, "How in a civilized world could such things happen? It was incomprehensible; why did those who knew of the massive slaughter turn a blind eye and allow it?"

These accounts prompted Rachel to become an attorney. She graduated Barnard Law School with top honors and exhibited passion and integrity to strive for justice in society. The pragmatic unperturbed manner she displayed in a courtroom cross-examination rattled opposing counsel and their clients. Rachel inherited the gift of Dora's magnificent hair and her petite frame from Nathan's family. This five-foot, three inch and 107-pound attractive auburn-haired woman was a natural and loved being part of the legal system.

"It's just like acting — one must learn the script," Rachel would say to colleagues when they praised her skills and expertise. Though outwardly modest, Rachel knew she could hold her own, even among the best of them.

After Lila's feast, David, Lisa, and Scott went to Blockbuster to rent some movies while the two siblings returned to their mother's bedside. She mumbled in German, sounding distressed while she slept, and Michael tried to bring her around.

"Mom, wake up! It's all right; it's just a bad dream. Everything is OK — you're safe, I won't let anyone hurt my best girl," he said, smiling. He placed his hand on her cheek as she wept.

"This burden has been on my shoulders every day. I remember it as if it were yesterday; he was born on January 25, 1942. It was a cold snowy night in Berlin and the hospital was crowded," Dora said. "There had been an accident on the *autobahn* and several cars spun out of control. I was in labor for nearly 36 hours. The doctor said Benjamin was stillborn, but I know it's not true," Dora said. "When I close my eyes, I can still hear him crying loudly."

"Mom, please calm down — getting upset isn't helping your condition, so try and relax," Rachel said, standing near Dora's bed.

Dora winced with each syllable she spoke.

"Stop talking to me as if I'm a child. I'm a grown woman and I know what I know."

Rachel was touched by her pain and couldn't think of a way to comfort her suffering. She began to cry. Dora became aware of her daughter's distraught state and made an effort to calm down. She looked at Rachel and patted the bed.

"Come, sit here. Please stop crying. Forgive me — this new medication isn't helping and I'm just not myself."

She sat beside her mother.

"Remember when I was little and we played the wish game?" Rachel said, her voice quivering.

Dora nodded.

"My one wish would be to see you ride Winston again. You had the poise and grace of a champion; I could sit all day and watch," Rachel said. The memory seemed to ease both of them. "Mom, if I could give that back to you, I would."

Dora smiled and held her daughter's hand.

"Rachel, you look tired. Go get some sleep. Michael will entertain me. I can't wait to hear the new scandals of the Royals," Dora said. "Please make me happy and take a rest."

Rachel did not argue. The two women hugged, and she walked toward Michael and grabbed his hand.

"If you need me—" Rachel said, but Michael stopped her before she could finish.

"We'll be fine. Mom's right — I think a little R & R is well deserved and would do you good," Michael said.

"—if you need me, I'm just a door away," Rachel continued.

He sat beside his mother.

"Promise me that you will look after your sister; she is going to need you once I'm gone. A mother feels and sees a child's pain and will do anything to take it away. Her brave front is transparent to me," Dora said. "All she's endured with the loss of Alon so long ago, and now my illness … be strong for her and the children."

"Mom—" Michael began to say, but Dora placed her finger gently upon his lips.

"Sha. Please just promise me."

"I promise." Dora smiled.

An hour later, Michael could tell that his mother had grown weary.

"Young lady, I hope that will hold you at least until the morning. It's getting late and I think you should take the advice you gave to your daughter," Michael said, after concluding the discussion on the famous Brits.

"OK, you win," Dora said, gazing at him with pride. "You have given me immense happiness. She grabbed his arms and pulled him closer to her.

"You are a wonderful mother," Michael said. He began to cry.

Two

The sun shining through the window woke Michael, who had been sleeping in the chaise next to his mother's bed. He got up and walked toward the bed, reaching for her hand. It was stone cold.

"Mom," he said, shaking her delicately. "Mom, wake up, Mom."

Dora remained still.

"Oh God, oh God, Rachel! Hurry!"

Within moments, Rachel entered the room.

"What, what is it?" she said frantically.

Michael was inconsolable and could barely speak.

"Mom's gone, Shelly. I woke up, came to her, and she was gone."

The children and Lila, after overhearing from the other rooms, came running in and looked at the bed. There they saw lying the motionless body of an amazing human being who was once full of energy. Michael and Rachel clung to each other, wanting to wake from this nightmare.

"We need to make arrangements and notify everyone," Michael said, trying to keep his composure. He remembered the promise he made to his mother — to look after his sister and the kids.

Rachel walked over to Dora's bed and held her.

"You're at peace, Mom. No more pain. Dad will take care of you, and Benjamin will finally be with you, too," Rachel said. "You'll be able to hold and care for him like you always wanted to do, and the hurt and longing will be over."

She paused.

"Thank you for being my mother and making me who I am."

"Sis, it's going to be all right."

With those words, Rachel pulled herself together, got up, and walked toward the window. She had been accustomed to sorrow from a young age. In life, she usually demonstrated a tough exterior, but now, the ache was too unbearable to endure.

Dora passed away late in June 1996. David went to his mother and she clung to him tightly.

"It's a beautiful day, which is a tribute to her. God has made sure to welcome his extraordinary child with open, loving arms. Your uncle is right — we need to notify the funeral home, friends, and family. I want to make sure her journey to paradise is perfect," Rachel said. "Lila, please cover every mirror in the house."

When an individual of the Jewish faith dies, all the mirrors in a home are required to be concealed. It was a time of mourning — not a time to exhibit one's vanity. The loyal housekeeper and extended member of the family cried as she looked upon both siblings.

"I really loved your mother. The Lord is lucky to have this fine woman in his arms," Lila said.

Michael contacted the Jewish Memorial Chapel in Yonkers to notify them of her passing. When Dora's condition worsened, she insisted that all preparations be made. Rachel, who protested at the time, was now relieved that she heeded her mother's request. Dora knew that the grieving process would be easier when the family already had the awkward details squared away, which were an unpleasant reality.

Her funeral took place early in the morning the following day. The clouds passing through the clear blue sky created a soothing atmosphere, and the warm sun on their skin provided a sense of comfort. The Landau family sat *shiva*, the Jewish tradition of being in mourning, at their family home in Scarsdale. Platters of smoked fish arrived from Murray's Sturgeon Shop in Manhattan; Dora had loved their smoked delicacies. When they lived in New York City, it was her favorite place from which to cater parties. Serving her favorite foods to their significant relatives, friends, and neighbors would have been exactly what she wanted.

After the seven days of grieving concluded, as per the rules of *shiva*, the Landau clan was left to themselves. The reality of her death set in with each one of them individually and left an indescribable emptiness. It was time for the family to stop dwelling on life's sorrows and forge ahead — the way their mother would have wanted them to.

Rachel asked her brother when he was planning to return to London. Michael was in no hurry to leave and enjoy being at his childhood home.

"Sis, don't you think it would be nice for us all to have this time together?"

"Of course — I love having everyone here. This is great for now, but soon you and the kids will need to return to your lives back in England."

"Shelly, Lisa, and Scott are on summer holiday."

Rachel laughed.

"'Summer holiday' — you sound so British."

"Rachel, cut it out!"

"Cut what out?" The smile left her face.

"Stop acting like everything is OK. I'm your brother, and you can level with me," Michael said.

"I'm fine. Really, I am," Rachel said, crossing her arms.

"No, you aren't."

"Let it go; what do you want me to say? That my rock — my solid ground — has been pulled out from under me? I don't want to think; thoughts can be cruel."

"Shelly, they can also be comforting."

"Don't placate me. Most of my memories are painful reminders of what will never be again."

"I'm sorry; it isn't my intention to upset you," Michael said. He walked away.

Michael and the children remained in New York until the middle of August. Despite the circumstances that brought him home, he hadn't realized how much he missed the states. But inevitably, the time came to return to England and attempt a restoration of normality in their everyday lives. Rachel drove them to the airport. She realized how comforting it had been while her immediate family surrounded her, and the thought of their departure filled her with sadness.

"Shell, if you need anything at all, you call me. Better yet, why don't you plan a trip with David during his winter break?"

"We'll see. It's his senior year, and you know how these kids are always making plans with friends. I love you, Michael, and I'll do everything possible to come see you," she said. "It's hard for me to believe he'll be graduating from Princeton in the spring."

"If David can't make the visit, how about coming on your own? We'd love to have you."

"Thanks, I really appreciate the offer, but let's see how busy my work load is over the next few months."

"You're heading back to the mean world of law?"

"Yes, it's time. When Mom got sick I took a leave and I'm ready to join the legal game again. It will be good for me."

"I agree with you. We need to brave the big mean world together. Take down the bad guys, little sister."

"Keep constructing those tall buildings, big brother."

They smiled at one another then embraced and kissed before he left the car.

"Kids, take good care of your dad!"

"We will."

"Goodbye, Aunt Rachel," they said, returning their sentiments with hugs.

"David, look after your mom."

"I will, Uncle Mike."

The two men shook hands and hugged one another. Scott and Lisa turned and embraced their cousin.

Rachel watched from her car as they entered the airport, and then drove away.

Three

Rachel's law office was located on Park Avenue and East 55th Street. Her family kept the East 68th Street brownstone they bought in the early 1950s. She stayed there and returned to Scarsdale on the weekends. Lila still resided in the main house on the estate. Dora and Nathan offered her residence in the guest cottage; they wanted this wonderful woman to have a place of her own. She made the choice to stay among the people who became her family. Lila anxiously waited for Saturday and Sunday, when she would welcome Rachel's company.

Since Dora's passing, the home had become quiet. When she became ill, Rachel returned to her childhood residence to look after her mother. Being back in Manhattan was a positive experience. She loved everything the city had to offer, from the theater, to concerts, to the most amazing restaurants in the world.

Now, her entire being was consumed with work, leaving little time to dwell on the hollow space she had in her life. During quiet moments Rachel would reflect, and Dora's days at Auschwitz often came to mind. Through the years, her father, Nathan, was haunted with the guilt and memory of his wife being imprisoned in a concentration camp while he was in America. He was always saying he never should have left her. The anguish, fear and terror he felt during those years without her, not knowing if she was alive, crippled him mentally. Once the war ended, his search began. He was unrelenting — leaving no stone unturned and using every resource available. Nathan had been fortunate, as the fur and diamond business established by the Landau and Stern families flourished in New York, even during the war. Money was no concern, which made his search for Dora easier.

By the grace of God she was found; he flew to Palestine to bring her to America, after an arduous search with the help of The Jewish Brigade Group, which was dedicated to organizing the exodus of Jewish refugees from Europe to Palestine.

He was shocked by the emaciated frame of a woman who stood before him. All that came to mind was his wife, who, in earlier years, stood tall and proud. Nathan raced to Dora in the refugee camp in an uncontrollable state of emotion and squeezed her close to him, never wanting to let go.

"God has given you back to me, my *eiches chayil*, and for this I will be grateful the rest of my days," Nathan said, expressing his love with the term for 'woman of valor.' "All the cruelty and pain you suffered should be washed from your mind and soul. The time has come for you to be happy again. I promise to make it so."

Dora was catatonic as Nathan held her in his arms. She was overwhelmed and in shock after her surreal experience at the camp. He understood the silence, and his calming words seemed to soothe and ease her aching. His support gave her a sense of safety and security, reminiscent of how things were before the war.

They returned to the states, and it took time for Dora, who had survived a gruesome ordeal, to regain her strength. She was malnourished for so long, having only been given small bits of food every day. Dora feared the long-term effects to her health. Rumors circulated that the Nazis wanted to sterilize female Jews to ensure that no procreation would be possible. They tried to accomplish this through the sparse food rations that were supplied daily. During the early stages of recovery, regular food at home made her ill. Supervised by a doctor who prescribed a balanced, healthy diet, she became stronger and was able to eat. Day by day, Dora became less afraid. As time went on, she returned to a normal life and regarded her home and family as a sanctuary.

God had a plan of his own. Despite the Nazis' efforts to annihilate the Jewish population, Dora gave birth to Michael Robert Landau. She was 30 when this miracle occurred on September 15, 1948, and she named him after her father, Morris. Once again on October 13, 1951 Rachel Sarah Landau made her debut into the world and she was named after Dora's mother, Rose. Jewish people name their children after loved ones that have passed away, and it is customary to use the first letter of the deceased person's name when a child is born.

Dora's mother and father always said, "Parents always strive to ensure that their children will triumph in life and surpass their own successes." These words never rang more true, since her children were their pride and joy.

This was a happy time and brought normality to the Landau home, which had been missing during the war. They were able to enjoy holidays and other family celebrations that were missed while she was at Auschwitz. Still, Dora felt the longing for a child lost to her in Berlin so many years ago. The memory lingered and always would. She told her husband about the night at the hospital, swearing their son cried out, but no one would believe her. Nathan tried to pacify her by saying it was another baby she had heard. This only angered and upset her. The marriage was loving and strong, but an invisible wall wedged itself between them because of their disagreement on the subject.

After a long, hard day at the office, Rachel was ready to call it a night when the phone rang. It was a friend she had grown up with named Cheryl Kaplan, now Cohen. They were the same age.

"Hey Rache, I wasn't sure you'd still be in," Cheryl said.

"You must have a good radar — I was just about to leave."

"How are you, Saunders?"

"I'm fine Cohen, how are you?"

"I'm hanging in there. Steven has been traveling a lot, leaving me with all the kiddy squabbles to referee. But thank God tomorrow I have a reprieve; I'm going to the Big Apple," Cheryl said. "The dress I bought for the Klondike Foundation Gala Fundraiser is ready and I need to pick it up at Saks. I was hoping we could have lunch?"

"Wow, a ladies' day out — now how can I refuse? What time did you have in mind?"

"Say 1 p.m.; I'll get the dress first."

"Sounds good, why don't I make a reservation at my favorite restaurant, The Four Seasons?"

"Perfect, I'm looking forward to catching up."

Cheryl Cohen traveled in New York society circles. Her husband was a successful entrepreneur who started a real estate empire in 1990. He was a man dedicated to his craft with a workaholic mentality. Unfortunately, his career left little time for his family and forced Cheryl to cultivate a separate life. She had mastered a balance between motherhood and charity event-planning. The couple coexisted, but primarily led their own lives. Rachel found her friend's relationship sad when she compared it to her own marriage; Alon had been the light of her life.

Later that night, Rachel was tossing and turning, hoping sleep would take over. No luck; she was thinking about her lunch plans with Cheryl and looking forward to it. They hadn't done this in quite some time. After all these years, they remained close, even when they disagreed. Once, Cheryl was having a meltdown and told Rachel she wanted to leave Steven, but didn't have the strength to be on her own. The charity event-planner feared being in the world as a single woman and mother. Cheryl made the painful tradeoff of wanting the comfort of having a marriage and family, even if it was without love.

"Strength? What strength? I didn't leave my husband, he left me. Don't compare the situations," Rachel said.

"Alon didn't leave; he loved you and died. Sorry; please calm down, what I meant was that you're tougher than I am."

Thoughts of her friend's words lingered in her mind as she was dozing, and Rachel realized that her resilience prevailed out of necessity.

In 1948, the United Nations declared that Palestine would be known as the state of Israel. Finally, a Jewish homeland — Dora and Nathan rejoiced in this glorious moment. When Rachel was three and Michael was six, they decided to spend their summers in Israel. The Landaus bought a lovely house designed by Bauhaus on the affluent northern side of Tel Aviv, near the beach. Evening sunsets were breathtaking. The people and atmosphere possessed a warm familiarity, which gave a refuge of hope for a new and better world. The children had an easy time learning to speak Hebrew, which helped them fit in with their peers. Michael was a more reserved child, and Lisa took on the same qualities. Whereas, Rachel was outgoing, vivacious, and always wanting to take center stage — just as she did in a courtroom.

Alon Saunders was fair-skinned with jet black hair and striking green eyes, standing six feet tall. Rachel and he lived in the same neighborhood in Tel Aviv. He was two years her senior, and an only child. His mother had died in childbirth. The young boy was shy, yet affectionate, with a smile that could melt your heart. She filled a void for him as they grew up together; they forged a bond that turned into an everlasting love. Their personalities were different as can be, yet they bettered each other. The Saunders and Landau families were close and encouraged the relationship between their children. During the year, Alon would sometimes come to New York on special occasions when the family didn't go to Israel. They wrote each other and kept in close contact about current events in their lives.

In Israel, it is required for men and women to serve in the military for at least two years once they turn 18. When it was time for Alon to enlist, Rachel became fearful. In early years, the land of milk and honey experienced turbulent times with its Arab neighbors. She feared for Alon's safety. In the summer, Rachel would visit him at the army base and they spent every free moment together. When he was called to active duty, she was even more worried and scared of the unknown. Prayer comforted her until the call came that he was safe. She still remembers his words: *"Ani ohev otach, chamuda,"* I love you, cutie.

Rachel started at Barnard College in the fall of 1969 and Alon joined a training program with Mossad, the Israeli Institute for Intelligence and Special Operations at the time — two paths running in different directions, yet intertwined to have the same destiny. They agreed to marry when she graduated. On May 24, 1973 Rachel Landau graduated with a BA in linguistics. Her family, friends and her future husband joined to celebrate this successful woman's accomplishments. Alon was very proud of his bride-to-be, supportive and admiring of her success. He had become a respected member of Mossad at the age of 24.

On August 15, 1973, a new chapter was about to begin in their lives. They were married in Israel and lived in Jerusalem. Rachel had taken a job as a translator at the U.S. Embassy which was exciting, educational and challenging, as she assisted high-profile dignitaries. At the same time, Alon's work kept him busy with highly classified government assignments. Respecting her husband's professional position, Rachel never probed, but she could read his face when he was immersed in a project that presented danger.

However, life prevailed and both were delighted. Two years after they got married, on August 7, David Adam Saunders was born. He was the spitting image of his father. Family is the core of the Israeli culture, and Alon spent all of his free time with his loved ones. Rachel stopped working and embraced her new role with enthusiasm and devotion. David was a little prince.

The couple was planning a second birthday party for David, and Alon was more excited than his son.

"I think it's *your* second birthday with the way you're carrying on," Rachel said, smiling.

She stared at him and her eyes beamed with a sense of worship. He put his arm around Rachel's small waist and kissed her passionately. They were overcome with emotion and clung to one another. Nothing needed to be said between the two — they defined the meaning of "my *bashert*," my soulmate. Dora, Nathan and Michael came for the celebration with Alon's father, Jacob, who never remarried. David was definitely the center of attention, "the king of this crowd." Both *sabas*, what David called both of his grandfathers, derived great pleasure from him and they helped open all his gifts.

Winter had passed and April was there; Rachel loved the warmth that came with the season. Alon was packing a suitcase, preparing for a new mission. She was scared and could read his fear. She tried to remain neutral while she studied him.

"Can't you skip this one?"

He showed a faint smile.

"Hey *chamuda*, I'll be back in a couple of days and take you and David to Eilat for the weekend. It's the perfect time of year to go."

"OK, good looking, it's a date."

It was a beautiful afternoon and the baby had just fallen asleep.

"What time do you have to leave?"

"Not until tonight," Alon said with a flirtatious grin, as he lifted Rachel and carried her to their bed. They made love, and held and caressed each other, wishing for time to stop so they could keep that moment forever.

The promised retreat to Eilat never came to fruition.

It was Thursday evening, and Rachel had been washing dishes when she heard the doorbell ring. She opened the door, and was shocked to see her childhood friend and Alon's Mossad colleague, Danni Hirsch, standing before her with a distraught look on his face.

"Why are you here by yourself? Where's Alon?" Rachel said, trying to keep her composure.

"Rachel …"

"Oh God, what is it?"

"I don't know how to tell you this …"

Rachel started to shake profusely with fear, and tears started falling from her eyes.

"No, no, no, this can't be happening. Where's my Alon?"

"Alon was killed."

Although usually void of emotion, Danni's lips began to quiver before he could get the words out. He came into the house and stood beside her.

"Just tell me what happened," Rachel said, not making eye contact with Danni.

"Let's go sit down," Danni said, placing a hand on Rachel's shoulder.

Danni explained that Alon had been killed in Haifa during a raid of a cargo ship containing illegal munitions. He had opened a crate insulated with a bomb and it detonated, killing him instantly.

Life as she knew it had ended. She lost part of herself that day too. No words could express the sorrow she felt. The thought of David being so young and left without a father was daunting. It was too early in his life to remember the wonderful man that loved him so deeply. Staying in Israel was not an option — there were too many memories that caused her pain. Rachel returned to Scarsdale to live with her parents.

Four

Having the love and devotion of her mother and father helped ease Rachel's sorrow. All of her focus and energy went into raising David, who filled the emptiness in her life. She always tried to protect and shield the child from harm, yet she allowed him to find his own way. At times it was hard not to interfere, even though independence was important. Rachel knew this was the way Alon thought he should be raised. Her son represented a treasured gift of their undying love. When he started elementary school, Rachel felt lonelier and needed to occupy her time. This was the way she coped with her life. The memories caused her anguish of what would never be again. Not allowing herself to reflect on the past would keep her numb. Without Alon's warm touch, nights were endless; she was not a sound sleeper and always longed for the comfort of daylight.

In the midst of the void that came with David starting school, Rachel continued to demonstrate her aptitude for learning. In addition to English, she spoke five other languages fluently: Hebrew, Arabic, French, Spanish and German. She was ready for a new challenge and decided to apply to Barnard Law School, and she was accepted. Sculpting a new career path gave her a feeling of creativity, like an artist — the plan was orchestrated perfectly. Rachel attended classes by day when David was in school, and the two studied together in the evening. He liked having a mom in school studying, knowing that he wasn't the only one burdened with homework.

Dora and Nathan were wonderful grandparents; they were always supportive of their family. Michael, now 33, had become a successful architect, having graduated from Rensselaer Polytechnic Institute in 1966. He and Rachel were a representation of everything Hitler had tried to bury and destroy in the Holocaust — they were two radiant and successful tributes to humanity.

After Rachel completed her law studies in 1985, she secured a job in the New York City District Attorney's office. The petite rookie thrived in her new role. She had a reputation for having an innate sense of style and fashion. Among her colleagues, she was given the nickname of "Courtroom Couture." Mrs. Saunders was admired, respected and above all, taken seriously. Rachel was a barracuda in the courtroom. However, as time went on, trying cases that dealt with heinous crimes became too difficult. So, she decided to open a private practice.

Her specialty was handling cases against apartment slumlords. It was a rewarding contribution — fighting for the underdogs, making sure that violations in buildings were brought up to code.

Rachel was down to earth and never put on airs. Her privileged background left her untainted, appreciative and unpretentious. Remembering the hardships her mother endured, nothing was taken for granted, and she raised David with the same values, explaining that it was important to respect everyone and never frown on their circumstances.

"We don't know what tomorrow holds for us. Embrace life's gifts and be kind to those who are less fortunate," she would tell her son.

The next day, Cheryl arrived to the restaurant first and was seated in the Pool Room. Rachel was well known at The Four Seasons. The ladies hugged when Rachel arrived.

"Sorry I'm late; my 10 a.m. deposition ran over time," Rachel said, taking a seat at the table.

"No worries, everyone took care of me very well, once they

realized the reservation was under your name. Look at you, Ms. NYC Attorney, that suit is gorgeous. I bet it's a Helena Krieger?"

"Very impressive, Mrs. Cohen, it is indeed a Helena Krieger."

"It's stunning. How is your handsome son?"

"David is doing well; it's his last year at Princeton and he's waiting to hear from medical schools. He wants to go to Yale. And how are my two godchildren?"

"They're flourishing, and they always ask about you."

The two continued to catch up, laughing and talking through lunch as if they were still teenagers. Time had gone by so quickly, Rachel didn't realize how late it was getting. She asked the waiter for the bill.

"Well Rache; I'm thrilled to have had this grown-up play date. I almost forgot to mention, you know, Helena Krieger is going to be at the Klondike Foundation Gala Fundraiser benefit next week. Why don't you come? It will be fun, and yours truly can guarantee you a seat at her table," Cheryl said. "Besides, I could use the moral support."

"You want moral support? Oh please, Cheryl; you are a pro at planning these events."

"Well, OK, maybe I don't need moral support; I would just really like it if you came. Believe it or not, Steven has promised to tear himself away from work and be there. Now, I know how much you would enjoy spending an evening with him," Cheryl said, the remark carrying a sarcastic undertone.

Rachel had never really liked Steven; she thought he was pompous and arrogant, and Cheryl knew it.

"Why didn't you say that in the first place? How can I pass up sharing a lovely auspicious occasion with your charming husband?"

They both laughed.

Cheryl told Rachel that the event would be the following Thursday evening in the Grand Ballroom at the Waldorf. Rachel asked if she had picked up her dress yet, and Cheryl expressed that she was very happy with it.

"Well, this is a great excuse for me to go shopping," Rachel said.

"Just don't get the Vera Wang black taffeta gown at Saks; I don't want it to look like we came from a fire sale."

"You got it; I'm more of a Versace kind of gal, anyway."

Again, the two were giggling like teenagers, both happy to be in the company of one another. Rachel returned to her office, looking forward to the upcoming occasion.

The Klondike Foundation was an institute that helped raise money for children with cancer. Rachel was glad she had accepted Cheryl's invitation. It was a worthy cause and she planned to make a generous donation in her parents' name. The prospect of meeting and sitting at the same table with Helena Krieger, a top designer, was thrilling. Krieger also happened to be a Holocaust survivor.

On the evening of November 17, Rachel arrived at the Waldorf. Place cards were left in the entryway of The Grand Ballroom. She grabbed hers and proceeded inside, wearing a magnificent Versace silk dasheen eggplant gown, and her hair was in a French twist. Heads turned when she entered. Her small frame was complemented by the form-fitting design of the evening dress, accompanied by a matching pair of spectacular Manolo Blahnik shoes. She had the elegance and refinement of a true debutante, with the ability to fit in with the affluent philanthropists.

A sudden tap on the shoulder made her turn. It was Cheryl. They embraced and each complimented the other's attire.

"Let me show you to your table," Cheryl said, leading the way.

As they were approaching the seating area, Rachel saw her. It was Helena Krieger, wearing a stunning midnight blue crepe gown, complemented by a dazzling blue sapphire and diamond necklace. Her hair was white as snow and tied in a bun, which gave her the regal look of Princess Grace. She was a striking woman, even at age 79, with the elegance and posture of someone in their mid-60s. Rachel thought that in her youth she must have been a real beauty.

Cheryl made the proper introductions.

"Madam Krieger, I would like to introduce you to one of New York's finest lawyers. She also happens to be a close friend of mine. This is Rachel Saunders."

"Madam Krieger, it is truly an honor to meet you," Rachel said, blushing.

"And, she is a very big fan and wears your fabulous collection," Cheryl added.

"Yes, it's true." Rachel glared at Cheryl.

"Thank you, my dear. I am thrilled to hear that such a lovely young woman appreciates the world of fashion, and that Versace dress looks stunning on you," Madam Krieger said.

The comment made Rachel feel embarrassed.

"Thank you, Madam."

"Please, call me Helena."

As the two sat together, Helena kept staring at her. She told Rachel that she looked like her sister, Anna, and Rachel felt the warmth and sincerity of the comparison. They discussed Rachel's beginnings as a linguist at the U.S. Embassy in Jerusalem, and the many times she was able to meet exhilarating and influential people. Helena then asked about Rachel's career as an attorney, and she explained that although she began working in the District Attorney's office right after law school, she now specialized in housing litigation, as the monstrous crimes became overwhelming and she didn't care for the politics.

"If you didn't play solely by their rules, you were not let into the club, so to speak. Now I am able to run my own show and defend the people who are worthy," Rachel said.

It was unusual for Rachel to open up to someone she had just met. For some reason, Helena gave her a sense of comfort and security, and she became uninhibited. They spoke for hours. Helena mentioned an upcoming trip to Europe to introduce her spring line in January. The tour would begin in Paris and conclude in Vienna, where she had a villa. Helena also touched upon the happy days she had spent in Germany before the Reich came to power. Rachel discussed her heritage and mother's plight from that era.

Steven finally arrived, and it was clear how thrilled Cheryl was to see him. He and Rachel, sharing disregard for one another, presented a façade of cordiality. Nevertheless, the event was a huge success; many people made charitable contributions to the foundation. Cheryl had outdone herself once again.

As the evening came to a close, Helena made it clear to Rachel how happy she was being introduced to her, and looked forward to meeting again at another fine gala.

"The pleasure was all mine. Helena, that would be lovely," Rachel said.

She leaned toward Rachel and kissed both her cheeks.

"Until we see each other again, dear heart."

Helena's adoring sentiment touched her deeply, and Rachel was sorry the glorious social event ended. She would always cherish this fond memory.

Five

It was May 2, 1997 — three weeks before David's graduation. He would be attending Yale Medical School that fall. Rachel was full of emotion; she was proud of her son's success, but saddened that Alon would not be there to share the happiness. Michael and the children would be at the commencement, with Jacob as the only surviving grandparent. Now 80 and frail, he would fly from Tel Aviv with Danni Hirsch, who had recently been recruited for the Kidon unit of Mossad after high-ranking officials had recognized his innate acumen for intelligence after serving in the Israeli Defense Forces. Growing up, he, Rachel and Alon were inseparable, like The Three Musketeers.

Since her departure from Israel, Rachel only saw Danni on a few occasions when he came to the states with his family. In more recent years, he escorted Jacob on journeys to New York. Danni was a wonderful person, although when it came to showing emotion, he was a stoic man. His character lacked the demonstrative magnetism that Alon had possessed. Rachel often wondered if this was a result of the covert operations to which he was assigned, yet she had a gift for making him feel at ease in her presence. There had been times she witnessed a warm, caring and unguarded side, like the day he came to tell her about Alon's death. Rachel never forgot the words spoken or look of despair on his face. Barely able to utter a sound, he managed to choke out, "Racheli, I'm sorry, so sorry." It was the only time she ever saw him shed a tear. He always called her "Racheli," an endearing way of saying her name in Hebrew.

Elated by her son's achievements, Rachel planned a wonderful party to be held at the Scarsdale home on the lawn in the backyard. Huge tents would be set up on the property surrounding Dora's incredible garden and gazebo. Rachel sought Cheryl's party-planning abilities to aid her in setting up. It was Sunday and the two ladies met at the Landau residence to coordinate the details, when Cheryl remembered suddenly that Helena Krieger had called to ask for Rachel's phone number as soon as she returned from Vienna.

"Are you serious or pulling my leg?" Rachel asked, astonished by the news.

"Even I wouldn't play a prank like this! I'm serious, she wants to get in touch with you," Cheryl said.

"Did she say why?"

"No, but remember I told her what a fan you were of her collection? Maybe she wants to give you a discounted rate on her new line. If she calls, you have to let me know."

"Which number did you give her?"

"Both home and office, I hope that was OK."

"Of course, now I'm curious," Rachel said, plucking a sunflower from her mother's garden.

The following Monday morning, Rachel's assistant told her that Helena Krieger was on the phone. Immediately she picked up the receiver.

"Madam Krieger, I am very happy and honored to hear from you," Rachel said.

"I thought we were past that, Rachel. I told you to call me Helena," she replied. Rachel could feel the smile in her voice.

"Very well, Helena. To what do I owe this pleasure?"

"I was hoping that we could meet at your office sometime this week. I have some things I would like to discuss with you."

"Certainly, are you available tomorrow?"

"Yes my dear, how about 10:30?"

"10:30 is perfect; I'm looking forward to it."

The next day, Rachel arrived to work wearing a sage green Helena Krieger spring suit. When Helena entered Rachel's office, she was pleased to see her new friend wearing one of her designs.

"Perhaps I should add you to the runway next season," Helena said, glancing over Rachel's perfectly put-together ensemble.

"I thank you for the kind words, but if I wanted to measure up to the runway models I would need to wear stiletto heels and I'd be afraid of falling over my own feet." They laughed.

In her office, Rachel displayed an exceptional array of beverages and breakfast pastries.

"Can I offer you anything to drink — coffee, tea, water or perhaps juice?"

"A white coffee would be lovely please, no sugar."

That was European terminology for coffee with a lot of cream. Rachel handed the hot drink to her, placing a neatly folded napkin with a demitasse spoon on the saucer. Madam Krieger admired the beautiful bone china Rachel used.

"Perfect!" Helena said, taking a sip. "Not many Americans know what a white coffee is." She placed the cup and saucer on the table, crossed her legs and folded her hands.

"I appreciate you taking the time to meet with me today, Rachel."

"It is my good fortune to have you here, Helena. Is there something I can help you with?"

"Yes, there is, and you are the one person I thought I could trust with this. I can see you are a kind soul and familiar with the bureaucracy of the legal system."

Rachel heard the desperation in her voice.

"Please tell me what's wrong."

"The evening we met, I mentioned my villa in Vienna."

"Yes, I remember."

"After my fashion tour ended, I spent several months there and have just returned last week. It has always been my safe haven and sanctuary. And while I was in Austria, I accepted an invitation to a banquet hosted by Baroness Deborah Von Heffner," Helena said, smoothing her dress with her hands. "It was that evening I saw him."

"Saw who?" Rachel said, leaning forward.

Madam Krieger's voice began to quiver.

"Gerhardt Dreschler."

Rachel had heard this name spoken by her parents. Gerhardt Dreschler was one of the Reich's loyal tyrants. He was only too happy to wreak havoc upon the Jews in Europe, being promoted to commandant at Treblinka. The officer idealized the Furor Adolph Hitler and was pleased to serve him.

Helena was trembling and Rachel found the accusation shocking and surreal.

"Are you sure it was him?"

"As God is my witness, it was. But his features are different now ... he must have had alterations to his face, but I will never forget those eyes — a menacing deep, dark grey, and a voice that resulted in bloodshed and misery," Helena continued. "I avoided contact with him but was close enough to have seen and heard the Baroness introduce him to someone as 'Werner Frece.'"

She began sobbing uncontrollably, shaking her head as she recalled seeing him. She told Rachel she would never forget the sound of his voice and his sincerity when he said, "It's a privilege to make your acquaintance."

Helena tried to gain her composure so she could tell Rachel the story. She explained that in 1939, her family owned a dress shop in Düsseldorf called *In Der Art* (In Style). Gerhardt Dreschler's wife, Elsa, was a customer who came to the store frequently with him. Helena recalled a time when she was going to accompany Herr Dreschler to a party hosted by Hitler. The Furor invited all high-ranking Reich members. Frau Dreschler raved about it, saying that she needed a brilliant ensemble for the special occasion.

Helena went on to explain that her sister, Anna, went to the back of the shop and came out with a beautiful brown velvet gown she had designed. Herr Dreschler was there with his wife. He laughed and said, "No, it can't be brown. I hate that shade; it's the color of garments worn by money grubbing haughty Jews."

He looked at Helena and continued: "All of you love to wear brown and strut around the streets in Mink coats thinking you are better than everyone else."

"However, the dress itself is lovely — can you get the fabric in black?" Elsa interjected calmly, as if her husband had not just uttered something so offensive. This was the disrespectful way the Nazis spoke to and treated them. They never retaliated or answered back out of fear.

Anna said that it should be in by the end of the week, and she assured them that she would call when it arrived at the shop.

The dress was dazzling; Anna had outdone herself by adding accents of detail that made it more attractive than the original creation. However, she was terrified in Dreschler's presence. Shortly after this incident he was stationed in Berlin.

"I will never forget those eyes; I looked into them three weeks ago in Vienna," Helena said. "He did not catch my glance. I can't forget his cruelty; I witnessed it first hand at Treblinka."

Helena paused before she continued the story, taking a sip of her coffee that had been sitting for far too long.

"Anna and I were separated from our parents before we were thrown onto the train. After the war, I tried finding out what happened to them, but my search was unsuccessful. I would like to reiterate that my sister was petrified of Dreschler, and since he was the commandant of the camp, he knew it."

They encountered his evil on a rainy day when the sirens summoned them to the yard. Dreschler noticed Anna as if she were a rabies-infected dog sniffing out his prey.

"Hey, brown-dress Jew, haughty whore, not so high and mighty now?" he said.

With that, Gerhardt Dreschler raised his pistol, pointed it at her, and the next thing Helena saw was her sweet Anna fall to the ground.

Helena started to scream, and he looked right at her and said, "And you, bitch, I will let live to be tortured by this memory."

He laughed and motioned to another officer, saying, "Lennart, do you have the camera?" Helena remained standing, numb as the other officer left to get the camera. He returned within minutes, and the Commandant posed. He placed his foot on top of Anna's face and Sergeant Lennart Bergmann began to snap pictures of Dreschler, one after another. He forcefully pressed his weight down on her and Anna's face became more distorted with each passing moment. Both men were immersed in the joy they were getting out of mutilating her helpless, motionless body. When the photoshoot concluded, Dreschler wiped the bottom of his shoe on the dirty ground. He looked at his photographer and said that he didn't want the sole of his shoe to have any trace of that diseased whore.

Rachel, now filled with emotion, embraced Helena, trying to relieve the agony of the wicked memory. It was evident that the Nazis had succeeded. Helena was taunted by the unimaginable recollection that she carried in her heart.

The civilized world would revel in the vision of capturing the miserable creature that was responsible for inhuman acts against so many innocent lives. It would be a victory and emancipation.

"The night we met, you mentioned working at the U.S. Embassy in Jerusalem some years back. Perhaps with the contacts you had, it would be possible to involve the right individuals in orchestrating his capture and bringing him to justice," Helena said. "I allow you to disclose all information about our discussion to anyone who can help. Please, I beg of you."

Rachel, astonished by the request, felt flattered and challenged at the same time.

"Helena, I left the Embassy over 22 years ago and haven't been to

Israel for over 20 of those years. It has been a long time since I had an alliance with this government, and I don't know how beneficial my involvement will be," Rachel said. "But, you have my word — I will do all I can. Have you told anyone else about this?"

"No — only you."

Six

*Michael and his family arrived in New York a week before David's grad-*uation. Rachel cleared her calendar so she could spend every possible moment with her family. Their company was comforting; both sib-lings were still coping with the loss of their mother and Rachel was still thinking about her conversation with Helena. Being together helped them heal.

The day before the graduation, Rachel went to the airport to pick up Jacob and Danni. They would be staying with the Landaus in Scarsdale. Seeing them made her think of a life that no longer existed. Still, she warmly welcomed them when the El Al flight from Tel Aviv to JFK was early. Both men looked tired, yet enthusiastic when they arrived.

Rachel embraced her father. *"Aba, birucheam,"* she said, welcoming him in Hebrew.

With a smile she turned to Danni and he hugged her.

"Hello Racheli, *ech aht?*"

"Hello Danni, I'm fine, *ech atah?*"

"I'm well enough."

The commencement ceremony was wonderful; David received top honors and a BS in biochemistry. After the commencement ceremony ended, the family returned to the home to celebrate his success.

Everyone seemed to be enjoying themselves. Rachel walked over to Danni and smiled at him.

"Are you having a good time?"

"It's a wonderful party, you have outdone yourself."

"Thank you, sir," Rachel said. "How are Sarit and the children?"

"Ronni is a fine paratrooper and Ariella will finish the army in early January," he hesitated. "But Sarit and I are divorced; it became final six months ago."

"I'm sorry."

"Don't be, not everyone has what you and Alon had. It's for the best; I could have been a better husband and tried harder. The job always came between us."

There was a moment of awkward silence before Rachel spoke.

"I want to discuss something with you and just haven't had a chance — it's been hectic with all the preparations for today."

"What's up?"

"Not now, let's talk tomorrow. Michael is planning on taking everyone to a game at Yankee Stadium and knowing we are not baseball fans, I thought it would be a good time to catch up."

"OK, tomorrow it is," Danni said, wondering to himself what was so important. Rachel smiled and waved as she saw Cheryl and Steven approaching.

"Rache, what a day. It's hard to believe David is a Princeton grad," Cheryl said, giving her a warm hug.

"You must be so proud of him," Steven added.

"I really am, but in my mind he's still 3, which would make me only 27." They all laughed.

Danni excused himself and went to sit with Jacob.

"You will have to excuse me, since I left the office early, I need to be home by 8:00 for a conference call," Steven said.

"No, of course I understand, thank you for coming."

He leaned towards Rachel and gave her a hug.

"I wouldn't have missed it." His sincerity was unexpected and refreshing.

"I'll see you later," he said as he turned to Cheryl, giving her a kiss.

After he left, she and Rachel walked over to get some food.

"So," Cheryl said, "did Madam Krieger call you?"

"Yes, you were right; she was flattered by my patronage and loyalty to her designs and offered to show me the upcoming line for next season. Good call, Cohen; you would make an excellent detective."

"Thanks Saunders," she said, smiling.

The next morning, Michael left with everyone for the game. Danni and Rachel were having a late breakfast outside in the gazebo.

After eating Lila's pancakes they needed to stretch their legs. The property was tremendous, allowing a lot of space to roam. They walked down to the stables that were now empty.

"OK, I'm curious — you looked very serious yesterday, so tell me what's going on."

She looked at him for a long moment before speaking. "What would you say if I told you I thought Gerhardt Dreschler was alive?"

He stared at her. "What makes you think he's alive?"

"A client of mine swears she saw him."

"Who? Please stop talking in riddles."

Rachel told him Helena Krieger's story and saw him pondering the notion.

"Come on Danni, it's possible. It wouldn't be the first time we heard about Reich officers changing their looks with cosmetic surgery after the war. I might add — with money they stole from the Jews. You have to admit, it could be true."

Staring at her again in silence, he continued to wonder.

"If it's true, what a discovery it would be."

"Imagine being able to make him accountable for what he did,"

Rachel added. "When Helena Krieger told me about all the misery and torment he was responsible for, it made we want to kill him. Being able to make the sick bastard suffer would be a satisfying moment."

"How long have you known about this?"

"Just a couple of weeks, and it's all I can think about. This would be huge for your career and make you a luminary legend."

"Racheli, I'll contact intelligence and see what they find on Mr. Werner Frece."

It was 1:30 a.m. in New York and 8:30 a.m. in Israel. Danni's cell rang; it was Yossi Maesel, a trusted colleague.

"Did you find out anything?"

"Yes, Werner Frece — late wife Brigitta, and he has a son, Alexander. Frece is founder of a crude oil refinery called W. A. Frece. Location — Austria in the Viennese Wine Country. Profit margin in 1996 — approximately 52.2 million U.S. dollars — several affiliations in neighboring countries, particularly with France."

"Thanks Yossi, I'll be in touch — and keep this between us."

Unable to sleep, Danni went to the kitchen for a drink and was surprised to find Rachel there too, stirring a saucer of milk on the stove.

"I'm having some hot cocoa, want some?"

"That sounds good, thanks." She noticed how preoccupied he seemed.

"Danni, is everything OK?"

"I spoke to a friend at headquarters and he found out that Mr. Werner Frece owns an oil refinery in Vienna. If it is Dreschler, the imposter has integrated himself into an affluent circle — the highest social aristocracy in Austria," Danni said, as Rachel handed him his cocoa. "The location he chose makes sense; a German can blend in without raising suspicion. He's calculating, shrewd and clever, except for one thing — if it's him, he may have been able to alter his physical appearance, but fingerprints can't be disguised."

As Danni relayed his findings, Rachel's heart was racing. She looked at him.

"If this turns out to be Dreschler, I want to be involved in trying the case."

He looked at her with complete surprise.

"Since I was a DA and a linguist, my participation would be advantageous. And your expertise as a crusader would make us the perfect team. I want to do this with you."

"You want to try the case?" Danni said, still shocked.

"Yes I do, I'm handing you an opportunity, Danni, that will secure your future. After this accolade, the bureau will refuse you nothing."

As they sat at the kitchen table drinking their cocoa, Danni explained that if Dreschler were captured, the extradition would be to Israel and the trial would fall under their jurisdiction. Rachel explained that there should be no problem; she had dual citizenship because she had been married to an Israeli, and had lived and worked there. All this would allow her to participate in the judicial system, and she was willing to team up with an Israeli co-counsel.

"Oh, you'd be willing, *geveret*? Very gracious of you," Danni said, referring to her as "madam" in Hebrew. "So, only duty would bring you back to B'aretz?"

Her eyes filled with tears as he posed the question.

"There is a bigger picture here — this isn't about me. The focus is to bring a ruthless killer to justice. If I can assist with the incarceration and prosecution of this devilish creature, I am willing to do so, even in Israel."

Knowing he had struck a nerve, Danni moved toward her as she turned away. Drawing himself back, he said, "I'd revel in seeing the animal hang."

Two days later, Michael and the children headed back to the UK. Rachel was saddened when they left, but she promised to try to make it to London before the end of the year. Jacob looked happy to be returning to his home. When they arrived at the airport, Rachel got out of the car to say goodbye to the men. Her father-in-law hugged and kissed her. She walked to the back of the car as Danni was taking out the suitcases.

"Have you given any thought to what we discussed?" Rachel said.

"Yes, I've given it a lot of thought."

"And?"

"I'm willing to run it by my superiors," he said, smirking at her.

Rachel was excited and without thinking, placed her hands on his face. She felt the heat in his cheeks. Sensing his own reaction from her touch, he removed her hands.

"Racheli, relax, I still need to convince the bureaucrats and it won't be easy."

"But you will, Danni, I know you will!"

Seven

When the plane touched down in Tel Aviv, Danni took Jacob home then proceeded to the Mossad headquarters. He entered the office of his superior, Liam Vuturi, the direct liaison to the Israeli Prime Minister. The two men had an in-depth discussion about the suspicion of Werner Frece being Gerhardt Dreschler. Danni told him about everything Yossi had found out.

His boss decided to set up a sting operation in Vienna to observe Werner Frece's daily routine. The suspect was under 24/7 surveillance for several weeks. It was Danni's project — he led the operation and all participants took direction from him. The team found out that Herr Frece frequently visited a restaurant called *Heurigen* located at a vineyard near his refinery.

Once becoming familiar with his daily routine, an agent posed as a busboy at the restaurant and the potential criminal's wine glass was taken by Mossad for fingerprint analysis. It was confirmed — Werner Frece was, in fact, Gerhardt Dreschler.

On July 15, 1997 at 8 o'clock p.m., Gerhardt Dreschler was met at the entrance of his home in Vienna. He was greeted by Danni and his team. To say he was irate and agitated when captured would be an understatement. After his incarceration, his home was searched thoroughly and no evidence of his past Reich affiliation was found. However, it was discovered that in December 1942, Dreschler moved his wife Elsa and son Kurt to Austria under the assumed names of Brigitta and Alexander Frece. Here, the brilliant and successful deception began. At the end of the war, he underwent extensive cosmetic surgery and fled to Vienna to start his new life.

That same afternoon, Rachel's cell phone rang as she was leaving the downtown Manhattan courthouse.

"We've got him!" Danni said. He could barely contain his enthusiasm.

"I knew you would do it. Now tell me what happened and don't leave anything out."

"No Racheli, *we* did it, and I promise you this will be your trial."

"They've agreed?"

"No, not yet, but you said it; I'm a luminary legend and the bureau will refuse me nothing! Believe me, the stage will be yours."

Immediately after they hung up, Rachel called Helena. They agreed to meet at the designer's penthouse for an early dinner. The East End Avenue and 87th Street residence was exquisite. It was lavish and decorated in a tasteful traditional motif. They sat in Helena's study, and she told Rachel that dinner would be ready shortly.

Rachel was restless and could barely sit still.

"Helena, I have wonderful news: Gerhardt Dreschler was captured and taken into custody. He is now being extradited to Israel."

She stared at the attorney in silence. Rachel got up and sat beside her. Finally able to speak, Madam Krieger grabbed her hand.

"Are you sure?"

"Yes, one-hundred percent sure. It's true — he's been apprehended."

Overcome with emotion, they embraced.

"Praise God, my child, I thank you. The nightmare is over."

"I know you're relieved, but it is going to be difficult for you to relive the terrible atrocities inflicted upon your family."

"When I was very young, my mother taught me that in life we endure hardships. The Lord never gives us more than we can handle. That horrible day at Treblinka, Dreschler chose life for me, but in reality it was God's decision," Helena said. "I wait for the day that the burden I carry will be unleashed — when I tell everyone about the venomous evils committed. Our goal here is to remind the world what occurred and make sure that a Holocaust never happens again."

Rachel arrived home at 10 o'clock and turned on cable news, where Dreschler's capture was being broadcast. Running across the screen the headline read: "Nazi Gerhardt Dreschler found in Vienna under assumed identity has been taken into custody and is being extradited to Israel." The news spread around the globe.

The following evening, Danni and Liam Vuturi were invited to join the prime minister for dinner at his home in Jerusalem. He was now part of the political circle he dreamed about. All engaged in deep discussions about Dreschler, Danni relayed how he and his squad executed their plan. When the moment presented itself, he talked about the upcoming trial and with confidence, mentioned Rachel.

"Mr. Prime Minister, I know you were made aware that the wife of a former Mossad agent gave us the lead on this case?"

"Yes," replied the prime minister, "Liam informed me that it was Alon Saunders' widow."

"Yes, sir, it was — she is a highly successful and respected attorney in New York City. Helena Krieger gave her the information on Dreschler."

"I know, her name is Rachel; she worked with the American Embassy here several years ago."

"That is correct; she was a professional translator who graduated from Barnard College with a law degree — a very intelligent individual, I might add."

"Danni, I see that you have a very high opinion of Mrs. Saunders."

"I do — Alon, she and I grew up together. Her family owns a home in Tel Aviv and they spent their summers and some holidays here. I know Rachel very well. She has excellent language expertise, and as a result of having worked successfully in the office of the New York District Attorney, Rachel would be an asset as our lead counsel."

A long silence fell as the prime minister and Liam eyed one another.

"Mrs. Saunders is an American citizen."

"Yes, and also an Israeli after marrying Alon, becoming *oleh chadasha* (a new immigrant). I also feel her participation would strengthen our alliance with the United States. It would show support of an effort to seek global justice."

The prime minister's eyes were set on Agent Hirsch.

"Perhaps you should plead the case, Danni; it looks like you have argued every point in favor of your client." The prime minister turned to Liam. "What do you think?"

"I think he's right. I met her years back at the U.S. Embassy. She is very charismatic and demonstrates a refined professional demeanor, which has assured success in the courtroom. I've heard her speak perfect German, which will help ensure nothing is missed or lost in translation."

The prime minister looked at Danni.

"When do I get to meet our lead counsel?"

Danni called Rachel when he left the prime minister's home.

"Congratulations, the case is yours!"

"If this is a prank, Hirsch, I'll never forgive you!"

"No, I'm serious! They agreed, just like I knew they would. After I sang your praises, they couldn't say no," Danni laughed. "I would be a good PR man for you."

"How much do you charge?" Rachel said, chuckling.

"For you, it'll be pro bono."

The timing of this worked out perfectly, as she anticipated hearing good news and hadn't taken on any new cases. He asked when she would be available to come to Israel and they agreed to meet in two weeks. Helena's profound analysis about God knowing how much one can handle put everything into perspective for Rachel. Perhaps this was the direction she was being sent in to free the demons that haunted her heart.

The Landau family hired a caretaker to look after their Tel Aviv home. Rachel contacted Nissim Katz and asked that he see the home was aired, cleaned and stocked with groceries for her upcoming arrival. Thinking about the prospect of returning to the place that held many happy childhood memories gave her a sense of comfort, yet at the same time she felt anxious. It was Wednesday, July 30 when the EL AL flight from New York touched down in Tel Aviv. To her surprise, the apprehensive feelings disappeared. Rachel navigated through the crowd in customs to baggage claim and found Danni waiting there. They hugged one another as he took her bag.

They exited the terminal and found his BMW in the parking lot. As they drove, Rachel observed the familiar atmosphere that she had blocked out of her mind for 20 years.

"Danni, how are your parents?"

"My parents are well, thanks, and have recently left on a cruise to France, Italy, Greece and Egypt. When I told them you were coming to Israel, they were disappointed about not being able to see you."

"Tell them I'm disappointed too, and I look forward to spending time with them on my next trip."

He paused and glanced at her.

"Does it look much different to you?"

"No, not really."

After arriving at her home, she walked out onto the deck that overlooked the sea. Rachel had forgotten how beautiful and serene it was there. She went back inside and moved around the entire dwelling slowly. She sat in the living room with Danni, and glanced at the old television, which reminded her of a story from her childhood.

"I was six years old and had an argument with Michael over watching TV. Each of us wanted to see a different show that was on at the same time, but we only had one set. My father, angered by the nonstop bickering, unplugged the set, removed it and placed it in the big closet next to the foyer," Rachel said. "He returned and sat on the sofa and continued reading his paper. Since he was always so easygoing, we were speechless when he did that. After a moment I walked toward him and said, 'Thank you, Daddy.' He looked at me puzzled and said, 'Why are you thanking me?' I pointed to the large vacant stand where the television normally sat and said, 'Because now I have a wonderful stage to sing a song for you and Mommy.'"

Danni smiled as she was telling the story.

"Then, I asked my father to please send Michael to his room. My dad wanted to know why he should do that. I told him because my brother caused a *ratekiss* and made me miss my favorite show. He said, 'What is a *ratekiss*?' I looked at him. 'Daddy, it's a big fight.' Trying not to crack a smile he told me, 'I think you mean *ruckus*, Rachel.' 'Well Daddy, he caused it.' My parents looked at each other and began to laugh uncontrollably as Michael told me sternly, 'I don't want to hear your stupid song!' and he walked out of the room." Danni chuckled.

"I remember your mother's apple strudel; it was the best."

In Scarsdale, the kitchen belonged to Lila and she remained there without the Landaus when they spent time in Tel Aviv. In Israel, Dora had complete reign and was able to exercise her culinary skills. No one made strudel the way she had.

Rachel jumped up.

"Let's go for a walk."

"You aren't tired?"

"I know I should be, but I'm not. On your feet, Hirsch. Let's go."

When they were kids Rachel had always called him 'Hirsch.' He enjoyed hearing the old familiar term. As they walked near the beach it became dusk. She studied the surroundings.

"Do you remember when you, Alon and I collected shells and we'd sit on the sand for hours comparing who found the nicest?"

"Yes, Racheli, I do — you always won. I remember you dove wearing goggles under the water again and again like a fish."

Looking at him recalling the fond memory made her happy. "God, look at that gorgeous sunset," she said, taking a deep breath, "And the pure clean smell of the air."

"Michael never wanted to join us. He still hates the water — it scares him. When he was about four, my parents had taken him to a poolside birthday party and a little girl was swimming, got a leg cramp and went under. Two people saved her; she was fine, however Michael never forgot it. I told him not to be afraid and that I'd go in the water with him. When I insisted, the more frightened he became. After a while, I gave up. I used to love losing myself in the grasp of the sea, yielding to the serenity I felt."

Danni, surprised at her openness, listened as she spoke. He was enjoying these unguarded moments with Rachel. After Alon died she only allowed herself to channel any sentiment through David, always showing him warmth and affection. Rachel's face became serious.

"The day Alon left for Haifa; he told me that on the weekend we would go to Elat and what a great time of year it was to be there. He never kept his promise and my love of the sea died with him on that final mission."

Not knowing how to respond, Danni stood silent. The momentary lapse of vulnerability reverted to her usual hidden emotion.

"The jetlag is beginning to hit me — could we go back?"

Danni nodded, realizing that the memory was painful for her, and they walked back to the house.

When they got home he said, "We need to be at the prime minister's home for lunch by noon tomorrow. I'll pick you up at 10:30. Sleep well."

Jerusalem was about thirty-six miles from Tel Aviv. The next day as they drove, Danni mentioned his superior, Liam Vuturi. He told Rachel that Liam recalled meeting her at the U.S. Embassy years ago, and he complimented her language skills. Rachel didn't remember meeting Liam, so she was surprised that he remembered her. She asked Danni what the prime minister was like, and he told her he was honest, to-the-point, and was looking forward to meeting his lead prosecutor. He assured her that everything would be fine if she just acted like herself. Danni also instructed her to address him as "Mr. Prime Minister Sir."

Liam was already there when they arrived. The introductions were made and he nodded his head and extended his hand out to Rachel.

"Mrs. Saunders, it's a pleasure. I had the honor of serving with your husband many years ago and he was a fine man."

"Thank you, yes he certainly was."

"I don't know if you remember me — we had met some years back at your embassy."

Rachel looked at him and tried to recall the occasion, and was embarrassed that she couldn't.

"Let me try and refresh your memory — the Israeli secretary of state was having dinner with the U.S. attorney general and chancellor of Germany."

Rachel chimed in, "Oh yes! Now I remember you accidentally banged your arm into the chancellor's water glass."

"I did, and it spilled right into his lap. I was mortified by what happened and he was a gentleman, graciously accepting my apology. Then I heard him mumble in German and you laughed. The chancellor looked in your direction; I still remember how you tried to disguise the reaction by coughing. At the end of the evening I asked you what he said."

Rachel interrupted Liam and started giggling.

"He said it looked like I peed in my pants." The three were laughing.

"Now I see why Liam was so impressed with your German language skills."

The prime minister entered the room.

"Please tell me what's so funny, I love a good joke."

Rachel was self-conscious as Danni introduced her to him.

Following Danni's advice word-for-word, she repeated: "It's an honor to meet you, Mr. Prime Minister Sir."

"The pleasure is all mine, Mrs. Saunders. Welcome to my home."

"Sir, please call me Rachel."

"Very well Rachel, do make yourself comfortable. It is an honor for me to meet the woman who played a critical role in facilitating the capture of Gerhardt Dreschler."

She was appreciative of his acknowledgement.

During lunch they discussed upcoming trial strategies. Rachel openly imparted her thoughts on the subject.

"A good attorney is organized with every detail. The jury needs to sense and envision the sinister acts of terror caused by this monster. To ensure this reaction, I want to go back to Germany, Poland and Vienna to find out everything I can on Dreschler. No stone will be left unturned. The people still alive that experienced his carnage and malevolence first hand will be our strongest voice."

"Danni and his staff will go to Europe with Rachel to guarantee her safety. The presence of Israeli agents would assure the cooperation of those trying to create obstacles in disclosing pertinent information on Dreschler. All barriers will be broken down, or a public global scandal will arise and show Nazi support against the innocent," Liam said.

At the end of the conversation the prime minister explained that he would announce Rachel's participation and position in the trial in five days. Until then, the status of the case was to remain classified. It was evident to him that she was bright, sharp and passionate about her vocation through the way she spoke about her plans for the trial. He felt reassured in his choice to make her lead counsel. Barring motions and other dilatory tactics, the trial would begin on February 1, 1998, giving her five months to prepare.

Eight

After they left their meeting with the prime minister, Danni looked at Rachel and grinned.

"It was obvious; the prime minister is crazy about you, and I knew he would be."

That evening, they had dinner with Jacob at his home in Holon, a suburb of Tel Aviv. Danni was the designated chef and prepared a wonderful barbequed meal. The elderly gentleman was happy to have them both there. An aid lived in his home and cared for him. In recent years he didn't have many guests and welcomed the company.

Rachel sat beside Jacob and he smiled at her.

"I am thrilled to see you, my darling. It's been a long time since you've come back to the Holy Land."

"I'm glad to be here, *aba*."

"How is my grandson?"

"Very well, he's starting medical school at the beginning of September."

"I'm very proud, Rachel — a future Dr. Saunders. Alon would have been too. Don't you think David looks so much like him?"

She nodded her head with a smile.

"Will you be staying in Israel a while?"

"I'll be here for three weeks."

"How is your law practice?"

"It's going well, thank you. I've decided to lighten my load in New York. From here I intend on going to London. I am looking forward to spending time with Michael and the children. He's always asking me to come for a visit, and I've decided to take him up on it."

"Now that's good news to hear, you should focus more on relaxing and having fun."

She was still jet lagged, so she was ready to go home and call it a night. Rachel kissed Jacob.

"I'll come and see you soon, I promise."

Danni dropped her off on his way home, and remembered he had an early meeting with his team.

Mentally weary and physically exhausted, Rachel fell asleep quickly, which was an unusual occurrence. Maybe it was being here now that subconsciously gave her comfort. For years she ran away rather than embracing the pain of the past. Rachel woke up the next morning with a burst of energy and feeling full of purpose. Unable to understand why, but not wanting to question it, she went with the mood and decided to visit Alon's grave. It would be her first time there since his funeral. Rachel hoped to receive the consolation she had searched for.

Before departing for the cemetery, Rachel approached the bedroom closet. On the top shelf stood a small box which she reached for and took with her. She rented an automatic car for her trip. Her first day alone in Israel was beautiful, but hot. Rachel welcomed the luxury of this serene quiet time. The cemetery was located in greater Tel Aviv and was called *Kiryat Shaul*.

Upon arriving, Rachel's heart began pounding and her legs became numb. Although petite in stature, she made up for it with her strength, and she sat for a moment, took a deep breath, then proceeded. Remembering exactly where Alon was buried, she walked to the grave and stood staring at the headstone. In Hebrew it read:

In Memory of Our Brave Hero, Alon Saunders: Beloved Son, Husband and Father.

Looking at the monument Rachel remained silent for several minutes before speaking.

"Hello, my love, forgive me for staying away so long. I've been angry that you left me alone to raise our son, who has grown up to be a fine, handsome young man. When David smiles, he is the exact image of his father and we can be proud. My thoughts are of us as we had been together every day and wish you were still here to hold me. They say time heals all wounds, but that is not true; my heart still aches."

She opened the box and inside was a compass that looked like a pocket watch. At the top of it there was a small knob, and when pressed it became released and unlocked. On the inside cover was a picture of Rachel and David when he was a baby.

"I bought this for your twenty-eighth birthday, only you left me two weeks before then. This gift was intended to provide you comfort and direction. Know that David and I are, were and will always be with you. Now I'm the one who is off course and needs your guidance in finding my path."

With those final words she kissed the compass, placed it back in the box and laid it on the ground at his grave. She got up, walked away and didn't look back.

On the drive home, Rachel stopped at the pharmacy to get some aspirin. Her head was throbbing. She was drained and decided to stop over and see Jacob. Hadas, Jacob's live-in aid, opened the door. He was sitting outside in the backyard. When he saw her walking toward him, he was overwhelmed with delight.

"You certainly kept your word; this is a lovely surprise."

With that she ran to him and held the elderly gentleman as irrepressible tears were streaming down her face. Rachel mentioned where she had been.

While sitting beside him on the outdoor wicker sofa, he pressed his lips against her forehead.

"Let it out, let it all out. I know how much you loved my son and now it's time to forgive."

"Forgive?" Rachel asked with a look of confusion.

"Yes, forgive him for dying and yourself for living. I have forgiven myself; it's time for you to do the same. When I lost Alon's mother the wound was unbearable. The loss of a child is even worse; outliving your son is unnatural. God asks us to grieve then endure and go on living. Once this is done, the refuge you desperately seek will be granted, I promise."

That was the first time Rachel allowed herself to experience the gush of emotion that was concealed for years, and now she desperately sought closure.

Composing herself, she got up. Hadas came outside.

"Mrs. Saunders, will you be staying for dinner?" she asked.

The aroma that transcended from the kitchen was wonderful.

"Yes, please, you must stay — Hadas is a fabulous cook and she is making *chulant* for Shabbat. Promise me you'll join us."

"I'd love to, thank you, *aba.*" she said, looking forward to the traditional Shabbat stew cooked in the oven consisting of meat, chicken, potatoes and beans.

Rachel excused herself and went into the house to wash her face. Jacob followed and sat in the living room. Striding through the home, she entered the hallway and saw a picture of Alon hanging on the wall.

"Rest well, my love," she said with a smile, looking at the image.

After freshening up she returned to the living room. Jacob was sitting in his leather arm chair and looked at her, tilting his head ever so slightly with an expression on his face that said everything will be fine. His appearance gave her a sense of peace. Later that evening they enjoyed a wonderful Shabbat feast. In addition to the *chulant*, Hadas made chicken soup, gefilte fish, sautéed vegetables and a wonderful noodle kugel.

After enjoying their delicious meal, Rachel didn't linger very long and went home. She thanked Hadas and kissed Jacob goodbye, promising to come back again soon.

While she was driving home, her cell phone rang and it was Danni. She told him she had an eventful day, but didn't go into detail, and he asked her to join him on his boat the following morning. To his surprise, she accepted his invitation, and he told her he would pick her up at 11.

The following morning, Rachel went to her top dresser drawer where she kept her swimwear. All the garments were outdated, but luckily there was one among the group that was brand new — a black Gottex suit. This didn't surprise her; even then she was a clothes horse. Though the style was a bit old-fashioned, it fit perfectly. Over it, she was wearing a beautiful salmon short outfit. Her bathing suit straps were still visible. The ensemble complemented her hair and eyes. Danni rang the bell at 11 o'clock sharp and she let him in.

"I made a pot of coffee, want a cup?"

"No thanks, I'm good."

He studied her then smiled.

"What are you grinning at, Hirsch?"

"It's nice seeing you dressed so comfortable and casual; I haven't seen you looking like this in years."

Rachel smiled, and the two headed to the dock.

Around Rachel, Danni was different. Perhaps it was their childhood history together. She was able to bring out a softer and gentler side in him. The callous exterior he showed to many people could also be attributed to the rigorous years he served with Mossad. It was easier to block out his memories of unpleasant events than to express tem. Placing a wall helped safeguard the reminder of such incidents, and nobody knew this better than Rachel, since she had also become an expert in hiding her emotions after Alon's death. In many ways they were the same — they both shared a common bond, and that was Alon.

It was a beautiful Saturday in Tel Aviv. They talked about the black tie dinner being hosted at the Israeli Consulate on Sunday evening.

"It starts at 8:00, so I'll pick you up at 6:30," Danni said. She smirked.

"All this chauffeuring service — I'm not used to it. Usually I'm the designated driver."

"Do you want to pick me up then?" She began to laugh.

"And steal you thunder Hirsch? No way, you may continue the driving; I'm actually enjoying being a passenger."

They arrived at the marina on Ben Gurion Street and walked toward Danni's sailboat. It was a beautiful 1990 Moody 376 called *Yahalom shel Hayam*, Diamond of the Sea. When he set eyes on the vessel, his pride and pleasure were obvious. As children his father had taken them all sailing. Danni's passion in navigating through the water was like watching a dancer performing. His grace, style and calm demeanor were effortless; he was a natural. When they were about 15 miles out, the captain shut off the motor.

"It's so peaceful here," Rachel said.

"Yes, I call it my tranquil escape. So, tell me what was so eventful about yesterday."

There was a long silence.

"Is everything OK, Racheli?"

"I went to visit Alon's grave for the first time in over 20 years, and afterward I only wanted to see Jacob. All the rage — every emotion I've held inside was released and that poor wise old man bore the brunt of it. He told me I needed to forgive, and that God asks us to endure and go on living."

Rachel and Danni had never really discussed what occurred until then.

"The day it happened, I wanted to die. We were assigned to different missions. I still think about it, he was supposed to wait for backup before proceeding on board. If I had been there, I never would have let him go."

"Listen to me Danni, it wasn't your fault. We both know that Alon had a mind of his own."

With that, he reached for and took her hand and gently stroked it. They shared a consoling, quiet unspoken release of sadness.

The sea displayed a hopeful vibrant shade of blue and looked like a movie background, yet it was real and inviting.

"Racheli, swim with me."

Hesitating, looking at him, she removed her top and then the shorts. Danni watched, his face clearly flushed. He was wearing a blue LaCoste shirt and matching shorts. Rachel returned his stare.

"Are you planning on going in like that?"

Embarrassed and aware of her knowledge of his gaze, he removed the garments and only his swim trunks remained. Then he jumped in and Rachel heard the splash.

"It's warm — come on now, it's your turn."

She took a long glance at the water and Danni. Standing near the front end of the boat Rachel positioned herself, dove in and felt a wet rush of bliss.

It was an instance where her sorrow was taken and washed away. She swam toward him. Looking intensely at one another, he put his arms around her and placed his lips on hers. Their mouths joined together as one, and awakened by the tender passion, they continued the gentle motion. The warm display of affection lasted for several minutes then she grinned at him.

"Very impressive Hirsch, very impressive."

He put his thumb and forefinger on the side of her chin and grinned.

"Likewise, beautiful."

They felt alive, free and allowed themselves to enjoy the magnificent splendor of the moment. Later on they walked in the Charles Clore garden located at the Tel Aviv shore and ate in a seafood restaurant on the beach. It was a perfect day.

The next evening Danni picked up Rachel at 6:30 sharp. When she opened the door he stood for several moments without a word.

"You look gorgeous."

He handed her a dozen beautiful long-stemmed yellow tea roses surrounded by baby's breath.

"Thank you, they are lovely."

"You're welcome; I remembered yellow roses were your favorite." She smiled.

"Hirsch, what a memory, and you look very handsome."

He was hypnotized and could not stop staring at her. Danni was wearing a black tuxedo and Rachel had on a strapless taffeta cream form-fitting Dior gown accented with black piping and a bow resting at the small of her back. The opened back was shaped like the letter V and highlighted her small frame and the front of the dress allowed the smallest hint of cleavage to show. Her hair was done in an up sweep.

They were a stunning couple. His salt-and-pepper hair, olive skin and blue eyes made him even more handsome than he had been in earlier years. The Mossad officer stood 6'2" and towered over the small attorney. He adored how petite she was.

Danni, still entranced, uttered, "You take my breath away."

She began to blush and he gave Rachel a soft passionate kiss.

It was agreed at the home of the prime minister that Danni would introduce her as his guest that evening. Due to the fact that he had been friends with, and she was the widow of a former Israeli intelligence agent, the explanation was feasible. When they arrived at the consulate a number of guests were already there. Dignitaries from all over the world had been invited. Several individuals watched them enter the room; many stood, stared and whispered, they looked like royalty. Yoel Agassi was a lieutenant in the Israeli Army. He walked toward them and said in Hebrew to Danni, "Aren't you going to introduce me to this beautiful woman?"

"I would like you to meet Lieutenant Yoel Agassi," Danni said in English. "Yoel, this is Rachel Saunders, she's visiting from New York City."

"It is a pleasure to meet you, Lieutenant."

"Likewise," he replied. Agassi didn't know who Rachel was, and since the introduction was made in English, the lieutenant had no idea that she spoke fluent Hebrew. Yoel looked at Danni and spoke in Hebrew. "Nice piece of ass, Hirsch," he said.

Danni was outraged at the crass comment and was about to respond. Rachel didn't give him a chance; she acknowledged the remark and answered in Hebrew.

"Lieutenant Agassi, I hope when you're caught in a dangerous situation, the sense in your head above supersedes all wisdom from the little one below."

His mouth dropped and the drink he was holding spilled. Danni's anger turned to laughter.

"Yoel, I forgot to mention that Rachel speaks six languages fluently, one of which is Hebrew. Would you please excuse us?"

Still amused, he looked at her.

"You are a piece of work, Racheli. You can clearly take care of yourself."

"I can, but at times it's nice to have someone looking after me as well."

As he led her, they scouted the ballroom together. The duo was seated with a diverse group of American and Israeli officials residing in and outside the state. A live orchestra played music. Danni asked Rachel to dance to a waltz, and to her surprise, he was a good dancer.

"You know, madam; it isn't polite to look so shocked, I've been known to cut a mean rug, as you Americans say."

She started to giggle. "You certainly do, Hirsch. I'm amazed again."

"Stick around pretty lady, because you ain't seen nothing yet."

It was about 1 o'clock when the social gathering ended. They waited outside and the valet pulled up with Danni's black BMW. They both got in the car and before driving away, he gently kissed her.

"I have the day off tomorrow, will you stay with me tonight?"

"Hirsch the night has ended, its morning already."

"OK, then spend the morning with me at my house."

Without falter, she nodded yes.

Danni's residence was charming and decorated in good taste with all modern amenities.

"Your home is beautiful."

"Thanks, can I get you anything to drink?"

"No, thank you."

They were seated in the living room. Danni removed his tuxedo jacket, leaned forward and kissed her. She graciously returned his display of affection.

"Hirsch, it's been … " she began, but had trouble completing her sentence.

"It's been what, Racheli?"

"It's been a long time for me, Danni. Alon was my one and only, I don't want you to be disappointed."

"You could never disappoint me, never; just being with you makes me feel complete."

Danni lifted her and took her to his bedroom.

"Are you sure about this?"

"I've never felt surer or more ready, I want you," she said, placing her arms around him. She unzipped the back of her gown. As he watched it fall to the floor, all that remained on her body was the cream-colored lingerie and stockings she wore beneath. Walking toward him, he lifted her on top of the bed.

She undid his bow tie and slowly began to open each button on his shirt. He removed the trousers and boxers. Her heart began beating fast; Rachel was aroused by his muscular physique, it was sculpted and toned. He then took off the remaining garments she was wearing and studied her small delicate body. Their hands were trembling as though it were the first sexual encounter for both of them. They were caressing and kissing, and then they made passionate and tender love. The motion as one was an experience of pure pleasure that lasted into the early morning hours.

They woke at noon. Rachel was at ease with him; no endless tossing and turning. He reached for her and pulled her close.

"Good morning, sexy lady."

"Morning passed about an hour ago, good afternoon handsome."

"Good afternoon, how do you feel?"

"Incredible, I feel incredible," she said with a gigantic smile. He kissed her.

"I'm afraid this is a dream and when I wake up you'll be gone."

"It's real and I'm not going anywhere."

"Are you hungry?"

"For your kisses," Rachel answered, biting his lip playfully.

"My girl, you are insatiable."

"Well if you want me to stop, just say so."

With that he pulled her on top of him.

"I never want you to stop."

She rested her head against Danni's shoulder and began caressing his chest.

"Hirsch, I never thought I could be this happy again. How about I make us something to eat?" she asked. Danni raised his eyebrows.

"Don't look so surprised, I know how to cook," she said.

"I thought you were only hungry for my kisses?"

"That's true but a girl can't live on kisses alone. Can you lend me something to wear? I just realized I have nothing except for the gown."

He gave her one of his T-shirts and it came down to Rachel's knees.

"Ariella has some clothes here; I'll find something for you to put on before I drive you back home."

Rachel went into the kitchen and found everything she needed to make shakshuka. It consisted of eggs, potatoes, onions, fresh tomatoes and tomato sauce. She remembered it was a dish Danni enjoyed eating when they were kids and knew how to prepare it.

"Don't come in here, I'm making you a special treat," Rachel said.

"OK, the kitchen belongs to you."

The house smelled wonderful.

"I know what you're making, can I come in now?" Danni shouted from the bedroom.

"Yeah, you big baby, come on."

"Wow!"

"I remembered that you liked *shakshuka*."

"This is a treat."

She gave him a taste from the pot.

"It sure is delicious — you can cook."

"It tastes OK?"

"More than OK, it's amazing," he said, giving her a kiss. "But you taste even better!"

After they ate, he cleared the table and loaded the dishwasher. He wasn't the type of man who expected a woman to be subservient to him. They went into the living room and turned on the TV and watched the news. The anchorwoman was talking about the capture of Gerhardt Dreschler and the upcoming trial, and she would relay all new information once it was known. When the program ended Danni shut the set and lifted Rachel.

"Let's go back to bed."

"I thought you'd never ask …"

Nine

That Tuesday the trial details were made public. The papers read, "American Attorney Rachel Saunders Appointed Lead Counsel in Dreschler Trial." Her background both in and out of Israel was disclosed in full detail. A press conference was held, she was probed, questioned and handled herself like an expert. Rachel felt as if she were a politician. The press found this new legal star to be refreshing, intelligent and personable.

As soon as the story broke, Rachel called her family and Madam Krieger; she wanted to tell them the information. David and Helena did not pick up and she left voicemails for both of them. Rachel was happy to hear Michael answer his phone.

"Hello, big brother."

"Well, sis, looks like you've hit the big time, now I know why you went to Israel so suddenly."

"Michael, please don't be angry with me, I was told my participation was to remain classified until the announcement was made. My legal obligation as an attorney was to keep this confidential."

"It's OK, Shelly, I understand. Why would I be angry? I'm really proud of you."

"Really?"

"Yes, of course I am, and I can't wait to hear about it when I see you."

"There's more, but I'll tell you when I get there."

"Are you OK?"

"Yes, truly I am."

"Alright Shell, see you on Wednesday evening."

Rachel sounded different to him; perhaps it was the excitement of the court case. Now curious, he wondered what else she had to say.

When she hung up her cell rang.

"Mom?"

"Hey kiddo, how was your trip?"

David had just returned yesterday from the Cayman Islands with a group of his friends.

"Great surfing, it was awesome. I was sleeping when you called; we got back late last night and I'm wiped out. How is Israel?"

"It's wonderful being here. *Saba* and Danni send you their love. I have some news."

"Oh, yeah?"

"I've been asked to be lead counsel on the Gerhardt Dreschler trial in Israel. The announcement was made today over here a short while ago."

"Wow, Mom. congratulations, this is huge! I'm so proud of you."

"Thanks baby, this is an enormous challenge that I'm looking forward to!"

"We'll talk when I get home next week, I miss you."

"Same here, enjoy the rest of your trip and send my love to everyone there."

That night Rachel stayed with Danni. While she was there, she received a call on her cell from Helena Krieger, who was thrilled to hear that she would play a very important role in Dreschler's downfall.

"This is wonderful news, God has chosen his messenger. I will help as much as I can and tell you everything I know."

"Thank you, Helena, I'm leaving Israel tomorrow and going to visit my brother in London for a week. When I get home, I'll be in touch."

Danni drove her to Ben Gurion Airport the next day. Saying goodbye they shared an open display of affection.

"I love you, Racheli."

Her eyes began to swell with emotion.

"I love you too, Hirsch." He gave her one last passionate kiss before they left each other.

While waiting for Rachel's arrival, Michael was bombarded by photographers and reporters at Heathrow Airport. Trying to make his way to the British Airways baggage claim area he answered the questions of the paparazzi.

"My sister's contribution will have a positive impact on this high-profile prosecution case." When she arrived the crowd besieged her. The flight was delayed two hours due to a bad storm in London; she was clearly tired and wanted to leave the terminal as quickly as possible. Turning politely to the reporters she said, "Ladies and gentleman I expressed my sentiments about the Gerhardt Dreschsler tribunal yesterday in Jerusalem. At this time I have no further comment, thank you all for the warm welcome to your country. I bid you all a good evening."

Seeing she was clearly not going to give any additional details, the hoard dispersed.

The siblings greeted each other warmly.

"Michael I'm exhausted, let's get the suitcases and go." He chuckled.

"What's so funny?"

"Suitcases ... how many, Shelly?"

"I have three, why?"

"You're traveling light this time."

"That's hilarious, Michael, ha ha."

"I'm disappointed — I brought the Jeep Cherokee; it accommodates five easily."

"Well I wish you would have told me that, I'll keep it in mind for my next trip."

On the way home he observed her.

"Even though you claim to be exhausted it is not evident," Michael said.

"I'm feeling pretty incredible."

"It shows."

Rachel explained that in a few weeks she would be flying to Europe to do some research on Gerhardt Dreschler. This would be the most visible case of her career, but she told Michael the trial wasn't why she felt so wonderful. She said she was in love with Danni Hirsch and assured Michael that he was divorced. Rachel shared her happiness with the brother she adored.

"Shelly, that's wonderful! I always thought he was a good guy and if anyone deserves to be happy, it's you."

Her week in England flew by; everyone had a wonderful time together. The vibrant nightlife there had a magical dynamic power. Rachel loved London's theater; here the stage exhibited an amazing energy like no other in the world. Before she left Michael hugged her.

"Be careful, little sister, and bring the bastard down. This is your moment to shine, and Mom and Dad would be really proud of you, Shell."

"Thank you, and I will."

David was starting medical school in less than a week. Rachel was looking forward to helping him get settled up in New Haven. The night she returned from England to Scarsdale, and David sat with her in the kitchen snacking on Lila's famous chocolate chip cookies.

"You know that this was my first trip back to Israel since we lost your Dad, and I went to the cemetery and visited his grave."

He looked at her with a sense of surprise, acknowledging how painful it must have been.

"Are you OK?"

She smiled. "Yes, I found the comfort I was seeking for a long time and wouldn't allow myself to embrace it, but finally I have."

"I'm glad, Mom, and Dad would be too; he would want to see you happy."

"I have more to tell you. Danni ..." she began, but David interrupted.

"Is Danni alright?"

"Yes sweetheart, he's fine. Danni and Sarit have gotten divorced, and I'm in love with him, David. We discovered that both of us have feelings for one another."

As the words came out, Rachel felt a weight being lifted from her. Elated at hearing the revelation he gave his mother a hug.

"That's fantastic!"

"You're not upset?"

"Why would I be upset?"

"It's about time; I want you to have someone special in your life."

She touched his face. "I do, and I have for the past 22 years."

"You know what I mean Mom, other than me."

"You're a wonderful child and will always be my very special treasured gift."

The Friday of Labor Day weekend David drove the car up to New Haven with his mother. Rachel was looking outside at the beautiful Indian summer day.

"I can't believe you're starting medical school. I'm so proud of you; your father would have been too."

He moved to a luxury apartment complex, it was a gorgeous 1200-square foot furnished loft and was in walking distance of the campus. That evening they dined at Galalios in the Park Plaza Hotel. The restaurant venue exhibited a lavish ambiance with a breathtaking view overlooking historic New Haven. This was a special time in her son's life, marking a new chapter and she was thrilled to share it with him.

The following morning they attended a welcome orientation and mingled with new students and their parents. Using her best judgment, she wanted David to have the experience of acclimating on his own. Rachel had him drive her to the Tweed New Haven Regional Airport that afternoon.

"I'm starting off with one leg up," David said on the way to the airport.

"What do you mean?"

"Not every med student has a famous parent — your notoriety on the Dreschler trial has made me a star. I met a really cute girl who gave me her phone number."

"That's wonderful! I feel like a brothel madam — happy I can help." They laughed.

At the airport terminal he gave her a big hug and she didn't want to let go.

"Good luck, take care of yourself, baby boy, and be happy."

"You too Mom, I love you."

"Right back at ya, kiddo."

Two new Saunders stories were about to be written. They were embarking on their own crusades and welcomed the challenges with open arms.

Ten

Madam Krieger met Rachel at her law office the Tuesday after the holiday.
They began their work together. Helena recounted in detail everything she knew about Gerhardt Dreschler starting with his life in
Düsseldorf and concluding at Treblinka. After a week of rigorous testimony, giving an accurate description of his acts of duplicity against
humanity, she signed her affidavit.

"Rachel, I have a favor to ask," Helena said.

"Certainly, how can I help?"

"I'm designing a suit for you to wear at the trial. Please indulge
me and model it when I appear in the courtroom, I believe it could
be critical to the case."

"What an honor — would you describe the outfit to me?"

"It's a surprise."

"OK, I can't wait to see your masterful creation!" Helena nodded
her head to Rachel, expressing gratitude for the kind words. "I'd like
to get your measurements and was wondering if you are available to
join me at my home for breakfast this coming Sunday?"

"I am, and I look forward to it."

After Helena's statements were finalized, Rachel reviewed other
information which was collected by Mossad that encompassed
Dreschler's days in Düsseldorf, Berlin and Austria. The next steps
were to physically go and see each location and retrace Dreschler's

past. The German, Polish and Austrian governments assured their cooperation during the investigation. Though relieved that Danni and his team were to accompany and safeguard her, she still felt apprehensive about the upcoming trip to Europe. Two of the countries signified a period in history which allowed inhumane atrocities to prevail over decency and civility. It was a time when the world turned mad. Her mother and Helena experienced firsthand and never fully recovered from bearing witness to the vile slaughter of innocent life; an unforgettable agony they carried with them always.

Rachel flew into Flughafen Düsseldorf International Airport in mid-September and was met by Danni and his team. She resided with him in a suite at the five star Hotel Nikko Düsseldorf, which was a ten minutes' walk from the old quarter. This area consisted of bars, restaurants and shops. It was a perfect place to blend in with the tourist crowd. The other six agents stayed at three neighboring lodges. Strategically residing in diverse nearby proximities was clever; it brought less attention to them as a non-collective group.

World War II caused massive structural damage within the city of Düsseldorf, making it difficult to view business and residential areas as they had appeared before the devastation. At the end of the war, only 249 Jews survived the annihilation. Rachel's reference to previously recorded information provided by Helena and Mossad helped her research Dreschler's past. All new taped documentation was transcribed and copied within Danni's unit. She went to diverse regions and collected facts about his past life. He grew up in the residential section of Pempelfort, which is northeast of the central district of Düsseldorf, and remained there with his wife until moving to Berlin in 1940. Gerhardt Dreschler worked as a carpenter and came from a family of humble means. His specialty was designing woodwork for inlaid wall shelving in private homes throughout the area, and was said to be a master at his craft.

A man named Frederick Grunwald was found with information provided by Israeli intelligence. He was a home builder that hired carpenters to work on the interior design of residences; it was a family business established in 1922. Dreschler worked for Grunwald's father Hendrik in the early 1930s; a certain mansion located in Pempelfort withstood the damages of war. It was one where Gerhardt Dreschler worked many years before, and all the original interior carpentry remained unharmed. The Lord Mayor of Dusseldorf arranged for Rachel and Danni to tour the inside of the home; Herr Grunwald was cordial to them and answered all questions asked. He gave a guided tour of the dwelling and spoke as they surveyed the premises.

"My father used to speak of a former employee named Gerhardt Dreschler. I remember him saying he was a quiet man who never engaged in conversation with the other workers, but his attention to detail was flawless. Dreschler was the most meticulous worker on his team; in fact, here is a wall unit he sculptured by himself," Herr Grunwald said, pointing to the wall.

The brilliant accent of detail stamped in the cabinetry was illuminated throughout the room, displaying octagonal shapes built into the wall. Herr Grunwald proceeded to demonstrate how some of the structures had small concealed flaps at the top portion of the design. If rotated clockwise, the doors would open and inside were vacant areas, allowing storage space. His artistry was clever, practical and subtle.

Rachel tried to comprehend what could turn a seemingly normal and talented person into a vindictive, hateful being.

Two weeks were spent in Dusseldorf; her days were filled with hard work collecting facts. Danni enjoyed watching Rachel review the data in the hotel suite; she wore glasses and sat at the desk with a laptop, evaluating the information gathered each day. Both kept a healthy balance between their professional and personal lives. In the evenings they went out socially and other private moments were filled with tender passion that had the insatiable intensity of adolescent lovers.

The next stop was Berlin. Rachel's mother and father had lived in the nearby suburb of Brandenburg located in Eastern Germany. With the fall of the Berlin Wall. this neighborhood was renovated to accommodate a vast tourist population whereby many estate homes were converted and made into upscale hotels and restaurants. Her parents' and grandparents' homes no longer stood there. She and Danni stayed at the Hilton Hotel Berlin which was about 15 to 20 minutes from The Brandenburg Gate. The same procedure as in Düsseldorf was followed. All the other agents settled in three different inns around the same vicinity.

More research was conducted and places visited; many areas were in ruins by the end of the war. Gerhard Dressler's Wannsee manor, located in another suburb of Berlin, survived the devastation, and the residence was lavish inside and out. He lived here with his wife Elsa, mother Kathryn and son Kurt, who was born at the home. His father passed away several years earlier in Düsseldorf and his elderly mother was in need of care and couldn't be alone; she died in May of 1942. Dreschler's house was situated in a nearby villa in the same neighborhood where they discussed "The Final Solution" — the plan orchestrated by the Nazis to annihilate the Jewish population. With his continued rise to power in the Third Reich, he was promoted to Captain and stationed in Poland at Treblinka. There, his reign of terror evolved when the camp opened in July 1942. Not to cause any suspicion, his wife Elsa and son Kurt remained in Berlin until the end of that year. Prior to his departure to Poland, Dreschler arranged for his family's relocation to Vienna. They lived under the assumed names of Brigitta and Alexander Frece.

Danni and Rachel went to visit Wilhelm Strasse where Gestapo Headquarters had been and took Berlin's Infamous Third Reich Sites Half-Day Walking Tour. When they returned to the hotel, Rachel sat at the desk reviewing the information collected there. She began comparing photos of him back during the war and after his cosmetic surgery. The transformation from Gerhardt Dreschler to Werner Frece was remarkable. He looked nothing like his former self — except for the dark grey eyes Helena spoke about. They were sinister and terrifying. Being in Berlin made her feel overwhelmed and uneasy; after staring intensely at the pictures she began to breathe heavily and sweat profusely. The fearful thoughts before the trip came to fruition as the location housed her family's suffering, especially for Dora. Danni was nurturing and tried to calm her. When she regained full composure, Rachel was embarrassed for her unprofessional reaction.

"You are a human being and you can't always control your feelings, especially after what your mother personally experienced," Danni said, sitting down next to her. Rachel put her head on his shoulder and broke down.

"I hate being here, it frightens me." He wrapped his arms around her.

"Don't be afraid — you're safe, I won't let anything bad happen." She felt comfort in the strength of Danni's arms.

"This is ridiculous; I'm acting like a child."

"Racheli, you are not."

"I need to pull it together, when I'm in the courtroom my equanimity is essential or else I'll be looked upon as a stereotypical hysterical woman who can't control her emotions."

"Well, you aren't in court now; allow yourself to be just a person, not a lawyer. You don't have to always be the strong one and I'm always here for you." He began kissing her, and the lust she felt for him was made clear as she opened his belt. Danni returned the overture and placed his hand under her shirt. Both consumed with a hunger wanting to satisfy and quench their cravings, so they could accomplish their purpose when they joined as one. It was the most intense gratifying moment they experienced together. Lying in each other's arms, Danni looked at Rachel as she returned the gaze with a big smile and placed her lips on his chest. He put his hand on her forehead and began to speak.

"Do you remember once when I was about 15 years old, you, me and Alon were at the park? He went to buy you a soda, I was playing soccer and Moshe Kushner kicked the ball away from me, and I lost my balance and fell."

"Yes I do, your nose was bleeding really badly."

"You ran out on the field, pulled out of your pocket a small pale yellow handkerchief that had purple embroidered flowers in the top corner, and placed it on my bloody nose. I gave the handkerchief to my mother to wash and she was able to get out most of the deep red color. Only a slight remnant of the shade was still there."

"What made you remember that?" When she posed the question he got up and went to his wallet, and folded inside where the paper money was kept, he pulled out that small pale yellow handkerchief.

Rachel stared at him in shock.

"My God, you kept that all these years?"

"Yes, it was that day I knew I loved you. I watched the way you and Alon looked at one another and felt your connection. I stood back and kept it to myself always until now." She was overcome with sentiment as the tears came streaming down her face.

"Danni, I had no idea."

"You couldn't have known, I was always good at hiding my emotions. When Alon died, I wanted to finally reveal my feelings, however I was married with a family and your grief ran as deep as your love. The day we swam together and kissed for the first time, I felt whole. I never loved Sarit the way I should have, you were always in the back of my mind." After speaking, Danni felt cleansed, and his confession left her speechless for several minutes.

"Hirsch, I love you."

"Marry me, Racheli, when this trial is over, we'll start fresh and I'll leave Mossad — you're all I want."

"I will marry you on one condition."

"What's the condition?"

"You have to buy me a new small yellow handkerchief." Before kissing her he said, "It's a deal, beautiful lady."

Eleven

It was on to Warsaw, Poland from Berlin. For Danni, the expedition was less explosive since he had the training and experience of being involved with difficult missions that dealt with death and devastation. He was able to remove himself emotionally from the situation, except for his reassuring compassion to Rachel.

The hotel chosen was Le Royal Meridien Bristol which was one of Poland's nicest, located near the Old Town. The atmosphere was upscale with European charm and elegance. They drove to Treblinka, which was approximately 60 miles northeast of Warsaw; their route was unfortunately a reminder of the trucks that brought innocent lives to their tragic destiny. The death camp no longer stood; only commemorative stones now lay throughout the site documenting where the unthinkable cruelty and suffering took place.

Danni snapped photos throughout the grounds; the monument where the gas chamber stood was surrounded by 17,000 stones — representative of how many people were killed there every day. Between 700,000 and 900,000 Jews were executed here by the end of the war. Viewing the site firsthand, they saw the unbelievable realism of human suffering that will never be forgotten.

Danni, to this point, had been less affected by their European visit, however, on the way back to Warsaw the quiet in the air was deafening. He finally ended the silence.

"What could we have done to motivate genocide against our people?" Surprised at his question and observation, Rachel looked at him.

"If things go badly in our lives we look for a scapegoat to make us feel better. To the Aryan race, the Jews were given the responsibility of Germany's economic collapse and Hitler selected us because it was effortless for him; it's easy to prey on those who are non-confrontational and submissive."

"We are said to be the chosen people, so why did God choose us to endure such hardships throughout time?" Impassioned by her words, Rachel continued.

"What I would like to know is why did they go so willingly? Why not fight back? Why allow the abuse? When I was little I once asked my father these questions and he had no answer for me. All I remember seeing was the look of shame on his face. Then I went to hug him and he began to quietly weep. I never brought it up again."

"I suppose viewing the circumstances abstractly is easier than actually living them. Racheli, when you're in the courtroom and bring all details to light, informing the world of Dreschler's acts, the panel will be captivated," Danni said.

"Hirsch, all I want is to see this imitation of a human being squirm like a caged animal."

Tomorrow it would be onto Vienna and this would be the final portion of the trip itinerary. When Mossad captured Dreschler they searched the house and found nothing. Now the villa would be viewed again as an exercise to understand how Werner Frece carried on a normal life here for 52 years. Perhaps the answer lie ahead.

It was October 20, 1997 when they arrived in Vienna. They stayed in a tourist location at the Steigenberger Hotel Herrenhof near the Hofburg Imperial Palace. The other group members were nearby. Their days were spent in the outskirts of the countryside. The Viennese wine country was magnificent; its picturesque atmosphere was gorgeous. Lion's Heart castle was located in a charming village that dated back a thousand years to King Richard of Lion's Heart.

Dreschler chose an incredible domain to wipe out the life that occurred before. It was a peaceful atmosphere located about 20 minutes from his crude oil refinery. Thus began the frightening return to real exploration. They uncovered that the processing operation had been shut down after he was arrested. Danni and his team combed every inch of the property, yet they found nothing. From there, they all proceeded to his residence. The landscaping on the outside of the villa was colorful and well-taken care of. The lawns were flawlessly manicured, and the inner lodging was immaculate in appearance. It was quaint yet upscale, and the carpentry was superlative and obvious throughout the house. Various family photos were displayed in different rooms showing his wife and child.

Alexander Frece owned a stud farm of Lipizzan stallions located in Piber, south of Vienna. The pictures clearly illustrated Gerhardt's pride in his son's breeding expertise. On several occasions during the trip, Rachel heard him speak on television publicly. He continued to believe in his father's innocence and tried to rally support, stating, "A grave error has been wrongfully proclaimed!"

In a soft spoken tone he recited these words: "If the trial is permitted to be conducted fairly, the truth will be told. My father shall be set free to return to his home in Austria and live out the rest of his days in solace. The State of Israel prides itself in being the land of peace and democracy. If these declarations are true, then justice will prevail."

Listening to him speak, Rachel thought he was bright and articulate, having a very warm demeanor that lacked the hatred exhibited by the previous generation. Strangely, she felt sorry for him. Under different circumstances, perhaps Alexander Frece would be someone she could like. It's much easier to be blinded by the truth and place ourselves in a state of denial, rather than to accept the fact that someone who loved and nurtured us could be a person responsible for committing unimaginable crimes.

After leaving the upper portions of the dwelling, they proceeded to the wine cellar which held a vast variety of reds and whites. Dreschler was a connoisseur, and it was evident in his supply. Nothing below was found; they looked at a large picture that hung on a wall next to his wine rack. He was holding a glass toasting at some sort of Gala honoring the refinery. A sign above him read in German: *We Drill to Thrive in Austria's Natural Resources.*

Next was a visit to Alexander Frece's ranch. A warrant was issued by the Austrian authorities allowing them to search the premises. He was told of their arrival and agreed to cooperate fully. The property was lovely and well kept. They were graciously greeted at the door by a blonde-haired, blue-eyed woman; it was Alexander's wife, Gretel. Frece had married her three years prior at the age of 52, and she had been 32. This was his only marriage. She held a little boy named Erik who was approximately two years old. They respectfully introduced themselves before entering the dwelling.

Mrs. Frece invited them in and seemed surprised to hear Rachel speak German so well. She led them to the living room. Shortly after, Alexander entered and nodded his head, acknowledging their presence. Dreschler's son handed his toddler a toy car he was holding and gave the child a warm smile. He was a very attractive man, standing at 6'1" with striking crystal blue eyes, grey hair and a fit body. His character appeared reserved, yet polite. The inner ambiance demonstrated an obvious Bulgarian motif. Walking them from place to place inside and outside, he stood and watched the quest for evidence against his father.

The three entered little Erik's room as one of Danni's men was searching through the child's belongings. He turned to Danni and shrugged his shoulders, "Nothing here."

Alexander Frece looked annoyed at the disorderly mess. Rachel noticed his expression. The man who searched the area was about to leave. She turned to the Mossad agent.

"I'm sure you're going to put everything back neatly in its place." Danni's subordinate immediately glanced at him and didn't look pleased with the attorney's remark. The Israeli Intelligence superior said to him, "Please make sure you put everything back exactly how you found it."

Once more the investigation proved to uncover nothing. When

they were ready to leave, Rachel and Danni thanked him for his cooperation. Alexander turned to her and said in German, "You see, madam, nothing; you found absolutely nothing. There has been a terrible mistake; the man you arrested is not the Nazi Gerhardt Dreschler. It is impossible; my father is a kind person and could never have committed these despicable crimes."

Looking at the desperation in his eyes she thought of an innocent child left to endure the sins of the father. Her maternal instincts gave her a sense of uneasy guilt and she wanted to say, "You're right, Herr Frece; please accept my apologies for the misunderstanding."

Unfortunately, Rachel was not able to convey these thoughts. Not wanting to sound abrasive or turning the knife any deeper to inflame his pain, her response was, "Herr Frece, all the evidence we've collected will be reviewed in open court and your father will have a chance to a fair trial."

Danni understood some of the conversation from his Yiddish dialect and saw how gingerly she answered him. Rachel handled the situation well and showed her humanity as a person — not as an attorney.

"Once more, we thank you for your courtesy, sir," Rachel said.

"If my father were accused of such horrible wrongdoings I don't think I could have been as polite and well-mannered as the Freces," Rachel said on the drive back to the hotel.

"It is part of their plan, Racheli, they want us to see how willing they are to cooperate. They're acting as though they have nothing to hide and want to show this incident to be a huge governmental error in judgment. Displaying anger and being uncooperative would only give credence to the accusations. Coming across the way they had was a smart ploy." She stared at him.

"Alexander Frece seems to genuinely be a good man. I saw the way he looked at the baby with true adoration. His annoyance at the disarray in his boy's room was obvious and he would have said nothing about it. Gerhardt Dreschler must have been a devoted and loving parent; it is evident in his son's character. Perhaps the sociopath mentality was deeply tucked away when he came to Vienna. The affliction upon innocent people was barricaded in the far corners of the sick man's mind; all hatred for Jews was never unleashed in the rearing of his son."

Suddenly there was an uncomfortable silence between them; Rachel sensed it.

"Hirsch, what's wrong?" He didn't respond to her question. "Danni, is something bothering you?"

"Racheli, from now on, if you have any issue with the way my team is handling a situation, discuss it with me in private. As their superior officer, they need to see that I'm in control of the assignment."

When his words resounded in her ears, she was clearly agitated by the chauvinistic remark and had no interest in concealing her feelings.

"My apologies, Chief, I didn't mean to emasculate you and take away your authority. The more I think about it, technically, according to your superior officer, you and the other group members were here to ensure my safety. In reality this trip is my show, but from now on, rest assured I'll remain in the background."

"Racheli, don't be that way." He had never experienced the wrath of her anger, and seeing this side she displayed was new and surprising for him.

"Be what way? It's that Israeli macho thing, I get it. Was my observation of the situation so threatening to your authority? I saw the other agent was angry when I made the remark. The bottom line is it was wrong for him to leave the space in disarray. Alon would never have —" she caught herself as the word came out but he completed the sentence for her.

"Go on, finish what you were about to say — Alon would never have what? Minded your interjection, felt threatened by you? Go on, please continue."

"I have nothing else to say."

The silence between them was daunting. She was unable to hold back her tears.

"I'm really sorry about what I said — it was wrong. Even though

I was fuming, mentioning Alon was hurtful. I don't want you to be like him. This was about us, no one else, please forgive me." He wiped the tears off Rachel's face.

"You were right."

"What was I right about?"

"The Israeli macho thing — I was wrong too. You should be able to say what you think to anyone working on this assignment. It's true — theoretically, it's your stage. Just so you know, I don't feel threatened by your views. I admire and respect them and always have. It makes me unhappy seeing you cry, and I certainly don't want to be the cause of the tears. Look at that, we had our first fight."

"Hirsch, I'm sure it will be one of many, and you want to know what the best part of having a fight is?"

"Tell me what?"

"I'll show you when we get back to the hotel."

"Is it all right if I pick up the speed?"

"Absolutely, step on it please."

The following day everyone returned on a commercial flight to Ben Gurion Airport.

Twelve

It was Monday in the middle of November when the European trip ended, which ran two full months. A meeting was held at the Knesset — the legislature of Israel, located in Givat Ram, Jerusalem. It was the place where parliament performed their daily duties. Since the government was given jurisdiction over the Dreschler trial, the prime minister was in attendance, along with Liam, Danni and Rachel. At the summit they discussed all the facts found during the mission. The panel consisted of an Israeli Supreme Court Justice named Abraham Messenger and two additional district court affiliates from Jerusalem and Tel Aviv. The prime minister would be in observance on days where key witness testimony would be heard.

At the conclusion of the meeting, everyone seemed very pleased with the outcome. Now was the time Rachel needed to methodically implement all documented timeline information from the beginning of Dreschler's rise to power as an SS officer, until the end of the war where his other journey began in Austria. Some of the witnesses that came forward and gave testimony about the agony they suffered at Treblinka were flown to Israel from New York, Los Angeles and Poland.

With legislative bodies presiding, it would be Rachel's role to narrate and present all collected evidence. She was given a large comfortable office at the Knesset next door to co-counsel, 52-year-old

Chayim Rabinowitz. He was a well-known highly regarded government attorney in Israel. In her absence, Rabinowitz collected the depositions and signed affidavits from the trial participants. After reviewing the documents, Rachel contacted each character witness directly. She found it amazing that everyone was willing to revisit their nightmare to ensure this incarcerated criminal be convicted and condemned for what he had done.

It was a little more than two months until the world would view her in the legal public arena. Thinking about the mental toll she endured from the trip kept her focused on the case. Her credibility was on the line — not only as an attorney, but as a woman. She needed to guard her feelings in the courtroom. Never before had Rachel questioned her composure while on stage. This case was different and touched upon situations hitting close to home. In her mind, she remembered the bitter atmosphere from the past and wished it hadn't existed.

Being back in Israel gave her a warm sense of comfort. A place she had previously forsaken was now a familiar refuge that gave her the strength and guidance needed to execute the task at hand. Rachel lived with Danni at his home in Jerusalem. His parents invited them for Shabbat dinner in Tel Aviv that Friday evening. She hadn't seen his family in over 20 years. Bella and Simon Hirsch emigrated from Moscow and came to live in Israel when it was declared a homeland for the Jews. Danni was a Sabra, a part of the first-born generation in the State.

His mother and father were crazy about Rachel and spoke about things they remembered from when their son was growing up with her. Mr. and Mrs. Hirsch knew about their plans of marriage and were thrilled about the relationship. The meal was incredible; Bella was a wonderful old-world cook. After dinner Rachel helped her clear the table and load the dishwasher.

"When my Danni is with you he lights up; I have never seen him look so happy."

Smiling, Rachel responded, "I love him and feel the same way."

Bella hugged her. "I would never try and replace your mother, if you ever need someone to talk to about anything, I'm always here to listen." This was a new experience; Alon's mother was never a presence in her life and she liked the warm maternal nurturing feeling being displayed. Rachel was touched. "Thank you, I will remember that."

They stayed in Tel Aviv that night at Rachel's house. The next day in the car on the way back to Jerusalem, Danni smiled at her.

"Please come with me, I have a surprise for you. Zip up your jacket." He drove to the park where they played as kids. It was a little chilly outside; even in Israel the temperature reflected the coolness of November. She followed him out of the car.

"Where are we going, Hirsch?"

"You will see in just a minute." He walked her to the stands of the soccer field and they sat where no other people had been present. A group of teenagers were playing soccer.

"This is the surprise; we're going to watch a soccer game?" He reached into his pocket and pulled out a velvet box then placed it in her hand.

"Go ahead, open it." Inside the box was a small pale yellow hand-kerchief and wrapped inside it was a beautiful 1.5 karat ring in the shape of a marquis stone. It was resting on a white gold band surrounded on each side by begets in a channel setting.

"Do you like it? If you don't, I'll take you to choose another."

"It's stunning; I love it, thank you."

"I thought this would be the perfect place to give it to you."

"It's wonderful, Hirsch and very romantic." They kissed.

On the way back to the car, Danni sneezed. Rachel handed him the new handkerchief.

"I'm beginning to wonder if it's me you're in love with or my yellow hankies." He laughed then lifted her off the ground as though she were a little girl.

"Rest assured, it's you I love." Rachel hugged him.

"OK, just checking."

The next day was Sunday and marked the beginning of a new week in Israel. She went to Ramat Gan to the home of Ida and Sam Horowitz, a 76-year-old couple who survived the Holocaust. Mrs. Horowitz was going to be a character witness for the upcoming trial. She was a frail woman weathered with time who met her husband after the war. They made a life for themselves in Israel. During her years at Treblinka, she was known as Ida Posner.

"Mrs. Horowitz, thank you for meeting me today, I wanted to review your deposition." Rachel read through the transcript and reviewed each detail with the old woman. Viewing Mrs. Horowitz's painful recollection of events was heartbreaking. Rachel stood beside her.

"You are a brave and courageous woman. Your family is looking down and is very proud that their honor is being defended, giving meaning to their death." The elderly lady smiled at the attorney. "Mrs. Saunders, I owe you my gratitude for what you are doing."

When she returned to the Knesset, Gerhardt Dreschsler's lawyer from Austria, Max Reinhart was waiting to see her.

"He insisted on speaking to you," the security guard said.

"Please come inside my office," she said, motioning to the door. "Can I offer you something to drink?" Surprised by her polite manners he answered, "No, thank you. I need a word with you Mrs. Saunders, I went to visit my client today and he wasn't wearing any shoes or socks. I was informed that a guard removed them, along with his blanket."

Rachel remained calm and stood quiet for a moment.

"Please be assured I will look into this matter."

Max Reinhart continued with a professional yet intimidating air. "This country is supposedly based on a justice system; I don't think this unlawful behavior towards a prisoner will bode well for Israel. It will be viewed as a place promoting complicity of wrongdoing. If the press were told, I think this democratic administration would be perceived unfavorably."

"Sir, for the record, threats don't bode well with *me*. If you do take this to the media I don't think your government will be very pleased with you. Austria wants this mess to go away. Your homeland welcomed, honored and housed a man who allegedly committed war crimes. Thank you for bringing this to my attention, I said I will look into this matter."

After he left she contacted Rimonim Prison where Dreschler was being held. Rachel identified herself and asked to speak to the warden, Zvi Artandi. When connected, she relayed to him in English what Reinhardt told her in a professional tone. He wasn't very cordial and sounded arrogant and self-important.

"Mrs. Saunders, what goes on at this correctional institution is not your concern. Your job lies within the courtroom, and that's where it ends."

"I see where you stand, Mr. Artandi." She hung up the phone. Rachel was incensed, opened the door and relayed to her secretary she needed to be taken to the penitentiary. A few minutes later her assistant, Orley, entered Rachel's office.

"The car is waiting outside for you."

Upon her arrival to the prison at the gate she identified herself to the guard.

"I need to see the warden immediately." Rachel was kept waiting for about 15 minutes before the automobile entered the inner perimeter of the institution. She left the car and walked through the front doors and was greeted by the warden.

"Mrs. Saunders?"

"Yes, Mr. Artandi?"

"I thought we said everything we needed to say to one another on the telephone." She looked at him and spoke in Hebrew very quietly so those in the vicinity were unable to hear her.

"Mr. Artandi, may I suggest we take this conversation behind closed doors unless you want your staff to bear witness to words they may be subpoenaed to repeat to several high- ranking government officials in a court of law."

Shocked by her tenacity and unfettered behavior he said, "Follow me please, Madam." As they entered his office, he shut the door and Rachel began to speak.

"Now listen to me. You are to make sure that Gerhardt Dreschler is given a blanket, shoes and socks immediately because we are a civilized, humane society and work under due process of the law. No matter how shitty the circumstances are, that is the way we do things and what separates us from them. If his son or lawyer mentions this publicly to the media, all Nazi sympathizers who believe the Holocaust never existed will show empathy toward Dreschler and perhaps even lash out and commit hate crimes towards innocent people. When these incidents occur and the prime minister knocks on this door to ask what happened, I have a strong hunch you won't be telling him what goes on at this correctional institution is not your concern."

They stood quietly staring at one another. Suddenly, Zvi Artandi picked up the phone and dialed a number.

"Bring Dreschler shoes, socks and a blanket now!" Rachel opened his office door.

"Mr. Artandi, I hope you enjoy the rest of your day."

All the concerns she felt about her emotional stability with regard to this case were washed away as she walked out of the jail. The situation was addressed and handled well. Her strength was viewed not only by the opposing counsel, but by another who, in essence, was supposedly on her side.

That evening when she returned home Danni was already there. As she opened the door he was standing in the entrance way waiting for her. Rachel smiled at him.

"This is a nice greeting." She dropped everything and threw herself in his arms. They kissed.

"Looks like someone had a good day. By the way, how was your afternoon at Rimonim Prison, make any new friends? From what I hear, your little impromptu visit made — what did you call it when you were six?"

"Oh yes — a big *ratekiss*."

"Did it now?"

"Well it must have if the warden ran like a little boy and tattled on me to Israeli intelligence."

"I didn't get the call, it was Liam and he told me Artandi said she may be *ha isha catana* (a small woman) however, she has *harbe chutzpa* (a lot of nerve)."

"Why didn't you call me, Racheli? I would have taken care of it."

"That's exactly why I didn't call you; I wanted to take care of it by myself. If I run to you every time there is a problem, I'll be looked upon as weak. As lead counsel for the state on this case, my credibility and competency can't be in question. When I walked out of Artandi's office today, I was on top of the world and felt like I had already won. The rush was incredible."

"You're incredible," Danni said.

Thirteen

The following day Rachel went to visit another witness named Saul Lieberman, who lived in Tel Aviv. Mr. Lieberman was 84 years old and in good mental and physical health. He was a tall, robust-looking man. In reviewing his deposition at his home, he came across as being very precise and clear about his recollections of the past. Each day he worked outside the camp leveling the ground at Malkinia railroad junction. They discussed what he experienced, and Rachel was eager for him to take the stand.

On the way back to Jerusalem, Rachel's mood was somber. Thoughts of his experiences were tangled together. She remembered when she asked her father, "Why didn't they fight back, Daddy?"

Mentally fatigued, Rachel arrived home and took a hot bath, just wanting to cleanse her mind. She heard Danni. He knocked on the bathroom door.

"That better be you, Hirsch." He opened the entryway; saw how drained she looked and walked toward her.

"Tough day, pretty lady?"

"It was, handsome, it was." Danni knelt down and kissed her. She smiled.

"Care to join me?"

"Now that's an invitation I can't refuse." Pressing herself against him in the jacuzzi tub felt warm and refreshing. He stroked her hair.

"Why so glum?"

"It was a rough afternoon reviewing testimony with a witness; I'm glad you're home." He put his arms around her.

"I love when you hold me, don't let go." Danni whispered in her ear, "I won't."

In his mind he was thinking about yesterday when she had the voracious appetite for power and control. All she wanted now was for him to acknowledge her need to feel safe and secure. Danni admired and respected Rachel's forceful independence, however, secretly he really preferred her soft, vulnerable feminine side and liked being the one she turned to for strength. It validated his masculinity and, in a sense, gave him the security he was looking for. They were enjoying the relaxing moments of solitude when her cell phone rang. She started to rise and he pulled her back toward him.

"Don't go, whoever it is will leave a message if they need you. Right now I need you, I want you." She didn't resist. When he said those words Rachel felt a warm excitement rise within herself.

"Take me, I'm yours," she whispered to him. The passion between them grew with a heightened strength each time they made love.

Later Rachel checked her voicemail, and there was a message from Helena Krieger's assistant. She listened in horror.

"Danni, Helena Krieger is in the hospital; she's had a stroke. I need to book a flight to New York tomorrow."

"I'll come with you."

"No, you don't have to do that."

"I want to."

It was mid-December on a Wednesday and the air was cold in New York. When they arrived at the hospital, Rachel was given permission to see Helena. The striking woman she met at the Klondike Foundation Gala Fundraiser was not the person lying in the bed before her. It had been a bad stroke, leaving the left side of her body paralyzed; she was barely able to speak.

Madam Krieger spotted Rachel; the excitement in her eyes was evident as she lifted her right hand ever-so slightly in the direction where her surrogate child was standing. Rachel walked to the bed and held her hand, and the ailing woman squeezed it.

"Is there anything I can do for you?" Barely moving her head, she motioned no. She tried to talk, but the words wouldn't flow.

"You need to relax," Rachel said. Slowly, she began again and Rachel realized that the word Helena was trying to say was "Dreschler." Out of frustration, unable to verbalize, Helena's eyes began to water.

"Stay calm, right now just concentrate on getting better — not on Dreschler."

Once again she tried to say his name, but Rachel stopped her. "Listen to me; I have everything in your signed deposition." Speaking softly into her ear Rachel said, "He won't get away, I promise. Helena, I will speak for you at the trial and be your voice." Her reassurance was soothing and seemed to quiet Madam Krieger's anxiety.

Danni and Helena's assistant, Trudy, were waiting outside in the hallway.

"How is she, Racheli?"

"Not well. The doctor's prognosis is grim as a result of her age. It will be a long healing process and they are not very hopeful she will regain her ability to walk again."

"Rachel, your being here means a lot to Madam. She looks upon you like her own daughter." As Trudy spoke the words, Rachel thought it was sad that Helena had no family left after the war. She never married. People react differently, perhaps due to the hardships she endured at Treblinka, her mind was in a state of disconnect of wanting to love and be loved again. It's possible her career filled the emptiness of loss left in her heart.

"I know this isn't the right time to bring this up, do forgive me," Trudy said, "Madam Krieger finished the suit she was designing for you and I wanted to know where to send it."

"To Jerusalem at the Knesset Building is the best place."

"Very well, I will."

They left the hospital and went to the Landau brownstone. Both were tired and jetlagged. Rachel was craving Chinese food and ordered dinner from a wonderful nearby restaurant.

"Now tell the truth, Hirsch — you can't get Asian food like this in Israel, admit it."

"I admit it, Lady New York." While they were eating she received a phone call; it was David. He called to ask about Helena, and Rachel updated him on the situation, and she asked him how his finals had gone. David was officially on mid-winter break and planned on spending three weeks in Israel. She was thrilled; it was a few days before Chanukah. Michael would also be coming for a couple of weeks with the children, as they were on vacation too. Everyone knew about Rachel and Danni's plans to marry. Her family wanted to celebrate the good news with them in person, and now was a perfect time. Even though she was heavily involved with trial preparations, Rachel always made time for her family, and even though she was saying with Danni, she made sure to spend time at the Landau home in Tel Aviv while they were visiting.

Danni saw how excited Rachel was when she spoke to her son. Rachel was sure that Lila would be happy to have the company. When the three arrived on Friday evening, Lila made a feast. This was the first time David had seen them as a couple. After dinner Danni excused himself from the table, and David was staring at Rachel smiling.

"What are you smirking at?"

"You're glowing, Mom."

"Oh, am I?"

"Yes and I think it's great, really great." He leaned over and kissed her cheek.

That night she told Danni to stay in the guest room because David was there.

"Racheli, are you serious? He's a grown man, I'm sure he realizes that we're not just holding hands."

"He may be a grown man, however, he's still my son and I want you stay in the guest room tonight. Please don't be angry."

"I think you're being ridiculous, but I won't argue with you." She gave him a hug. When David was going to bed he saw a light on in one of the guest rooms and knocked on the door. As soon as Danni opened it David looked puzzled.

"Did you have a fight with my mother?"

"No, why?"

"Well if you didn't have a fight with her, why are you sleeping in here?"

"Oh because you're home."

"That's crazy," David answered.

"I thought so too and I told Racheli that you were a grown man."

"Yeah and what did she say?"

"Her exact words were, and I quote, 'He may be a grown man, however he's still my son.'"

David walked to Rachel's bedroom and knocked on the door.

"Hey, Mom; can I come in?"

"Sure, kiddo — is everything ok?"

"Why is Danni staying in the guest room and not in here with you?" She began to blush at the question.

"Why are you asking me this?"

"I think having him stay in the guest room is silly. Come on Mom, give me a break — I'm not five." Rachel stayed quiet. "Tell you what, if I decide to bring home a bride-to-be she can share my room," David added. Rachel regained her speech.

"Please don't do me any favors."

"I thought it was worth a shot."

"Well, you thought wrong."

"Can I tell Danni the coast is clear?" Feeling her face getting flushed as she was uncomfortable discussing this with him, she said, "Yes David, goodnight."

Danni entered the room with a grin.

"Get that look off your face Hirsch; you can sleep here tonight but absolutely no hanky panky."

His smirk turned to an expression of disappointment like a child being refused a cookie. Rachel smiled, "Maybe just a little hanky."

His grin returned. "I'll take what I can get."

Fourteen

The next evening they all flew from JFK and arrived in Tel Aviv on Sunday afternoon. Rachel went home with David and drove back to Jerusalem the following day where she resumed her trial preparations. With those residing outside the state, she conducted her interviews via conference calls. When the date of the trial drew near, the people would be flown to Israel and Rachel would then meet them in person. Everyone that came forward recalled the horrible tales of Dreschler's wicked domination over their lives. Each night she wanted to step into the abyss of unfeeling ignorance and numb her mind of the pain and suffering.

Wednesday, December 24 was the first night of Chanukah and her last work day until after New Year's. On Thursday evening, Rachel went to the airport to pick up Michael and his family. She drove to their house in Tel Aviv. After she married Alon, Dora undertook the project of having their Israel home remodeled and made larger. Rooms were added and a third story was built, which featured another kitchen, formal dining room, large parlor and a new outdoor balcony that overlooked the gorgeous beach.

That Friday she hosted an incredible Shabbat Chanukah dinner. It was a true holiday celebration. The Hirsch children, Ronni and Ariella, arrived at the same time as their grandparents. Danni went to pick up Jacob, as they entered the house the elderly gentleman smiled and looked around.

"Where is my grandson the doctor?" David went and hugged his grandfather.

"Here I am, *saba*."

When Rachel was in the kitchen alone she was joined by her father-in-law. "*Aba*, can I get you anything?"

"No, sweet child, thank you."

"I wanted to spend a few minutes alone with you."

She studied his demeanor. "Is everything alright?"

"Everything is fine, I'm very happy about you and Danni; it is as it should be. Now it's his turn; I know he's always loved you."

His remark surprised her.

"Even though I'm an old man, I'm not blind. I know Alon would want you to be happy."

"David told me the same thing," Rachel replied.

"Listen to the Saunders men; you are blessed with a wonderful child." He kissed her on the forehead and went back in the living room to join the others.

Dinner was delicious; Rachel prepared a combined Shabbat and Chanukah menu. They ate chicken soup, gefilte fish, tossed salad, brisket, potato pancakes and zucchini pie. Everyone enjoyed and praised the meal, even though the successful lawyer was not known for her culinary skills. The day Rachel stayed with Danni at his home in Jerusalem she remembered the look on his face when stating, "I'll make us something to eat." The family seemed surprised that the food was so good and she sensed their astonishment, especially when her nephew Scott looked at her in shock.

"Wow Aunt Rachel, you made all this? It was really good."

"Thank you, but it's not nice to seem so surprised!" she answered in a joking way. "Wait till you see what I have for dessert." She went into the kitchen and brought out one tray with *sufganiyot* (jelly donuts) — a traditional Israeli dessert for Chanukah. Rachel then laid a second serving dish on the dining room table. It was Dora's strudel. As a child, observing her mother preparing it was memorable. Rolling out the long piece of dough then adding the filling, tucking and folding, layer after layer.

Michael tasted the strudel.

"Shell you made this? It's delicious and really tastes like Mom's."

She looked at Scott. "Like father, like son."

Lisa walked over and hugged her aunt. "Thank you for a nice Chanukah dinner."

"Now that was a sincere compliment. You're welcome little cutie; can you do me a favor? Please open the wooden storage chest in the corner and take out a plastic tablecloth so I can set up the coffee and tea in the other room."

"Sure, Aunt Rachel, but there isn't a table cloth in here."

"No? Hmm that's strange." Lisa looked at her smiling, "Just lots of presents with everyone's names on them."

"Really, I wonder where they came from. I have an idea, Lisa, why don't you hand them out?"

"OK."

Sitting next to Rachel, Michael looked at her with an emotional reminiscence of their childhood. When they were growing up, sometimes the family would spend Chanukah in Israel. On these occasions, Dora and Nathan hid all the gifts in that storage chest.

"How did you find the time to do this?"

"Oh, I did a little shopping here and there over the past few weeks and hid everything in the car."

"Between all you're doing preparing for the trial, you're something else."

"It's not often we're all together for the holiday and I wanted to make this one special."

"Well you have." Michael kissed her and said, "Come on guys; a round of applause for the hostess." Rachel stood up and took a bow.

"Let's go everyone, get to it, open your gifts."

David was given a stethoscope, Lisa a CD player, Scott a new computer scanner, Jacob a handsome pipe and smoking tobacco,

Bella a lovely Hermes scarf, Simon a golf putter, Ronni a Hugo Boss leather wallet, Ariella a fashionable Coach purse and she gave Michael a lamb's wool sweater. The evening was wonderful and while they were opening their presents, Rachel looked around the room feeling lucky and full of pride — thinking how pleased her parents would have been to see the whole family together and thriving as one.

As they thanked Rachel for her thoughtful generosity, she walked over to Ariella.

"Your father told me how much you like Coach and I thought this would be a good color."

"It will match pretty much everything." Ariella looked at her. "It's really nice, thank you." The lack of enthusiasm in the young girl's voice was obvious and gave Rachel the impression she didn't like it.

"If you want to choose a different one, I've enclosed the gift receipt in the box."

"No, that won't be necessary — this one is fine." Danni was annoyed at his daughter's attitude and was about to say something. Rachel subtly grabbed his arm and chimed in.

"Ariella, enjoy it." Danni's daughter clearly wasn't receptive to their relationship. Ronni seemed to be happy for the couple, but his sister wasn't good at hiding her animosity and it made Rachel feel very uncomfortable.

Ariella motioned to her brother.

"We'd better get going." Looking at Rachel she smiled, "My mother and other grandparents are expecting us."

Ronni's glare at his sister clearly showed how angry he was by her rudeness.

"I'm really happy you were both able to join us." Ronni gave Rachel a hug and kiss, thanking her for a wonderful evening; then he embraced Danni. Ariella kissed her father and turned to Rachel.

"Thanks for a nice time," she said, and she walked out of the house. As they approached the car, Ronni expressed his annoyance at her.

"Why did you act that way? Rachel was nothing but nice to you, I could tell that *aba* felt bad and was embarrassed by your behavior."

"I don't care; it's *eema* he should be with — not her."

"Ariella didn't you see how happy *aba* is with Rachel?"

"Ronni he shouldn't be with her; it's wrong."

"Why is it wrong?"

"She's not our mother, that's why."

"You know that things between *eema* and *aba* were bad for a long time. They were always fighting and both of them realized the relationship wasn't working. Can't you at least try for *aba*?"

"Come on, it's getting late," was all she said.

After they were gone, Rachel and Danni were alone standing in the hallway.

"Racheli I want to apologize to you for the way Ariella was acting."

"I understand, her feelings are normal, seeing you with me instead of her mother is difficult." Rachel subtly changed the subject. "I just realized something; everyone got a present except for you. Now, handsome, come with me."

She grabbed his hand and led him to her father's study.

"Racheli, what are you doing? We have a house full of people."

"Hirsch, focus, you have a one-track mind. Just follow me." On the desk in the room was a box. He looked at it, then at her.

"Well go on, open it." There were all different colored handkerchiefs with his initials monogrammed on them.

"You never seem to have a handkerchief, so now you have several in different colors and won't need to take any of mine."

"Thank you, I really like them."

Rachel looked around the room as though she were confused.

"Anything wrong?" She walked behind the loveseat and leaning against it was a beautiful cherry wood sofa table.

"Hirsch, can you come here for a minute please?" Lying on top of the sofa table was a long wooden crate and attached to it was an envelope that said *For Hirsch*.

"Looks like this is for you too."

"What, more handkerchiefs?"

"I don't know, you better see." Danni removed the top part of the crate; on a wooden stand was the most magnificent miniature replica of his boat. He was speechless for a long moment.

"How did you do this?"

"Your father gave me a picture of it and I had it blown up, and the designer worked from the photo. See, look on the front; it says *Yahalom shel Hayam*, Diamond of the Sea."

"How did you get this in here?"

"I didn't, it was delivered last week when we were in New York. Our family caretaker came to the house and made sure it arrived safely."

"Racheli this is unbelievable, I love it and you even more."

"Well you better love me more." He kissed her. "Don't worry, no competition, my beautiful lady."

"Wait, now it's your turn," Danni said.

"What's my turn? You just gave me this gorgeous ring."

"That wasn't for Chanukah; I'll be right back stay here." He went to the hallway closet, took a small wrapped package out of his jacket pocket and walked back to the study. He placed it in Rachel's hand.

"This is for you, my lady."

"Thank you."

"Don't thank me yet, first see if you like it." Inside was a box with a diamond bangle bracelet with the same detailing that was outlined in her engagement ring.

"My God, Danni, this is gorgeous."

"Turn it over." Engraved on the back in Hebrew it said *I love you. -Danni.*

"I love you too and don't care how many people are in this house tonight. Hirsch, not only will you get some hanky but there will be plenty of panky!"

Fifteen

It was January 4, 1998; the holiday was over and Rachel returned to the
Knesset building. She continued preparing for the rigors of the task
at hand ensuring all facts were accurately documented. The Gerhardt
Dreschler trial was beginning in a little less than four weeks. Rachel
met with another witness named Ethel Schultz, whose maiden name
was Altman. Dreschler's mother's health became increasingly worse
and she needed professional care. He hired someone to look after her
at his Wannsee home. A private German nurse was very expensive. If
you hired a German Jew, the cost was practically nothing. Dreschler
went to the Jewish Hospital in Berlin looking for a medical registered
nurse to stay at his house. Whenever an SS officer entered the establishment, everyone became uneasy. A woman named Ethel Altman
from the hospital staff began working for the Dreschlers.

Another grueling reenactment of an iniquity from long ago left
the prosecuting counselor mentally drained. When she departed
the residence of Ethel Schultz in Rishon LeZion, all she looked
forward to was a relaxing evening at home. Suddenly she realized
that tonight Danni was hosting Ariella and her boyfriend, whom
he never met, out to a dinner celebration. Her twentieth birthday
had just passed and he wanted to do something special. She was
released from the army, having served two full years. After the
arduous day Rachel experienced and knowing how Ariella felt

about her, she didn't want to join the festivities. Regrettably that wasn't an option; her absence would make Danni feel bad and even though the girl didn't like her, it would be viewed as a snub. Either way, Rachel was in a no-win situation.

Danni was already home when she arrived.

"Hey handsome, you smell good."

"Yeah?"

"Very, yeah" Rachel answered with a smile. "What time will Ariella be here?"

"We decided to meet at the restaurant." They met at an intimate seafood, steak and barbeque bistro located in West Jerusalem. Ariella warmly greeted her father and politely said hello to Rachel. She returned the cordial formality.

"Happy birthday, Ariella."

"Thank you; I would like you to meet Erez Hadar." He was a handsome, tall Sephardic young man with olive skin and light brown eyes. Rachel nodded her head.

"It's very nice to meet you Erez, I'm Rachel."

"Yes, it's nice to meet you too."

Danni shook his hand and Erez looked at him. "Sir, it's a pleasure, I have heard so much about you."

Then he gave his daughter a small box and said, "Happy birthday, *motek*, (sweetheart), this is from us."

When she opened it, inside was a gold bracelet with her name written in Hebrew. Hugging Danni, she said, "I love it *aba*, thank you."

"You're welcome; I told you it's not just from me — it's also from Racheli." All she said was, "It's beautiful."

Changing the subject, Rachel asked Erez how the two met.

"We met in the army. Erez completed his active duty a couple of months ago and he's going to attend The Hebrew University of Jerusalem next month."

"That's great," Danni replied.

"What are you planning on studying?" Rachel asked.

"Architecture is really my interest and passion."

"My brother is an architect," and Danni added, "Not just an architect — but a famous one."

"Really, what is his name?"

"Michael Landau."

"Are you serious? Michael Landau is your brother?"

"Yes, he is." Ariella felt left out of the conversation and tried to change the subject.

"I'm starving; let's order." Erez ignored her interjection. "Your brother has designed some incredible buildings in London."

Rachel smiled. "He certainly has. If you like, I can arrange a telephone conversation and he can help guide you in the right direction of certain classes to focus your studies on."

"Do you mean it? That would be fantastic, thank you, Rachel."

"You're very welcome Erez. I'm going to be speaking with him tomorrow; can I give him your phone number?"

"Are you kidding? Of course you can." She took out a pen for Erez to write down his information.

Again Ariella chimed in with, "Let's order."

Danni glared at her childish, rude behavior. Rachel noticed his expression and tried to lighten the moment.

"You heard the birthday girl, let's order."

They were studying the menu and Ariella was annoyed.

"Oh now that *she* says let's order we're ordering?" Erez gave her a look and her father was ready to blow a gasket. Rachel got up.

"That's it; I can't do this tonight." She extended her hand to Erez. "It's been a pleasure meeting you." Danni stood and Rachel stopped him.

"No, please stay, I'll see you later." He followed her outside. "Go back inside; I just want to go home alone. I didn't want to come tonight and I shouldn't have, I said I'll see you later." There was a cab stand by the restaurant, and she hopped in one and it sped away.

When Danni went back inside he looked at Erez.

"Can you please excuse us for a moment?"

"Yes, sir."

"What the hell is wrong with you? I didn't raise you to act this way," Danni said once Erez left the table. "Rachel is and has always been nice to you."

"Don't you mean Racheli?" Danni was beyond the point of fury.

"Now you listen to me, my child."

"I'm not a child," she said, interrupting him.

"After this evening's performance, you most certainly are. I love you and always will but I am very ashamed of the way you acted tonight, and also at Chanukah. Let me make this clear, I love Rachel and with or without your approval, I'm going to marry her. I want you to be in my life however, I will not tolerate you treating her disrespectfully again."

He got up from the table and motioned for Erez to return. Danni shook his hand.

"You'll have to excuse me, I need to leave, but it was very nice to meet you."

"Thank you, sir, it was nice meeting you too."

"Dinner is on me, order whatever you like." Danni threw down a wad of money on the table and then walked out.

As Ariella watched her father leave the restaurant, her eyes began to water. She looked toward Erez for sympathy.

"What got into you tonight?" was all he said. She began to cry.

"Oh, now you too? You only like her because her brother's a big deal architect."

"That's not true," he replied defensively. "The way you described her, I thought we'd be eating with a monster; she was nothing but gracious and actually quite charming. Rachel went out of her way to be nice to you and to be honest; I don't blame her or your father for leaving."

Ariella, still crying, got up in a huff and left. He went after her.

"I'm sorry, I know you're upset and I don't want to hurt you more, but it's important that you realize she's a nice woman. My own mother hasn't asked me what classes I'm taking at the university, and a stranger showed true interest. It's obvious she's a good mother and clearly wanted to have a relationship with you."

Ariella stopped and put her arms around him. "I want my father and mother to be together."

Erez held her.

"And I wish that we lived in a perfect world, but we don't. You've told me how unhappy your parents were, yes?" She nodded in acknowledgment.

"Don't you see what you're doing Ariella? I've never met your father until tonight and I can see that he really loves you. The way you're acting is tearing him up inside, and after what happened tonight, I understand why he left. The army is supposed to strengthen and prepare us for life, but you still need to grow up. I realize that seeing your parents together would be wonderful. The brutal truth is it's not an option, and Rachel makes your father happy. So you need to think about how important his happiness is rather than what you wish could be," Erez said. He kissed and held her. "I know how warm and caring you are, that's why I fell in love with you."

She became calmer in his arms. "I love you too; forgive me."

"It isn't me you need to ask forgiveness from."

Rachel heard the door open and wasn't looking forward to the scene that was about to play out. She was wearing her pajamas and lying on the sofa in the den. Danni entered the room.

"I'm very sorry about what happened tonight." She was quiet. "Are you OK?"

Still, she spoke no words. "This will never happen again," Danni said. Rachel finally broke the silence.

"I shouldn't have left like that, it was a long day and my tolerance level is low."

"You're apologizing to me? You have nothing to be sorry about and have always been very gracious where my daughter is concerned. I don't know what's gotten into her."

"I do and I've told you, I'm not her mother, she hates the fact that you're with another woman. It's not your fault that Ariella doesn't like me, you can't force her to."

"Well I told her that with or without her approval I loved you and we were going to be married. I also said that I wanted her to be a part of my life but wouldn't condone her insolent attitude toward you."

"Ultimatums aren't good options to give our children." He came and sat on the couch where she was lying.

"I stated a fact, it wasn't an ultimatum." Rachel sat up, kissed and wrapped her arms around him.

"I'm exhausted," she said. He carried her to bed.

The next day Rachel made sure her schedule was light. David was returning to school on January 6, so Rachel went to Tel Aviv and spent his remaining time in Israel with him. The suitcases were already packed for the next day's flight. Looking at the luggage gave her an empty feeling. She loved having him there. It was the first occasion they had been there together since he was a baby. During some past summers, Dora and Nathan brought him to Israel for a few weeks, but Rachel never joined them. Though she wanted him to stay, he needed to resume his own life back in the states. They spent a relaxing and mellow evening together at home. Danni came to say goodbye and left shortly after; he wanted to give the mother and son some private time.

She called her brother and told him about Erez. Michael said he'd be more than happy to give him a call and make some course study suggestions. Then David got on the phone and his uncle wished him a safe trip back. The following morning Rachel took him to the airport. Before he left, David told her how special the holiday had been and that he wouldn't forget it. When he departed, Rachel proceeded to her office in Jerusalem.

Sixteen

It was 12:30 p.m. when Rachel arrived at the Knesset. There was a little Palestinian boy standing outside the building. She wondered why he wasn't in school. He was watching a trailer where a man was selling sandwiches, sodas and juice. She saw how the child looked at people coming and going with the afternoon treats. Realizing he was hungry, she walked toward him and spoke in Arabic.

"What would you like to eat and drink?" The shabbily dressed child looked down shyly and didn't answer her. Rachel tried again. "Come on now, tell me." Timidly, he pointed to a turkey sandwich on pita and a Coke. Rachel smiled.

"Please make it two turkeys and two cokes," Rachel said to the vendor. He nodded and seemed surprised at her generosity toward the Arab child. The little boy was happy and responded with, "Thank you, Miss."

"You're very welcome young sir. What's your name?"

"I'm Mustafa."

"It's nice to meet you Mustafa, I'm Rachel."

"That is a very pretty name."

"Thank you, why aren't you in school?"

"Today class ended early because of teacher meetings."

"I see, well, enjoy your lunch and have fun this afternoon."

"I hope you enjoy your lunch too, Rachel, goodbye." She waved as the child walked away.

"It was a very nice thing you did Mrs. Saunders," the vendor said to her before she entered the Knesset building. The lawyer was surprised he knew her by name and she then thought of all the notoriety on the trial.

"No child should go hungry."

"Enjoy the rest of your day, ma'am."

Rachel spent the afternoon alone in her office prioritizing case details in chronological order of relevance. It was almost 4:15 when Orley knocked on her door.

"This box just arrived from New York and Ariella Hirsch is here to see you." She was shocked to hear about her unexpected guest.

"Can you please put the box in that corner and ask Ariella to come in?"

Rachel saw how uncomfortable Ariella was when she walked into her office and tried to make her feel welcome.

"Hi, this is a nice unexpected surprise; can I get you something to drink?" Near her desk was a small refrigerator loaded with all types of beverages.

"No thank you, I'm fine. I wasn't sure you'd even see me.

"My door is always open to you, is everything alright?"

Ariella stood still, feeling sheepish. "I want to apologize for the way I treated you the other night, and also at your home on Chanukah."

"Apology accepted, I know that wasn't easy for you and appreciate the fact that you came here."

"Your brother called Erez today and he was thrilled. It was really nice of you to talk to him about my boyfriend."

Rachel acknowledged her sincerity. "You're welcome."

"My father is very angry with me," she said, and began to cry. Rachel felt bad and brought her a tissue.

"Your father loves you very much, he'll calm down and everything will be fine."

"Why are you being so nice to me?"

"I was hoping we could be friends like we were before I became involved with Danni. I don't know about you, I could use a drink; will you join me?"

Before Ariella could answer they heard a loud explosion and the room shook. Rachel was startled. "Are you OK?"

"Yes, I'm alright."

"My God, what was that?" She opened the door and people were out in the hall screaming, "A bomb went off in Sacher Park."

It was located near the Knesset. Sirens sounded in the building and over the intercom a voice was yelling, "Everyone evacuate the premises immediately, I repeat evacuate the premises immediately."

They walked down the stairs with the others and went outside. There were fire engines racing toward the park. It was a horrible, frightening scene. Police cars lined the street and told all pedestrians to leave the area.

"Ariella, call your mother and tell her you're OK. I'll call Danni and let him know that we're going to the house." She did as Rachel asked while they walked quickly to the car. The traffic was bumper to bumper. It took an hour and a half until they made it there.

Rachel turned on the television and the reporters said, "It was a terrorist attack. A suicide bomber from Hamas blew himself up at Sacher Park. Twenty-five children were killed and fifty more were injured." As they watched, Rachel saw a child she recognized lying among other dead children. It was Mustafa. She was stunned.

"Oh my God."

"Rachel what's wrong?"

"That little Palestinian boy, I know him."

"What, how do you know him?"

"He was outside the Knesset building earlier today, he looked hungry and I bought him lunch. His name was Mustafa. Oh my God, how could this happen?" Rachel was hysterical, and memories of Alon became vivid in her mind again, and she was devastated.

Ariella looked at her. "I'm very sorry." She went into the kitchen and brought Rachel a glass of water. Her cell phone rang.

"Hello Racheli, are you and Ariella home?"

"Yes we're here, where are you?"

"I'm at Sacher Park, it was Hamas."

"Yes I know, they announced it on the news."

"You sound upset."

"I'm fine, Danni; we'll talk when you get home. Just promise me you'll be careful," she began to cry again. "I want to call David and leave him a message on his cell that we're alright."

"Good idea, and don't worry about me, I'm fine."

"Can I speak to Ariella?" She handed Rachel the water. "Thanks, your father wants to speak to you. I'm going to call David and then take a shower, excuse me please."

"Hello, *aba*, where are you?"

"Hi, *motek*, I'm at Sacher Park. Racheli sounds upset, is everything OK with the two of you"?

"Yes, *aba*, it isn't what you're thinking." The question Danni posed made her feel bad, however, it was valid under the circumstances of her behavior. "There was a child in the park that Rachel recognized on the television, a Palestinian boy."

"Ariella, I don't understand." She told him the story that Rachel had told her earlier.

"Racheli has a nurturing, kind, warm heart."

"I know she does, *aba*, today I went to her office and apologized for the way I've been acting." She paused and became emotional. "Can you forgive me too?"

"Yes, of course, I love you, *motek*, and I'm happy you're both together and not alone. Did you call your mother?"

"Yes, Rachel told me to when we left the building."

"Would you like to stay with us tonight?"

"I would really like that; I'll call *eema* back and let her know."

After Rachel left David a message, she took off her watch. It was 7 o'clock. He'd be flying for another four hours. She went into the bathroom and got undressed, and let the warm water run over her still-shaking body. Rachel couldn't get the image of Mustafa out of her head. His smiling face when the vendor handed him the sandwich and soda was vivid in her mind. This innocent child was just like those who also perished during the Holocaust that weren't Jews. She couldn't stop trembling.

After the shower, Rachel went downstairs to be with Ariella. As she approached the kitchen the aroma was incredible.

"Wow, something smells wonderful. What are you making?"

"Chicken schnitzel, chips and salad." The table was beautifully set.

"You didn't have to do all this."

The young girl smiled, "I wanted to. Are you feeling any better?"

Rachel nodded yes. "I heard the phone ring when I was upstairs."

"It was *aba*; he's on his way home and also invited me to stay here tonight, I hope you don't mind."

"Why would I mind? This is your home." Ariella turned to Rachel and hugged her. She was surprised and caught off guard, but she returned her affection.

"I'm very glad you're here."

Danni walked in and was pleased at the scene he was witnessing.

"Can I join you ladies?" He embraced and kissed his daughter. She was happy to feel the reassurance of his love again and Ariella began to cry. Rachel was standing behind her and she smiled at him acknowledging their reconciliation. Danni realized she felt embarrassed by the emotional display.

"If you want something to cry about, I'll start to sing, that would bring anyone to tears." Danni said. Ariella started laughing.

Danni walked to Rachel with a greeting of warmth and affection.

"Look what your beautiful daughter made for dinner."

"Ah, schnitzel. Let me wash up." It was a warm atmosphere in the house — no hostility or animosity. Reflecting on the events of the day, a silly family squabble seemed so insignificant. After dinner Danni helped them clear the table. They all went into the living room and continued watching the news. Three more children were declared dead when they arrived at the hospital, bringing the total to twenty-eight. Ariella excused herself to call Erez; she hadn't spoken to him since the horrible incident occurred.

"Go ahead, *motek*, and by the way, I really like him."

"So do I," Rachel added. She smiled at them. "He's a good one, I think I'll keep him."

"Ariella told me that she apologized to you today, and she also told me about the Palestinian boy. I'm very sorry." Her anguish was apparent when looking at him.

"His name was Mustafa. I asked if he was hungry, and shy and embarrassed, he looked away. All I wanted to do was make him feel at ease."

"You could charm anyone, I'm sure you did."

"Before he left me I told him to have fun, he said thank you, smiled and walked away. It's unfair, why was a sweet innocent child killed?"

"Those fanatics have no regard for any life, Racheli, even when their own people are killed." Individuals living in Israel have become accustomed to hearing about and seeing tragedies of this magnitude or worse. In her mind she thought, "I'll never get used to this, ever," and she felt the same emptiness when Alon was taken away so long ago.

Rachel's cell phone was ringing off the hook. First Cheryl called to check in, then Michael from London, then David finally returned her call when he got off the plane. She assured all of them that she and Danni were OK, and once she got off the phone, she told Danni she was going up to bed.

While walking to their bedroom Rachel stopped and knocked on Ariella's door.

"I just wanted to say goodnight."

"Goodnight Rachel, sleep well." Danni was coming up the stairs. "Goodnight, *aba*."

"Night, *motek* have sweet dreams." As they entered the bedroom Danni shut the door. He began to kiss her and it was clear he wanted more. She looked at him.

"Would you be angry if I took a rain check?" He was unaccustomed to hearing her say those words.

Danni smiled. "I am not angry; this is one rain check I'm looking forward to cashing in on."

During the night Rachel had a bad dream and began to cry in her sleep. Danni woke her.

"Racheli; wake up." When she opened her eyes she was in a pool of sweat.

"What's wrong?" Rachel was breathing heavily, crying and didn't answer him. "Are you alright?" She nodded yes, got out of the bed, walked into the bathroom and shut the door. Rachel turned on the sink, ran the cold water and splashed it over her face. After regaining her composure, she went back to bed. Danni was sitting up waiting for her.

"Can I get you anything?"

"No thanks. I'm fine now; sorry I woke you."

"Was it about the little Palestinian boy?"

"His name was Mustafa and I'd rather not talk about it." He went to hold her, but she pulled away.

"Try and get some sleep, Danni."

The Palestinian conflict was a delicate spot for Israelis. In her mind she wondered if it had been an Israeli child that she knew, would he have addressed him by name rather than nationality.

Seventeen

The next morning Rachel was lying in bed awake looking at Danni as he began to stir. He woke up and asked her how she was feeling. Rachel expressed that she was a bit tired, and he encouraged her to take the day off since it was Friday, and everything shut down early in Israel in preparation for Shabbat anyway. She protested, explaining that she had too much work to do and that she would be just fine after a cup of coffee.

Remembering how she pulled away from him during the night, Danni kept his distance from her. Usually when they woke they kissed and spooned for a while. This morning was different; there clearly was distance between them. Rachel got out of bed, went to the bathroom and quickly came out.

"I'll make us a pot of coffee." Danni was having trouble reading her. He felt as though she was placing a barrier between them the way she had all those years before accepting Alon's death. Was this all because of yesterday?

After showering he went downstairs and found Rachel in the kitchen sitting drinking her coffee and in deep thought. When Danni entered the room he startled her. She got up and went to pour him a cup.

"That's OK, I got it." With that, Rachel grabbed her own mug and gave him an unaffectionate robotic kiss. "Have a good day, be careful and I'll see you tonight." Before he could answer she was up the steps.

Rachel took a quick shower, got dressed and knocked on Ariella's door. She woke her up to ask if she needed anything before she left for work, and Ariella said no, but told Rachel about her plans to meet up with Erez for lunch in Tel Aviv. Rachel thanked Ariella again for the wonderful dinner she prepared the night before, and Ariella smiled.

While in the car, Rachel thought again about the Israeli culture adapting to the crises set before them. Ariella had plans to meet Erez for lunch as if a bombing at Sacher Park hadn't happened the day before. Thoughts of Alon today were brighter than they had been in recent months. Even though his demeanor was softer than Danni's, he also took in stride the Middle Eastern turmoil and accepted the stringency of their society. It was something instilled in these Sabras from birth. It was hard for Rachel to understand and adapt to this attitude.

When arriving at the Knesset there was extra security at the building inside and out. She entered her office and saw the box in the corner that Orley had brought in yesterday. It was from Helena Krieger's assistant, Trudy. Orley knocked on the door to ask if Rachel needed anything, and they both lamented about the previous day's events, hoping that today would be uneventful.

It was almost noon and as much as Rachel tried, she couldn't concentrate. Orley buzzed her on the phone.

"Mr. Danni Hirsch is here to see you."

"Please send him." She was surprised by his impromptu visit. He shut the door.

"Hey Hirsch, to what do I owe this pleasure?" His manner was very serious and business-like.

"I wanted to let you know his name was Ahmed."

"Who is Ahmed?"

"His name was Mustafa Ahmed. I was told this morning that his parents came to the morgue last night after seeing him on television." Rachel looked at him.

"Thank you Danni." As he glanced at her eyes the life that gleamed in them over the recent months was fading again.

"I thought you'd like to know that a condolence note was sent to his — excuse me — I mean, Mustafa's family, just as was done for all the other Israeli children who were killed." Now her eyes were not only dull, they were also filled with tears. In his face the hurt was expressed from her coldness toward him during the night and again this morning. Rachel composed herself as best she could and nodded her head.

"Thank you again for letting me know." Then, feeling a tear fall on her cheek, she turned from him.

"I'll see you tonight."

Still looking away she heard him twist the door knob. Rachel quickly walked toward the entryway.

"Please wait." He released his hand and turned around. Danni saw her tears and pulled out one of the pocket handkerchiefs she gave him for Chanukah and wiped her eyes. She slightly smiled.

"Would you look at that, your hanky has come to my rescue for once."

"I don't think you want any rescuing from me, Racheli." She not only saw the wound of her actions in his expression, but also spoken from his heart and she felt awful.

"I owe you an apology — last night I was upset and took it out on you."

"No, you were angry at me because you think I don't care that Mustafa, a Palestinian boy, was killed. Just so you know I am affected by any innocent person being cheated out of life. Especially by the stupidity of someone else's sick twisted actions causing it. I also find it difficult to show sympathy to those who won't acknowledge that we do and have the right to exist here in this country. For this, I will not apologize to you or anyone else.

"I've lived with and have watched their hatred all my life and witness awful things that I hope you will never see. Those who deny our existence have caused these unspeakable actions against us. Please don't question my sense of integrity or humanity again; I find it hurtful."

She grabbed him firmly. "I won't, I promise."

He didn't reciprocate her affection.

"Please forgive me, I love you so much." With that he held and pulled her closer to him.

"Sometimes I'm not sure if you do." His insecurity was made apparent and stemmed from her love for Alon, whose presence was with them last night and this morning.

When those words fell from his lips it was as though a knife had cut through her. She looked at him, reached up and placed her hands on his face.

"Never doubt my love for you; my heart is yours." He knew that was only half true and she read it in his expression. "Danni, you also have to understand that I won't ever forget Alon."

He interrupted, "Or stop loving him."

She shook her head. "No, I will always love him and it's not the same as being in love with him — he's the father of my son. When something happens like Sacher Park, it brings it all back — the pain and sense of loss stirred inside me. I'm not saying it to hurt you; I see the look of doubt in your eyes. Please know what I feel for Alon is different than what we have. You woke me from a long sleep; just your touch makes my heart race. When you hold and make love to me, I feel an ecstasy that I've never felt before."

He was shocked by her words; Rachel was blatantly telling him that he was a better lover than Alon.

"Every day I thank God for you, Hirsch; don't ever doubt my love."

He kissed her. "OK, no more doubts. Last night when I was dreaming, you were right, it was about Mustafa, but the nightmare also encompassed some of the testimony I've been hearing regarding things Dreschler did — unthinkable things."

"What time is it?

"It's almost one o'clock."

"Racheli, have you eaten?"

"No."

"Let me take you out to lunch; the day is pretty much over."

"I'm not hungry, all I want to do is go home. Again, you were right, I shouldn't have come to the office. All day I couldn't focus on anything."

Danni called to check in at work to make sure there was nothing critical going on, and his coworker said no, but Danni still said he would be reachable on his cell if he were needed. Rachel shut her laptop and told Orley to go home early. They walked outside the building.

"I called Ariella before; she's meeting Erez for lunch and then going home to see her mom."

"Yes, I know, we spoke before I came to the office this morning. Where is your car?"

He pointed across the street. "I'll see you at home soon." After Rachel went to the garage, Danni spotted a flower vendor and bought her a beautiful bouquet of yellow tea roses. Danni owned two automobiles; she drove his white Mercedes sports coupe and he used the black BMW. When Rachel arrived, the black BMW was already there. She opened the front door of the house and lying on the table in the foyer were the yellow tea roses. As she was turning around, he was right behind her.

"The flowers are gorgeous, thank you; let me put them in water." Danni lifted her. "The flowers can wait, I can't."

He carried her upstairs to their bedroom.

The words she said to him repeated in his mind. *When you hold and make love to me, I feel an ecstasy that I've never felt before.*

"Racheli, I want you so much."

"You have me, Hirsch. I'm yours." A male ego is a strange mechanism; though Danni felt insecure about Rachel's feelings for him, she validated his masculinity and skills as a lover. With that, all his uncertainties subsided. Rachel nestled herself close to him and they both slept serenely. When they woke at 8:30. Danni smiled then kissed her.

"My beautiful lady, did you sleep well?"

She grinned. "Like a baby, and you?"

"After the workout you gave me, nothing would have woken me."

"You know what they say, Hirsch: A stimulating workout is good for the soul. Thank you for an incredible afternoon, handsome."

"The pleasure was all mine, my love, all mine. It was amazing Racheli, you're amazing."

"Well I don't know about amazing, but I'm starving. And get that look off your face, this time I mean for food, I didn't eat anything today. Aren't you hungry?"

"For you always, yes I'm very hungry too." Rachel sensed the revelry in his voice and was happy he felt reassured of the love she felt for him.

"A pizza would be perfect; I wish we were in New York, nothing like New York pizza."

"It's Shabbat, so everything is closed, but I have a frozen pizza. Not New York caliber, but it is really good."

"Hirsch, then frozen pizza we shall have."

"I want to take a quick shower, will you join me?" He followed her into the bathroom. She lathered him with his soap; one that smelled just like his cologne, and he loved the attention. They behaved like playful innocent children, laughing and splashing one another. Rachel accepted the events of the day before, she realized the concept of the Israeli culture is that life goes on and you must embrace every moment. We can't change the past; we can only learn from it and strive to make the future better. This was true of the Holocaust — always remember those who perished and never allow the future generations to forget. Making them aware will ensure the impiety is never repeated or revived again.

Danni threw on a pair of sweatpants and grabbed a blue T-shirt from his drawer. Rachel looked at him.

"Can I wear that?" Smiling he handed it to her. He thought of the first time they made love when he gave her another one to put on.

"It definitely suits you, very cute!"

"Thanks." They went downstairs. She put the beautiful flowers

— now a bit wilted — in water and hoped to revive them. The couple set up plates, cups and drinks. When the pizza was done, Danni brought it into the living room and he opened a bottle of wine.

"No wine for me yet, my stomach's empty. Let me eat something first, I'll start with the iced tea." As he poured her a cup, she set the pizza on their plates.

"Bon appetit."

Even though Rachel was little, she had a healthy appetite. Danni was amazed at what the petite lady could consume and it never showed on her, even at age 46. He was looking at her and began to laugh.

"What's so funny?" He took a napkin and wiped the tomato sauce off Rachel's nose. "Nothing, you're like a kid."

"Thanks, Hirsch — the pizza is pretty good, not like New York, but it isn't bad."

She started on her second piece. "Racheli slow down, you're going to get sick."

"I'm fine, can't keep up with me?" She went to pour herself a glass of the red merlot. He took the bottle from her and poured it for her. She held the glass by the stem, swirled, smelled it and then took a sip.

"It's delicious, very smooth." Rachel knew a lot about wine and Danni loved how worldly, refined and cultured she was.

"That was delicious, handsome."

"You're full?"

"Aha."

"How about you?"

"I'm getting there." She got up, put on the television and flipped through the channels.

"I don't want to watch the news if you don't mind, something funny would be good."

"Yeah; *Friends*, great show." He loved her enthusiasm and followed her every move.

"What?"

"I enjoy seeing you like this."

"Like what, Hirsch?"

"Hyper and full of energy, it reminds me of when we were kids."

"You think I'm hyper?"

"Yep, that's why everything you eat doesn't stick and gets burnt up."

"So tell me, what happens if it starts sticking, will you still love the plumper me?"

"I'd love you no matter what."

"Sure, you say that now."

"I say it always."

She suddenly felt light headed after drinking two glasses of wine.

"The wine is hitting me." Giggling, she said, "My fingers and toes are numb, pour me another glass please."

"I think you've had enough, Madam Lush." Still giddy, she said, "That's funny."

Danni was amused by her silly behavior and lifted Rachel onto his lap.

"You have very pretty eyes, Hirsch, and a really cute nose." She placed her forehead on his. "You smell good, too." Then Rachel put her head between Danni's shoulder and neck.

"Where is my wine?"

"I really think you had enough, just sit back and relax."

"Okey dokey, smokey." He started laughing. "We don't need to watch a comedy, you're providing one yourself."

"It's warm in here." Her face was hot as she rested on him.

"No, it's very comfortable; I think it's the alcohol." He had never seen her tipsy before. Even though she drank wine and knew much about it, Danni didn't recall seeing her have more than one glass. Perhaps the second drink was more than she could handle. Rachel closed her eyes and fell asleep while lying on him. He lifted and placed her back on the sofa then cleaned up. When Danni returned she was still in a deep sleep and he carried her upstairs and Rachel didn't stir until the morning.

When Rachel finally woke up, Danni pointed to the glass of water he left next to her, and she didn't seem to remember the events that had transpired the night before.

"You were very entertaining after the two glasses of wine you drank."

"What did I do?"

"Nothing bad, it was fun to watch. Honestly, you really don't remember?"

"I remember feeling lightheaded and sitting on your lap."

"You told me that I have pretty eyes and a cute nose."

"Well, you do."

"Racheli you were comical; I enjoyed seeing you let your hair down."

"Did I do anything crazy?"

"Not crazy, just adorable, and very childlike."

"I really drank two glasses of wine? Usually, I only have one."

"Not only two but you requested a third. I took control and didn't give it to you — it's fine, but sometimes it important to unwind."

"Unwind maybe, but unravel, no."

"It was memorable."

It was a chilly Saturday morning when Rachel got out of bed. The box from New York was on the chaise. She opened it, and the suit was magnificent. Rachel tried it on and studied its detail. It fit perfectly; Helena Krieger outdid herself with its design. The garment was indeed the most ideal ensemble to wear while she interrogated Dreschler on the stand.

Later that afternoon, Rachel called Cheryl to wish her a happy birthday.

"Hello, Cohen."

"Rache?"

"Yes, I just called to say hi! Oh come on, Cheryl, happy birthday! Have many more!"

"Thank you."

"Do you have anything special planned?"

"Yes, I am going to the theater with the children."

"That's great, and I have something funny to tell you. Last night

Danni told me I was plastered after I drank two glasses of merlot and I don't remember."

"Oh, I believe it."

"What do you mean you believe it?"

"Now come on Rache, I remember when we were younger, if you had more than one drink it was over," Cheryl continued, laughing between words, "you are a pretty funny drunk."

"You sound like Danni; he said I was very entertaining."

"What did you do?"

"I told you, I don't remember. This morning he seemed very amused."

"Rache, do you remember the jazz club we went to in college?"

"God, please Cheryl."

"You do remember! You had three martinis and decided to ask the Maître de if you could entertain the crowd. Apparently *Raindrops Keep Falling on My Head* was your favorite song."

"OK, Cohen, enough."

"I still think you're a good singer, and so did everyone else in the audience."

"I get it, not more than one glass of wine."

"Thank you for making me laugh on my birthday."

"You're welcome, I'm so happy my stupidities can make you happy, talk to you soon, enjoy the show."

The next call Rachel made was to the hospital in New York where Helena Krieger was staying. Almost one month had passed since she was admitted after having her stroke. Rachel contacted Helena's doctor every few days to check her progress. Dr. Burke told Rachel that Madam Krieger was doing much better, and she would be released on Monday. She would be taken to her home in the city, and a nurse would be on the premises providing round-the-clock care. Although she was recovering, the doctor explained that she would need extensive speech therapy in order to be able to express herself, and time would only tell regarding her mobility, which, Dr. Burke expressed, seemed grim at the moment.

But Rachel and the doctor both knew that Madam Krieger was a resilient woman. Rachel thought of all Helena had endured and lived through. She certainly was one who tolerated the most strenuous hardships life had to offer.

Eighteen

That Monday Rachel sat with her second-chair attorney Chayim Rabinowitz and sifted through many affidavits throughout the morning hours. It was early in the afternoon when she received an unexpected visit from Gerhardt Dreschler's lawyer and son. The lead prosecuting attorney was polite. Max Reinhart wasn't very receptive to her courteous behavior; she sensed it and knew something must have happened. Rachel extended her hand.

"Good afternoon Mr. Frece. Gentlemen, please come into my office, can I get either of you something to drink?"

"No thank you, Mrs. Saunders — let me get to the point," Reinhart responded.

"Go ahead."

"Mr. Frece went to visit his father this morning at Rimonim Prison in a rental car. When he came out, the tires were slashed and there was writing on the windshield in Hebrew. A security guard smiled and translated the words to him, it said: 'Go home, son of the Jew killer.'"

Rachel looked toward Alexander Frece; he was uncomfortable, intense and staring at her. Max Reinhart continued.

"There is no other proof than this; the security officer who proudly told him what it said had black ink on his hands. Now, you and I both know that not having seen him commit the act and only Mr.

Frece's observation of the ink on his hands would be considered to be circumstantial. He requested to see the Warden and was abruptly denied access to him."

Alexander Frece interrupted him. "Mrs. Saunders, Mr. Reinhart told me that you were the one responsible to seeing that my father was given shoes, socks and a blanket. Thank you for that. We came here today in the hopes that you would be able to have this current situation addressed."

Rachel saw the desperation in his eyes. "You're welcome, Mr. Frece."

Once again, 'the sins of the father' came into her mind.

"Mr. Frece, please write down the name of the rental company and I will contact them on your behalf; you won't be held accountable for the vandalism. Without question, I personally will look into this incident."

Max Reinhart was surprised at her civility toward Alexander Frece. Her demeanor toward him was much nicer than what she displayed to Reinhart in the past. The knife cuts both ways; Alexander Frece was openly non-confrontational or condescending toward her.

Before going to Rimonim Prison, Rachel called Danni and told him what happened. His involvement this time wouldn't be regarded as an act of weakness on her part. It was clearly a hate crime. He picked her up and drove to the facility. When they arrived both were escorted inside immediately, unlike her previous visit. While parking they saw a guard on duty in that area. Rachel glanced at his hands and, low and behold, the black ink Max Reinhardt described was still visible. Danni noticed it too. When they walked past him, he smiled and tilted his hat at them in an arrogant, pompous manner. Rachel saw the name on his uniform: Menasha Gold. They entered the prison and the warden was in the lobby just as he had been before. He wasn't happy to see Danni.

"Please, will you both come into my office?" he asked. When they entered, he shut the door.

Zvi Artandi looked at Rachel with his usual superior deportment.

"Does Max Reinhart run to you every time he has a problem?"

"Warden, I don't remember mentioning that I was here at the request of Max Reinhart."

His face went red.

"I'm impressed, you are very good at this game; it just so happens that is the reason why we have graced you with our presence. Perhaps if you took control of your staff, Mr. Reinhart wouldn't have to turn to me for help."

Danni looked at him. "Zvi, this is bad. The guard outside has black ink all over his hands. He's too arrogant to wash off the evidence."

"Danni, you don't know that he did it."

"OK, we'll play the parking lot security camera and see; I know there is one, play it now! My people know in every prison where the hidden surveillance cameras are and the only other person made privy to their locations is the warden. Zvi, there better be a tape or your job will be on the line for tampering with evidence. I do hope you have it and don't fuck up your career for a worthless piece of shit like Manasha Gold."

With that, the warden took the tape out of his drawer and put it in the VCR. The video confirmed that Menasha Gold did, in fact, vandalize Alexander Frece's rental car. Danni glared at the warden.

"Zvi, I'm placing him under arrest for vandalism and the act of performing hate crimes, make sure you fire Gold before I take him into custody," Danni continued, "The press is going to have a field day with this when they interview Max Reinhart and Alexander Frece. They are going to say that the Warden at Rimonim Prison wouldn't address the issue when asked to do so. This is what your response will be: the reason you wouldn't meet with Mr. Frece was because you had no comment until an investigation took place and the facts were reviewed. Once the misconduct was identified, the culprit was taken into custody and relieved of his duties at the correctional center. Is that clear, Warden?"

Zvi Artandi looked at Danni and nodded.

"You better get your staff in hand or you won't have a group to govern," Danni said.

Danni was right; when they returned home the vandalism was being broadcast all over the news. The press interviewed individuals who were Holocaust sympathizers and they commended Menasha Gold for the act, saying it was justifiable. Rachel was infuriated that the crime committed was being noted as an act of heroism and she expressed her feelings. Alexander Frece was being unfairly judged and persecuted for his father's crimes.

"Look, Racheli, in the eyes of the world he's the child of a twisted evil son of a bitch; it's understandable that the world views him in the same light."

"So what you're telling me, Hirsch, guilt by association is acceptable? Condemn someone blameless just because of who they know?"

As he listened to her retort, Danni still couldn't understand why Rachel always felt an allegiance to Alexander Frece and it bothered him.

"I don't understand why you feel sorry for this man."

"Not just this man, I would have the same empathy for anyone being tried for a crime they hadn't committed."

"Racheli, you can't save the world, no matter how much you want to. It's impossible."

"I'll say it again; his father was a Nazi bastard, and yes, I suppose the thought in the mind of others is that the apple doesn't fall far from the tree. But come on, Danni! We both met him in Vienna; he is nothing like Gerhardt Dreschler."

"I've told you, it could all have been an act, and if I were a gambling man, I'd have to make a safe bet that Max Reinhart will call him to the stand as a character witness. If this does happen, you're going to have to cross-examine him whether you like it or not. Not doing so will show prejudice for the defense against the prosecution."

She hated what Danni was saying but knew he was right.

"Don't worry; I'll do what needs to be done." Again, Rachel saw his annoyance at her empathy toward Alexander Frece. To some degree, she couldn't understand it either. There was something about him that incited compassion in her. Perhaps it was her innate perception of reading people; perhaps it was his charm; perhaps it was his demeanor of sanity in a world of insane behavior.

They were sitting in the living room and Danni changed the subject.

"What time are you flying to New York on Wednesday?"

She got up from the sofa and sat on his lap. "At 9 in the morning, and I land on Sunday in Tel Aviv at 5." Rachel kissed him. "Will you be able to take me to the airport?"

"You don't have to bribe me with kisses." She went to get up, but he pulled her back to him and reciprocated her affection. "Forget it, keep bribing me."

"When I get home tomorrow I have to pack; I'm going to work through the day on Wednesday and I want to be ready before my trip."

"Remember, you're only going to be gone four days, not four months."

"You're a riot, Hirsch. If you would let me finish, I was going to say that I have to pack a carry-on only; everything I need is at the brownstone. What's the matter, getting too weak to carry my luggage?"

"Racheli, carrying your suitcases is like a workout at the gym."

"Oh really, well perhaps I'll save you a trip to the gym and take more than a carry-on."

"Please, don't do me any favors." He started laughing. She didn't look amused. "I'm teasing you."

"A little tip: Never make fun of my travel wardrobe."

Danni saluted her. "Yes, my lady, I'll remember that. Now where were we?" With that, he continued kissing her.

Nineteen

It was mid-January in New York. Snow was on the ground and the air was cold. As much as Rachel missed the city, she hated the winter weather. When exiting the El Al arrivals terminal at JFK, a car was waiting outside with a name sign in the window reading *SAUNDERS*. On the way into Manhattan, Rachel called Danni to let him know that she arrived safely. Then, she listened to a voice mail message from Trudy. She said that Madam Krieger was looking forward to her arrival on Thursday, and that she had arranged for a lovely brunch.

Rachel didn't deal well with jetlag and was wound up. She ate on the plane but was still a little hungry. According to her stomach it was breakfast time. The driver stopped at an all-night store near the brownstone and she picked up a box of cereal with a container of milk. The townhouse was cold and immediately Rachel raised the heat up to 85 degrees to allow it to warm up faster. She put on her flannel pajamas and ate her snack.

She walked into her bedroom and surprisingly saw a message flashing on her answering machine; most everyone knew she was away.

"Hello Mrs. Saunders, this is Dr. Heffner's office calling to confirm your 8:30 appointment on Thursday, January 15. If you are unable to make it, please let us know." The appointment was scheduled for the following day, but she had completely forgotten to cancel it when she went to Israel. However, she decided to keep it since it coincided with this trip.

The next day, the doctor greeted her warmly.

"Hello Rachel, good to see you."

"Hello, Dr. Heffner, it's nice to see you too."

"I feel like I'm treating a celebrity; perhaps I should ask for your autograph, with all the media coverage about this big trial in Israel."

"I'll leave my signature on the check I write you today."

"How have you been feeling?"

"Well thank you, though the last few months have been a bit stressful at times, I'm alright."

After he poked, prodded and did his yearly series of blood work, the physician said he'd call tomorrow with her test results. The only thing found last year was an elevation in Rachel's cholesterol.

"Doctor, the best way to reach me is on my cell — I'll leave the number with your nurse." His office was always busy and she was there over two hours before leaving. It was 10:45 when Rachel looked at her watch and hopped in a cab to Helena's home. She couldn't have timed it better — it was exactly 11 when the taxi arrived at the highrise.

After a warm greeting from Trudy, Rachel immediately went into Helena's bedroom. Her color was back, and Rachel was happy to see that Madam looked better than she had during their last visit. Rachel sat in a chair beside the elderly woman's bed. She leaned down to kiss Helena on the forehead and grabbed her hand. It was evident that the fashion mogul was thrilled in her presence.

"Helena, you look beautiful, I'm so happy to be here with you." She was able to nod her head slightly to acknowledge Rachel's remarks. The housekeeper wheeled in a magnificent large cart with eggs, assorted smoked fish, bagels and dessert pastries. A beautiful table had been set in the bedroom for the meal. Everything looked wonderful. Trudy fixed a plate for Helena and went by her bed to feed the designer.

Rachel made a gesture to take the plate. "Please, let me."

Trudy obliged. Helena's eyes filled with tears, embarrassed that she was unable to eat by herself.

"Come now, no need for tears, I didn't prepare or cook any of this, I'm sure it's delicious." Trudy smiled and a faint smirk emanated from Helena's face. Rachel had a gift of giving people a sense of comfort. Her kindness always put them at ease.

When lunch was over, Trudy left the two women alone and went into the living room.

"Are you tired, Helena? Would you like to take a nap?" Rachel asked. She shook her head slightly to motion no.

"I owe you an apology; I haven't thanked you for the superb suit you made for me. I love it. You have outdone yourself; it's gorgeous."

Slowly, she began to try to articulate Dreschler's name, and it was difficult for Rachel to understand her words. But she knew what Madam was trying to say.

"Yes, in about three and a half weeks the inquiry will begin."

"Come — I want to come, I am better," Helena said with slurred words.

"Helena, I don't know if coming to the trial is a good idea after what you went through five weeks ago. Don't worry; I told you I will be your voice."

"See him — I want to see him." Rachel didn't know how to respond and saw that she was getting agitated.

"Let me speak to Dr. Burke." Helena stared at Rachel intensely. "Let's see what the doctor says, now you need to rest and get some sleep, I'll be back tomorrow around noon if that's alright?" Answering in a tone that lacked clarity, Helena said yes. Rachel kissed her and walked out of the bedroom.

"Trudy, have a good afternoon, thanks for everything. I'll see you tomorrow."

"You're very welcome Rachel, is there anything special you would like for lunch? Madam Krieger's chef, Charles, would welcome preparing any favorite dish of yours."

"Please, don't go to any trouble on my account."

"No trouble at all, Madam Krieger was really happy today. You have a wonderful, kind way with her." Rachel smiled.

"Trudy, whatever Charles prepares will be fine, have a good afternoon." When she left the penthouse, a feeling of intense sorrow broke her heart when she remembered the once-regal lady who refused to be defeated by the hardships forced upon her. Helena's determination to endure and be at the trial gave credence to the woman's remaining inward strength.

On her way home, Rachel stopped at D'Agastino's Supermarket and bought a few things. It was almost 3 p.m. in New York and 10 p.m. in Israel, so she was feeling the jetlag. Before she fell asleep back at the townhouse, she made sure to call Dr. Burke.

"Hello, Doctor, it's Rachel Saunders. I spent some time today with Madam Krieger and I agree she's doing much better. May I speak with you for a moment on a strictly professional level?"

"By all means, Mrs. Saunders, please do."

"I'm sure you're aware of the trial in Israel regarding Gerhardt Dreschler."

"Yes I am, and of your participation."

"Madam Krieger strongly expressed an interest in being at the proceedings. You and I both share a hippocratic oath of confidentiality. I think Helena's strong determination to recover from the stroke is driven by her desire to be present at the tribunal. I was hoping if we transported Madam on her private plane cautiously, you would allow the journey if you feel she's up to it."

"When would this trip take place, Mrs. Saunders?"

"If she arrived in Israel the second week of February, that would allow her time to settle in comfortably, which would be a month from now. I assure you, she'll receive the finest health care there."

"I have no doubt, that country is noted for its medical advancements. Let's see how she does over the next few weeks, and if Madam

Krieger continues her positive progress, I may allow her to make the journey."

"Thank you, Doctor, that's wonderful news."

"You're very welcome, Mrs. Saunders; I'll be by to visit her later this afternoon and the speech therapy begins tomorrow."

"Very good, enjoy the rest of your day, Doctor."

"Thank you, Mrs. Saunders. I bid you the same, goodbye."

Rachel was pleased to hear that the doctor was open to the possibility of Helena making the trip. She hoped Helena would continue to make progress so she would finally be able to confront her demons.

Just as Rachel went to lie down, Cheryl called her, and she picked it up even though she was ready for bed. The conversation was short; Rachel explained that she was suffering from jetlag, so they quickly confirmed their dinner plans for Saturday, and Rachel promptly fell asleep.

When she woke up it was 11 p.m. in New York and 6 a.m. in Tel Aviv. Rachel called Danni to say good morning, and she told him about her meeting with Helena, how she expressed her desire to be at the trial, and her subsequent conversation with the doctor. Danni wondered if it would be wise for Helena to do so much traveling in her delicate condition, and Rachel assured him that she would only go if the doctor gave her the green light. Danni said he would make all the necessary arrangements if she were to make the trip. Rachel was reminded — yet again — how much she loved Danni. After they hung up, she felt a sense of emptiness. Soon after, she went in the kitchen and fixed herself a bowl of cereal since her body thought it was time for breakfast.

Again, she picked up the phone and dialed.

"Hey Hirsch, it's me again. I had a very important question to ask you, what are you eating for breakfast?"

"That's your important question?"

"It certainly is. You know that breakfast is the most important meal of the day."

"I was just about to pour myself a bowl of cereal."

"Oh really, what kind?"

"Quaker Granola, why?"

"No way."

"Racheli, are you OK?"

"I'm fine; it just so happens I'm having the same here right now and you know how much I hate eating by myself. Could we have breakfast together? This way you wouldn't seem so far away. When we hung up before I felt like something very important was missing, and you're the something. There, I said it — you should be reveling in this moment where I'm bearing my soul to you."

"Pretty lady, I felt the same way, and the pleasure would be all mine if you dine with me this morning. I wish you were here; my coffee isn't as good as yours."

"I hope that isn't the only reason you're hungry for my absence."

"Racheli, you know it isn't'."

"Well, maybe I need to hear it."

"Are you sure everything is alright"?

"Yes."

"When you come home, I'll show you how much I missed you."

"I'm smiling. Have a wonderful day, handsome, speak to you tomorrow."

Even though she didn't fall asleep until 2, Rachel felt more rested than she had the previous morning. When she got out of bed, her cell phone rang.

"Hello, Rachel? It's Dr. Heffner."

"Good morning, Doctor. Is everything OK?"

"I just got your blood work back from the lab; can you stop by my office today?"

When he said the words, Rachel felt a knot in her stomach. Last year when her cholesterol was a bit elevated, he had just told her about it over the phone.

"Is something wrong?"

"No, however I'd rather talk to you in person if possible. I have an opening at noon."

"Alright, Doctor, I'll see you then."

Rachel was nervous, and after thinking for a moment she remembered her lunch plans with Madam and called her to reschedule. She asked Trudy if it would be possible to change lunch to dinner, and she said it wouldn't be a problem. Not even taking time for her morning cup of coffee, she took a quick shower, got dressed and hopped in a cab.

"Mrs. Saunders, I'll let Dr. Heffner know you're here," the receptionist said when Rachel entered the office.

Oh God, she thought, *even though he said everything was alright, it must be bad if the nurse is interrupting him to announce my arrival.*

A few minutes later he popped his head into the waiting room.

"Rachel, right this way please." Once she was seated in his office, she looked at him.

"Doctor; please tell me what's wrong!"

"I told you, nothing is wrong — you're pregnant!"

Rachel went silent and stared at him blankly for several minutes before finally uttering, "I'm what? That can't be."

"Yes, you are approximately three weeks pregnant."

"How can that be?"

"Do you really need me to explain it to you?"

"No, I don't mean that. I'm 46 years old; how can I be pregnant?"

"At this age, some women are very fertile — even more so than when they were younger. I wanted to tell you the news in person instead of over the phone. It's a lot to take in. And by the way, your cholesterol was much better this time."

Her thoughts were racing.

"Last week I had two glasses of wine and I now know I shouldn't have in my condition. Also, I would not have taken this trip here now, since flying during your first trimester is not recommended."

He smiled and was pleased at her instinctual maternal concern.

"Don't worry, I'm sure you're fine — it's very early, however, at your age you will need to be very careful and have an amniocentesis. Here is a copy of your bloodwork; give this to your OB/GYN."

He assured her it would be OK to fly back to Israel that Sunday since she was in the early stages. She was shocked, and she couldn't stop thinking about what Danni would say when she told him.

Twenty

Rachel arrived at Madam Krieger's penthouse later that afternoon. Her speech therapist was leaving and the evening nurse had just arrived. Trudy escorted Rachel to Helena's bedroom before leaving for the night.

"Hi, did you have a good day?" Rachel said, sitting next to Helena.

She replied with difficulty. "It was a long day."

"Are you feeling any better?"

"Yes."

"I just saw your speech therapist leaving, how did it go?"

"It isn't easy for me."

"Be patient with yourself and the words will come."

As Rachel sat and helped her have dinner, she seemed more comfortable with Rachel's assistance than she had been before. After they ate, Helena looked into Rachel's eyes.

"What's wrong?" Helena asked.

"Nothing, why?"

"Far away, you look far away." It was difficult to understand her speech. The lawyer was growing accustomed to the sounds and was able to decipher most of what she had to say. Rachel changed the subject.

"Helena, I spoke to Dr. Burke yesterday and he said if your progress continues as it has, he may let you fly to Israel for the trial." When she heard Rachel's words, a look of excitement appeared on her face. "But you have to promise me that you won't push yourself too quickly. I told him that if you came the second week of February, you would have time to settle in since Dreschler probably won't testify until the third or fourth week of the trial."

"I will be there."

Rachel smiled. "I believe you will. When I spoke to your doctor I told him you would fly to Israel on your private plane. Danni will make sure everything is organized when you arrive."

"How is Mr. Hirsch?"

"He's well," Rachel said with a smile.

"Please let me see your ring." She lifted her hand to show the diamond engagement band.

"It's beautiful. When are you getting married?"

"Hopefully, shortly after the trial is over."

"You seem excited."

"I am; he's a wonderful man and I love him very much." Rachel began to cry.

"What's wrong, please tell me," Helena said softly.

"Just between us?"

"Yes, just between us."

"I found out today that I'm pregnant."

Helena smiled as best she could. "That is wonderful news, why the tears?"

"What if he isn't happy when I tell him?"

"Of course he'll be happy, he loves you. Are *you* happy about the baby?"

"Yes I am, especially knowing the baby is a part of him. This is going to sound crazy, but I've only been gone two days and I feel as though we're apart for weeks and I miss him so much. I can't believe I'm talking like this."

"It's good that you are. I think of you like a daughter. You're a good girl and I want you to have joy always. You'll see, when you tell him about the baby, he'll be very happy."

Helena asked Rachel when she was flying back to Israel, and Rachel told her she was going back on Sunday. However, as soon as the words came out, it dawned on her that maybe she should return earlier — she didn't want to wait to tell Danni the news.

"I don't know if it's my hormones or just a spontaneous whim, but I want to go back tonight."

"Call, call the airline and see." Rachel grabbed her cell phone and dialed Continental Airlines since they flew directly to Israel, and EL AL had no scheduled trips on Friday due to Shabbat. The only available flight was from Newark, and she didn't care about the price of the ticket even though it was more than the one she already had.

"Go," Helena said. It was 7 p.m. and the flight was going to leave at 10:50, so Rachel was going to have to skip dinner.

She looking at Helena. "This is crazy," she said.

"It's not. Go home, child." She hugged and kissed her surrogate mother.

"Thanks, I love you." With that, Helena began to weep. The words rang true; in her heart, Rachel was going home.

Helena's doorman hailed a cab for Rachel, and she rushed to the brownstone to pack. She asked the driver to wait outside for a few minutes and then to take her to Newark. No more than fifteen minutes later, Rachel was back outside and in the taxi. Realizing she and Cheryl had plans for Saturday night, she quickly called her and explained that she had to return to Israel that night, but didn't reveal the big news. Cheryl said she would let Rachel make it up to her. And with that, she was on her way to the airport.

Twenty-One

On Saturday afternoon, the plane arrived at Ben Gurion Airport. As Rachel exited customs, she turned on her cell phone and there were messages from Danni, and he was wondering why he hadn't heard from her in a few hours.

Outside the terminal she hopped into a cab, told the driver where to go and dialed Danni on her cell.

"Hello, beautiful."

"Hey handsome, where are you?"

"I'm at home; I've been trying to reach you. I was worried."

"Really, you were?"

"Yes."

"I slept later and my cell phone was off. But Hirsch, I sent you a little something that should be arriving to your house in about fifteen minutes, so don't go anywhere."

"Nothing will arrive here in fifteen minutes, Racheli. It's Shabbat — no deliveries." She almost started laughing.

"Now that's a shame, they promised me it would be delivered today."

"Maybe it will be here on Sunday; I'm not working until Monday. I'll be home until I come to pick you up at the airport. Are you going to tell me what it is?"

"Nope, you're going to have to wait."

Just as she hung up, the taxi turned into the cul-de-sac where Danni's house was. When she got out, Rachel rang the bell. He opened the door and had a look of shock and confusion on his face.

"Hirsch, I told you to expect a delivery today, don't you know by now never to doubt my words?"

While standing in the doorway, he lifted Rachel and gave her the most passionate kiss.

"Now that's one hell of a greeting, I missed you and needed to come home, tomorrow seemed like an eternity."

"You never cease to amaze me." She started to laugh.

"What's so funny?"

"Oh, just what you said, if you think this is amazing, wait, you haven't heard anything yet."

"What are you talking about?"

"Can we go inside please? I think we've given the neighbors enough of a show."

He put her down, grabbed her carry-on bag and shut the front door. She walked into the kitchen and Danni followed her. Rachel poured herself a glass of Perrier.

"Ah, that's good."

"I can't believe you're here, would you please tell me what's going on?"

He sat down and she sat in his lap. Her eyes filled with tears.

"Racheli, what's wrong?"

"Nothing, I'm just really happy to see you." Even though it was her early stages of pregnancy, she was hormonal and couldn't decide how to tell him.

"All the time I was on the plane, I was trying to figure out how I was going to say this."

"Say what?"

She stared at him. Again he repeated, "Tell me what?"

"When I was in New York, I had a doctor's appointment; it was my yearly physical."

His face turned serious. "What's wrong? Please tell me."

"The doctor did the usual blood work and …"

"Yes, please tell me what?"

"Are you ready for this?"

"Racheli, just tell me."

"I'm pregnant. Approximately three weeks," Rachel said. "Ta-da!"

Danni's grave expression turned to the biggest smile she had ever seen. "Are you sure?"

She nodded. He was delighted; filled with joy and began to cry. The only other time Rachel saw him get so emotional was when Alon died.

"I was worried how you'd feel about a baby at our age." He placed his hand on her stomach.

"I feel incredible; it's the most wonderful gift, thank you."

She felt his sentiment and was pleased. "No need to thank me, you helped. This wonderful gift is ours together." She kissed him.

"How do you feel?"

"Good, really I do."

"Have you had any morning sickness?"

She started to laugh. "No, it's too early, but I didn't have it with David during my entire pregnancy. It's been such a long time since I was expecting a baby — almost 23 years to be exact. Now we'll see if your word holds true, Hirsch."

"What are you talking about?"

"One thing I do remember before I went into lush mode last week."

"I still don't know what you're talking about."

"Do you recall me asking if you'd love me even if I became chunky? Your answer was that you would love me no matter what, but now we will really see."

"I can't wait until you're huge," he said joyfully.

"I don't want to rain on your parade, but I didn't get huge the last time, just plump."

"Well, then I can't wait until you're overly plump."

"Just getting plump would have been sufficient, thank you. I don't want to tell anyone else yet, not until after the trial. If the media gets hold of this, they would have a field day.

"No one else except you and me," Danni replied.

"Oh, and Helena. I told her the day I found out because I needed someone to talk to."

"OK, no one else except you, me and Helena." He paused. "Are you hungry?"

"No, I ate on the plane and I'm messed up again with jetlag."

"Come on, I was going to barbecue a couple of burgers. We'll eat in here since it's cold out. Danni knew how much Rachel loved barbequed food.

"I'm going to go upstairs and change while you dazzle me with your cooking expertise."

When she came back, the table was neatly set and a gorgeous salad was placed in the center.

"Everything smells good. Oh yum, you got the pickles I like."

The bell rang and they looked at each other.

"I'm not expecting anyone."

"Looks like you forgot to call your girlfriend when I was upstairs and tell her I came home a day early."

"You're right; I got very involved with the food." Rachel went to answer the door. It was Ronni, Danni's son, and a girl was with him. He looked surprised to see Rachel and immediately hugged her.

"Hi Rachel, I thought you weren't coming home until tomorrow."

"I surprised your Dad and came a day early. It's wonderful to see you, Ronni."

"Thanks, it's good to see you too." She glanced at the young lady who escorted him.

"Hello, I'm Rachel. It's very nice to meet you," she said.

The girl smiled. "Hi, it's nice to meet you too. My name is Gila."

"Excuse me, Rachel, this is my girlfriend Gila."

"Please come inside."

"I spoke to my father earlier today, he sounded lonely with you being away, so I thought we'd surprise him and come over."

"You're a good kid." They all walked to the kitchen. Danni hugged Ronni.

"This is a nice surprise."

"I was telling Rachel that when we spoke earlier you sounded lonesome. Aba, this is my girlfriend, Gila."

"Hello Gila, it's very nice to meet you. I'm Danni, welcome."

"Thank you Mr. Hirsch, it's very nice to meet you."

"Please, call me Danni."

"This is a treat and you're just in time for dinner. It's nothing fancy, we're having hot dogs and burgers. Gila, how do you like your burger?"

"Medium-well please, thank you."

"Ronni, I know you like yours burnt."

"Thanks, Aba."

Gila was a pretty blonde who was about 5'6" with blue eyes. She was friendly, yet on the shy side. Ronni, now 24, was a paratrooper with the 35th Brigade of IDF. He trained all new incoming soldiers and was dedicated to his position. Danni was proud of his accomplishments. Their personalities were different; his son's emotions were less guarded.

They ate a wonderful meal; everyone seemed to be enjoying the evening. Rachel felt like it was a double date with another couple and kept the thought to herself. Danni may have gotten a kick out of the observation; however it may have embarrassed the other pair. Ronni and Gila gestured to help clean up, but the host and hostess told them to leave everything and they would take care of it.

"Thank you, it was a wonderful evening," Ronni said as they got ready to leave.

"Yes, thanks for having me to your home; it was so nice meeting you both."

Rachel gave her a hug. "Come again."

Danni kissed her. "Yes, please do."

Once Ronni and Gila drove away, the two went back to the kitchen to finish cleaning up. Danni was reluctant to have Rachel help, but she insisted that she was fine. The last time Ronni brought a girl home was in high school, so Danni was surprised and realized he must really like her. They finished cleaning up the kitchen and went to bed.

Upon waking Rachel called Dr. Ari Kashan, who was the physician who delivered David. He happened to have a cancellation for the same day, so Rachel decided to take the appointment. She went downstairs to find Danni sitting in the kitchen, and told him she was able to get in at the last minute for that afternoon.

"Great, I'll join you."

"Really?"

"Of course, I don't want you to go by yourself."

Rachel smiled and poured herself a bowl of cereal. When she was finished, she went upstairs to get ready and they headed to the doctor's office.

Before Dr. Kashan examined her, they sat together in his office.

"Rachel this is a lovely surprise. I knew you were in Israel preparing for the Dreschler trial, but I didn't think I would see you."

"Surprise! I would like you to meet my fiance, Danni Hirsch." It was the first time Danni heard her refer to him as her fiance, and he liked the way it sounded.

"Mr. Hirsch, it's a pleasure to meet you."

"It's nice to meet you too, Doctor."

"Rachel, tell me — how is David?"

"David is great; he's in his first year at Yale Medical School."

"That's terrific, so what brings you here today?"

"Doctor, at my age I'm going to have a baby. In case you were wondering, this handsome man is the father." Danni glanced at her — not amused — and was embarrassed by Rachel's remark.

The doctor laughed. "I had a hunch." Dr. Kashan extended his hand. "Congratulations, Mr. Hirsch."

He smiled and reciprocated the gesture. "Thank you, Doctor."

Rachel told Dr. Kashan she was three weeks pregnant, and explained how she found out while in New York when she went for her yearly physical. As she explained, Rachel gave the doctor a copy of the blood work.

"I arrived in Israel last night, if I had known I was expecting; I never would have gone to New York. Over a week ago, I also had two glasses of wine and would not have done that either."

"That's not a problem; it's only the very beginning of your first trimester. From this point forward we will regulate what you do. Go into the examination room and change."

"Racheli; I'll be in the waiting area." She seemed disappointed and looked toward the doctor.

"Dr. Kashan, even though it's early, are you going to do a sonogram?"

"Yes, I am."

"Can Danni come in and see that?"

"Certainly, Mr. Hirsch, please do. First I'm going to give you an internal exam." The doctor sensed Danni's discomfort as he uttered the words. "Mr. Hirsch, how about you wait in my office and I'll come and get you when we are ready to do the sonogram?"

Danni looked relieved. "Sounds great, Doctor, and please call me Danni."

"Rachel go change, I will keep Danni company in the meantime."

The two men chatted briefly while Rachel changed. Danni explained that he and Rachel weren't going to mention the pregnancy to anyone yet, which Dr. Kashan understood of course, since it was still so early. He also told the doctor about Ronni and Ariella — ages 24 and 20 — so he understood that times were different when his ex-wife had been pregnant. Husbands usually didn't go to the doctor with their wives, so it was nice for Danni to be more involved than he had been before. But Dr. Kashan could sense that with the newness of the experience came uncertainty for Danni.

"Danni, I know this time is a different experience for you; are there any questions you may have that I can answer?"

He became quiet and sheepish when Dr. Kashan posed the question.

"You can ask me anything, really," he continued. Danni paused.

"When my ex-wife was pregnant, she told me that her doctor said it wasn't a good idea for us to ..." Danni trailed off.

"To what?"

"He said it wasn't a good idea for us to be close with one another during that time." The doctor laughed.

"It's perfectly alright for you to have intercourse with Rachel during her pregnancy."

"Is it really?"

"Yes, so long as she is feeling OK, it will not harm the baby."

"Thank you, Dr. Kashan."

"You're welcome; I'm going to examine Rachel now."

As he sat in the doctor's office, Danni was thinking about what Sarit told him when she was expecting their children. He wondered if her doctor said they shouldn't have sex or if she didn't want to. From the discussion they had the night before, it was clear that Rachel's relationship with Alon during her pregnancy with David was different than it had been between he and his ex-wife. Sarit never seemed to enjoy the intimate moments they shared.

The door opened.

"Danni, I'm ready." He followed the doctor into the room where she was lying on the examination table.

"Dr. Kashan, is everything alright?"

"Yes, just fine." Danni smiled and took her hand while the doctor was rubbing gel on Rachel's stomach. Then he began the sonogram, and pointing to the tiniest speck on the screen, he said, "There it is."

The two were filled with emotion as they viewed the monitor.

"Looks good, ladies and gentlemen; it looks very good. Rachel, I want to see you back in three weeks and we'll do an amniocentesis because of your age, and then we'll do another three weeks after the first one. I'm also prescribing prenatal vitamins, please take one every morning."

"I will, doctor — whatever you say."

"Try and take it easy, but as long as you're feeling well, you can continue to be close with one another." The doctor smiled as he referred to Danni's wording.

"Thank you, Dr. Kashan."

"You're very welcome." He shook Danni's hand again. "Good luck to you both."

Twenty-Two

A week had passed since her appointment with Dr. Kashan. Rachel was getting ready for work and suddenly felt nauseous. Danni watched as she ran to the bathroom. He stood by the door and waited for her to come out, but just as she said she was OK, the uneasy feeling in her stomach returned and again she raced back inside. Upon her second exit, Danni was standing with a glass of ginger ale and a package of crackers. He suggested that she stay home, but she protested, as there was still a lot of work that needed to be done. She took a few sips of ginger ale and nibbled on a cracker, hoping to settle her stomach.

Rachel sat and waited until the queasiness subsided. Rachel smiled.

"See, I'm feeling better."

"How about I drive you?"

"No really, it isn't necessary."

"Promise me if you don't feel well, you'll come home."

She raised her hand and was firm in her decision. "I promise." But she knew that nothing would keep her from her task.

When Rachel arrived at the Knesset, Chayim Rabinowitz was there waiting for her in his office. She knocked on the door.

"Yes, please come in."

"Good morning, Chayim did you have a nice weekend?"

"I did, and you?"

"It was very enjoyable, thank you." Chayim was a quiet reserved gentleman who had never been married and devoted himself entirely to his profession. His legal reputation was steadfast; her co-counsel was precise in following protocol and procedures. When he was asked, he gave Rachel guidance on various regulations of the state. She was unfamiliar with certain policies and had some reservations about procedural matters. His knowledge was a critical contribution and the lead prosecutor learned a great deal from him. Chayim was well-aware that Rachel was running the show, although she never presented herself as such. He thought she was bright and intuitive; each one's personality complemented the other. Their collaboration made them a powerful team.

"Rachel, I think our witness order of appearance in the courtroom is perfect."

"I agree, Chayim, and if everything stays on track as we project, Dreschler will be called to the podium three weeks into the trial."

That same Sunday at Rimonim Prison, Max Reinhart met with the commandant. Even though Mossad had proven he was not, in fact Werner Frece, but Gerhardt Dreschler, the defendant insisted his attorney address him as such.

"Werner, it's important for us to call your son to the stand as a character witness. We need to let the presiding inquiry counsel see what your life was like after the war."

"No, Max, he's been through enough and knows nothing of my past years in Germany," Dreschler said.

"I've been saying for several months that you need to enlighten him, and you need to do so before next Sunday. When the prosecuting witness testimony comes to light, whether it is true or false, he cannot appear shocked in the courtroom," Reinhart said. "The bottom line is you were an SS officer of the Third Reich; it's a known fact, and the state has solid evidence proving so. All I can do is try to portray you as a soldier whose actions were predicated on following procedures specified by your superiors. He must testify, so talk to your boy; say you were obeying government regulations. Make sure Alexander knows it was a time in your life you weren't proud of."

"Understand this; I don't want to say anything, Max," Dreschler replied.

"In order to represent you to the best of my ability, you must speak with your son. Not calling him to testify would be a big mistake. He is the one witness who can show you as a caring, loving and nurturing individual. Besides, the woman acting as head counsel for the state—"

"What is her name?" Dreschler interjected.

"Rachel Saunders. I don't think she'll be rough on a cross examination. It was evident when I saw her speaking to him; she was sympathetic and somewhat delicate in her approach, trust me on this. The only other person that will help give some credibility to a gentler side of you would be the nurse who took care of your mother when she was ill, and her not being of Aryan descent should work to our advantage," Max sighed. "This is all I have to show favor of your moral fiber."

"Very well, Max, I'll allow you to call Alex to the stand. But if that Saunders woman takes my son apart, be prepared to counter her argument."

"I don't think that will happen."

"I mean it, Max, you better be prepared."

That evening when Rachel returned home Danni hadn't arrived yet. She went upstairs to change into her silk pajamas, then proceeded to the living room and turned on the T. V. She laid down on the sofa and dozed off. Suddenly Rachel was stirred by his kiss and wrapped her arms around him.

"Hey, handsome."

"Sorry, I didn't mean to wake you."

"It was a nice way to be woken up."

"Racheli you look tired, are you feeling better?"

"Yes, stop being such a worry wart."

"What about dinner?"

"I'm not too hungry, I had some soup for lunch. I'm glad to be holding that down at least."

"You have to eat more," he said sternly.

"Why are you angry?"

Danni didn't answer.

"Hello, I asked you a question, why are you angry?"

"I'm not."

"It seems as though you are."

"I see you're tired and pushing yourself."

"No, I'm not. I feel fine."

"You weren't this morning, I don't know if this trial is such a good idea."

"What do you mean?"

"Maybe you should sit back and let Rabinowitz be first chair."

"Are you kidding? You can't be serious."

"I am. The situation has changed, now you're expecting a baby."

"I don't need to be treated with kid gloves. Last time I was pregnant, I worked well into my eighth month."

"That was different. It was over 23 years ago and you weren't 46."

Rachel started to cry and went upstairs. As soon as the words had flown out of his mouth, he knew it was a mistake.

Danni waited about a half hour before he went upstairs to the bedroom. The door was shut; he knocked and heard no response. At that point, he pushed it open and waved a white napkin. Rachel didn't acknowledge his gesture. When Danni entered the room she had tears in her eyes as she glared at him.

"Go ahead, say it — I'm a jerk, not just a jerk, but a very sorry one."

Trying to keep a serious face, she turned her head away from him.

"Nope, it's too late, I saw you crack a smile."

"It's true, you really are a jerk and don't have to remind me that I'm old."

"You're not old."

"To be having a baby I am."

"Apparently God doesn't think so or he wouldn't have willed it. My words came out wrong; all I was trying to say was the last time you were pregnant your body reacted and responded differently."

"I would never jeopardize the well-being of the baby for this case. Right now, I can handle it. If that changes, you'll be the first to know, but until then, please don't ask or even suggest I back away. After all the preparations I've made for this trial, how could you even suggest I turn the reins over to Chayim?"

"Racheli, I said I was sorry."

"No, what you said was that you're a sorry jerk, and yes, I forgive you."

The next day at Rimonim Prison, Alexander Frece arrived from Vienna. His plan was to stay in Israel until the conclusion of the trial. He met with Gerhardt Dreschler privately in a small room, and outside a guard stood watch.

"Hello Papa, how are you?"

"I'm fine my son, how are you and your family? How is little Erik?"

"He's growing quickly, and Gretel and I are confident that you will be coming home soon. Are they treating you well?"

"Well enough, did you have a good trip?"

"Yes."

"Alexander, I need to speak with you, it's about what you're going to hear at this tribunal."

"Papa, you don't have to say anything; I know it's all lies."

"Please let me finish, it's not all lies," Dreschler paused. "When you were a baby, I was an SS officer under the Third Reich."

As Dreschler spoke he saw the look of shock and disbelief on his son's face.

"I was just a soldier following orders and did what I was told to do. After the war I wanted to leave the past behind and start again. You need to know this before next week. When you hear stories told in the courtroom, people may fabricate and exaggerate what happened. It's important to me that you realize the things they say aren't true. Only remember that I was an officer obeying rules established by the administration, do you understand?"

Alexander stared at his father for a long time without saying anything. Dreschler repeated, "Do you understand?"

"Yes Papa, I understand," he said, but he found himself at a loss for words. Dreschler changed the subject.

"How is your hotel?"

"It's very nice."

"You look tired; perhaps you should go there and get some rest, we can speak again tomorrow." He was relieved at his suggestion to cut their visit short; it was a lot of information to process. Why hadn't he mentioned this when he was arrested; why pretend? Alexander had many questions to which he wanted answers, but all Frece knew was the man in a cell at Rimonim Prison was his flesh and blood, and he loved him.

Despite what Max Reinhart had advised, Dreschler did not express any remorse about his past. Over and over the words of his attorney played in his head: *Make sure he knows it was a time in your life that you weren't proud of.* Dreschler thought if he told him this, it would be an admittance of guilt and wrongdoing. He would never utter those words to his son.

That afternoon, Orley knocked on Rachel's door.

"Mr. Alexander Frece is here to see you."

Now what has Warden Artandi done? Rachel thought to herself.

"Thank you Orley, please show him in."

Her assistant ushered Alexander into Rachel's office.

"Hello, Mr. Frece."

He nodded. "Mrs. Saunders, hello."

"Can I get you—" she began.

"No, I don't want anything, thank you," he interrupted. He stood quietly for a moment trying to search for words. Rachel waited for him to speak and saw he was clearly flustered.

"Mrs. Saunders."

"Yes?" Alex wanted answers but couldn't ask the questions, and realized coming to see her was a mistake. What was he thinking, what could he ask her? Nothing, it would show distrust and disloyalty to his father.

"Mr. Frece, is something wrong? Did you have a problem with the car rental agency?"

"No, that's what I came here to tell you, today when I picked up an automobile, the company told me that I was released from all liability damages on the original car. I wanted to thank you for taking care of that for me."

She thought the in-person visit was odd; he could have called her.

"I'm very glad to hear that, is there anything else?"

"No, that's all, Mrs. Saunders."

When he left, Rachel was puzzled. She was sharp and felt there was more to Alexander Frece's impromptu appearance at her office. His body language showed him to be visibly anxious in her presence. He had something else to say that had nothing to do with his rental car, but the question was what was the true reason?

Again there was a knock.

"Danni Hirsch is here," Orley said.

Once he entered and the door was closed, Rachel raced to hug him.

"Hey handsome, this is a nice surprise. My day has been filled with unexpected visitors."

"Oh yeah, who else was here, your other love?"

"Wow, I see you're psychic, that was my first guest this morning and then I had another before you came." Rachel laughed. "Alexander Frece left my office about twenty minutes ago."

"What has Artandi or his staff done now?"

"My thoughts exactly, but it had nothing to do with the prison. He came to thank me. Mr. Frece picked up his car rental today and the company confirmed he would not be liable for any damages made to the previous vehicle. But Hirsch, I don't understand why he didn't call instead of coming here in person. I've been a lawyer a long time and there was more, I could swear to it, he was clearly ill at ease."

"Racheli, that's understandable, why would he feel comfortable with the person who can help ensure his father is sentenced to death?" Rachel stared at Danni for a long while before replying.

"It's Dreschler who has guaranteed the nails be placed in his coffin — not me, I'm just the messenger."

Twenty-Three

It was Sunday, February 1, 1998, marking the beginning of the Gerhardt Dreschler trial. The media frenzy had taken on a life of its own all around the world. Rachel hadn't slept well; she tossed and turned before morning came. She would be in the spotlight — a place she faced with trepidation and anxiety, but nevertheless relished in. Danni woke, smiled and turned to hold her.

"Good morning, my sexy prosecutor." She clung to him.

"I didn't sleep at all last night." He saw she felt unsettled and nervous, and tried to lighten the moment.

"Hey pretty lady, I know that song."

"Stop Danni, no jokes!"

"Well, my love, this is serious. Whenever you call me 'Danni' instead of 'Hirsch,' it's a severe state of affairs. I have every confidence that you will do a spectacular job. You are a wonderful lawyer who always uses her knowledge and expertise to achieve victory in a court of law. Never doubt what you can do; this is your moment to shine."

With tears in her eyes, Rachel felt his sincerity and was comforted by his words.

"Thank you Hirsch, I love you very much. Now I need to get up or I'll never make it to the courtroom this morning."

When they arrived at the Knesset, Rachel was bombarded by reporters. Politely she answered their questions.

"Ladies and gentlemen, if you will all please excuse me now; I need to make my way into the building." Danni stayed close to ensure the media allowed her to pass. As they entered the courtroom, it was full. Some journalists were allowed inside to view the proceedings. Television stations requested permission to film, but Rachel would not relent to their requests. The government agreed with her and the motion was denied; none would be allowed. She argued that such a grave case and the misery attached to it deserved more than turning it into a soap opera. People testifying should not be put under any direct media scrutiny. The trial would be handled in a dignified manner.

Danni took a seat in the open forum area with his peers. The prime minister and Liam Vuturi were sitting next to him. Alexander Frece was located on the left side of the defense table. Rachel made her way to the front; all eyes were gazing at the attractive attorney. Her reputation as "Courtroom Couture" was clearly evident upon her debut appearance. She wore a magnificent St. John navy blue and light grey tweed suit with matching Charles Jordan navy blue shoes, which carried accents of the tweed material on the tips and backs. Rachel conducted herself with poise and confidence while walking down the aisle and didn't glance at the spectators. She was warmly, yet professionally greeted by Chayim Rabinowitz. Across from them at another table, Max Reinhart was seated next to a vacant chair.

The room was vast, and Rachel looked toward all three individuals on the panel to which she would be recounting Gerhardt Dreschler's despicable actions. Each member wore a headset that would translate in their native language the entire trial dialogue. In addition, a large projection screen was present in the area where other viewers sat. A court stenographer was stationed near the inquiry counsel. The stenographer also wore a headset to ensure she was ready to transcribe into Hebrew the multitude of words that would be spoken. Her dictation appeared on the wide screen so all audience members could follow the proceedings comprehensively.

Everyone in the large room heard the banging of the gavel by the

Israeli Supreme Court Justice as he tried to silence the spectators. When all were quiet, Judge Abraham Messenger began to speak.

"Guests and participants, I call this tribunal to order." Looking at the bailiff he added, "Please bring the defendant into the courtroom."

Today was the first time Rachel physically laid her eyes on Commandant Gerhardt Dreschler. The 84-year-old former SS officer stood six feet tall, weighed approximately 180 pounds and looked younger than his years. As the defendant entered and approached his seat, he deliberately stared at Rachel. Looking straight at him, she was relaxed and did not heed to his attempted intimidation. Danni watched with pride as Rachel handled herself like a pro. Max Reinhart gave Dreschler the headphones as he made himself comfortable, placing them over his ears to listen as the translator would relay all verbal terminology.

Rachel moved to the center of the room and began to speak in English.

"Participants of the Inquiry Counsel governed by the state of Israel, I bid you good morning. We are all gathered here today to begin the criminal trial against commandant Gerhardt Dreschler for atrocities committed during World War II — crimes against humanity. I will prove beyond a reasonable doubt through multiple witness testimonies that Gerhardt Dreschler, who has lived under the assumed name of Werner Frece since the conclusion of the war, is immoral and scandalous in the eyes of the law under the rules of civility."

Danni observed with pride as he listened to her opening summation. In his heart he knew she was a good attorney, but never experienced her superlative skills firsthand in a court of law. The woman whom he deeply loved was marvelous; she commanded the domain with a stance that showed her to be in full control. The razor sharp talent of a DA emerged in that courtroom. Alexander Frece listened to her speech; this woman did not sound anything like the demure person whose office he sat in days before. Her modest behavior disappeared and became nonexistent within the walls of the legal arena. As he sat and observed, he was astonished.

Rachel walked to her seat and Max Reinhart took the stage and spoke in English.

"Good morning, commissions of the state, we are gathered here today in accordance with your magistrate's regulations; I will prove to you all beyond a reasonable doubt that commandant Gerhardt Dreschler was acting under the governance of his superior officers during World War II. Any refusal to follow those instructions would have resulted in his court martial under German law." Pointing at Gerhardt Dreschler, Reinhart continued, "Over the next several weeks everyone will see this man, a devoted father and highly respected citizen of Austria, who was only acting under the sworn duty to his former country."

When Reinhart sat down, Rachel stood holding multiple copies of a document that listed the individual prosecution witnesses. Walking toward the panel, she explained the information being handed to them.

Most of the day was spent outlining a foundation to the committee. She explained how the prosecution would proceed and present facts. The discussion lasted for several hours and then Judge Messenger adjourned for the day.

When Gerhardt Dreschler was exiting the courtroom, he half-smiled and tipped his head to Rachel. Danni saw this and wanted to wipe the superior smirk from his face. She remained unfettered. As Dreschler left, he heard her respond to his arrogance. In perfect German, Rachel said, "Until we meet again tomorrow, sir."

When the words rang out, he turned and his dark, cold grey eyes peered through her. He hadn't expected any verbal response, nonetheless one in German. She thought the expression on his face was priceless. Rachel wanted him to know that she was by no means jesting with him. His posture showed his discomfort; he wasn't amused by her remark. It appeared that the tyrant became the one who was intimidated.

As the first day came to a close, Rachel was mentally drained, but it didn't outwardly show when she exited the courtroom. In the hall were hordes of reporters waiting to speak with her and Max. After answering their questions Rachel dashed outside with Danni. When they were far enough from the public spectacles he pulled over and stopped the car. She looked at him puzzled.

"What's wrong?" He was staring at her with admiration.

"You were unbelievable today." She smiled.

"Really?"

"What do you mean, really? Racheli, I was so proud of you. I knew you had a gift and your words were captivating; when you started speaking this morning everyone in that room was entranced. The performance you gave was mesmerizing."

She held him and spoke softly into his ear. "You're my unexpected gift."

They rode in silence the rest of the way home. Rachel rested her head on his shoulder; nothing else needed to be said. Hearing Danni's praise and validation gave Rachel a pleasure that she wanted to revel in.

That night she received a call on her cell.

"Hello, Mrs. Saunders, it's Robert Burke."

"Hello, Dr. Burke, is everything alright with Helena?"

"Yes, I'm sorry if my call alarmed you. I just wanted to let you know that Madam Krieger has made remarkable progress and can fly to Israel next week. I gave her the news earlier today and said you would be in touch to finalize the arrangements."

"That is wonderful news; I'm sure Madam was thrilled."

"Yes, she was very pleased, and after only having a little over three weeks of speech therapy, her strides have been vast."

"Doctor, if things go according to my plan, I was hoping we could organize the trip to depart from New York this coming Saturday."

"That's fine with me, Mrs. Saunders; have a good evening."

Twenty-Four

The trial was actively underway and the proceedings were proving to show a long, arduous progression of events. Every Sunday court only ran until 1 p.m., and every Friday until noon, but on Monday through Thursday, it was supposed to run until 4 p.m. Since this was Rachel's first trial in Israel, she wasn't used to this schedule set before her. She began by presenting witness testimonies; everyone who saw the revulsion executed by this madman wanted to overtly confront him. These individuals were eager to show he was no longer in control, and their fears were left behind at the death camp.

When Rachel and Chayim prepared for the trial, they thought it best to start slow. The strategy was to begin questioning people who observed the abuse that other prisoners endured by Dreschler. Then gradually, the prosecuting counsel would build up momentum with other witnesses who recalled the direct violence they encountered on a daily basis. The witnesses gave endless statements documenting various acts of terror. The inquiry counsel listened and, at times, asked questions about what they heard.

Rachel studied Gerhardt Dreschler's behavior as multiple former prisoners of the death camp spoke aloud. He was clearly unaffected, a cliché reaction of a true sociopath able to remove himself of any guilt or responsibility. She also observed Alexander Frece's deportment. He was clearly ill at ease with the explicit words being spoken about his father.

The man had been in a state of denial for several months, not wanting to believe the person who raised him was a former Nazi. For this she felt truly sorry, and her thoughts were constantly encompassed by the hope that Max Reinhart wouldn't call Dreschler's son to the stand.

On Sunday afternoon, Danni drove Rachel to Dr. Kashan's office for her first amniocentesis. As he stuck a needle into her belly she looked away and held Danni's hand tightly. She hadn't a high threshold or tolerance to pain.

"Is everything OK, Doctor?"

"Yes Rachel, you're doing well." He continued the exam and gave her a sonogram.

"Perfect, young lady, keep it up."

"Doctor, can you tell the sex of the baby?"

"I have somewhat of an idea, but to be sure, I would rather wait until your next visit to confirm it."

"Can you tell me what your hunch is?"

"Racheli, let's wait until the doctor knows for sure," Danni said.

"No, I can't even if you're wrong, please give me a clue."

The doctor began to laugh. "I think it's a girl." She and Danni looked at one another smiling. Rachel grabbed his hand again and squeezed it, and this time her grasp was out of excitement.

"Now, I would like to speak to you on a personal note for a moment — I think you're doing a fantastic job in the courtroom and wanted to let you know that."

"Thank you very much, Dr. Kashan, it is kind of you to say so."

"The pleasure is all mine, I'll see you next month."

After leaving the doctor's office, they headed to the King David Hotel in Jerusalem to see Helena, who had arrived late the night before on her private jet with Trudy and a nurse. An Israeli speech therapist would come to visit her daily. Danni made arrangements for Madam and the other two women to stay in the Royal Suite, which had three bedrooms, a living room and dining room. He spared no cost to ensure that she had every necessary comfort.

When Danni and Rachel arrived at the hotel, Trudy opened the door and greeted the couple warmly. She directed them to Helena's bedroom, and Madam was elated when they entered. Rachel walked to the bed and kissed her cheek. With great difficulty she moved her hand and placed it on Rachel's arm.

"I see someone is showing off what they can do," Rachel said. Helena gave her a faint smile and slight nod. The elderly woman extended her hand toward the direction where Danni was standing and he moved closer.

"Madam Krieger, it is a pleasure to meet you."

With the slightest bit of clarity she replied, "Mr. Hirsch; it's my pleasure, and please call me Helena."

He grabbed her hand. "I will, only if you call me Danni. Are you comfortable in this suite?"

"Yes, everything is perfect; thank you."

"You're very welcome, if there is anything you need, do let me know and I'll make sure you have it. If you ladies will excuse me, I need to go downstairs for a few minutes. I'll be back shortly."

After Danni left the room Helena's nurse excused herself. When they were alone, Rachel shut the door. Helena looked at her.

"I see why you wanted to rush home to that charming handsome man." Rachel began to blush. "Was I right, dear heart? The baby, was he happy when you told him about the baby?" Rachel gave her a big smile. "Yes, you were right, he was thrilled. I also told him that you are the only other person who is aware of my pregnancy."

Helena smiled. "How could he not be thrilled? That's wonderful, and I was thinking about the suit I made for you, in case it doesn't fit now and needs to be released, the seamstress at my Tel Aviv store can do some alterations."

"No need to worry about that, with all the morning sickness I've been having, I lost two pounds, so I think we're in good shape where the suit is concerned." Helena's facial expression turned serious. "The doctor said it's perfectly normal with the way I've been feeling; don't worry, you sound like Danni," Rachel said, sitting in a chair near her bed. She changed the subject. "Your speech has really improved; Dr. Burke told me how well you've progressed. Now I see it for myself, I think you are amazing."

"So are you; the media is saying that Rachel Saunders is 'the masterful public prosecutor of the century.'" Rachel was visibly uncomfortable with the praise being given to her. "I'm just relaying the facts to the inquiry counsel," Helena said. "Don't be so modest, especially with me. Your knowledge and passion for your profession is something you should always take pride in, never forget that."

"Thank you, last Sunday was the first time I laid eyes on the cold-hearted bastard." Helena was surprised to hear her use that terminology. After the words came out, she was embarrassed. "Forgive my vulgarity; I never should have said that to you."

"No need to apologize, what you said was true."

After lunch Rachel told Madam she'd come by to see her tomorrow evening. "It isn't necessary, you might be tired, I'm being well-cared for, no need for you to be rushing here after a long day."

"I love spending time with you." Madam Krieger looked toward Danni. His response was, "No use arguing with her, she'll see you tomorrow evening."

Outside the hotel, Rachel grabbed Danni's hand.

"Helena likes you a lot."

"The feeling is mutual; she and I have something in common."

"What's that?"

"We both love you."

"Hirsch; I'm really feeling much better; you won't believe what I'm in the mood to eat even though it's cold outside."

"Tell me, I'll get you anything."

"I could go for a vanilla fudge ice cream cone." He started to laugh.

"I remember once when we were kids at the park your brother was eating a vanilla fudge ice cream cone," Danni said. He paused to see if Rachel recalled the incident.

"Yeah, and …?"

"Racheli, you really don't remember? Michael needed to go to the bathroom and asked you to hold his cone. I think you were about nine years old at the time; the ice cream cone was dripping all over." She began to giggle.

"Yes, the ice cream cone was dripping all over me and I started eating it because I was getting sticky."

"By the time he came back, you finished his cone."

"I sure did, boy was Michael mad, remember what I said to him? 'It's not my fault, next time wait until you finish your cone before you go to the bathroom!'"

She was laughing so hard, tears began to trickle down her cheeks. Danni again pulled out one of the handkerchiefs she gave him and wiped her face.

"Well handsome, that's the second time these new hankies have bailed me out of trouble."

"We go back a long way, my adorable little girl."

"Oh, little girl, huh?"

"Yes, in my eyes, I still see that adorable nine-year-old little girl wearing the blue and pink short set with matching ribbons in her pigtails eating that cone."

She reached up and kissed him. "You never stop surprising me, Hirsch, never."

"Your nose is cold, let's go to the car, there's a great ice cream place near the house; I'll get it for you on the way home."

"Wait, I changed my mind. Now I want a sundae instead of a cone. A vanilla sundae with butterscotch sauce, hot fudge, lots of sprinkles and whipped cream, you can't forget the whipped cream."

Danni got a kick out of Rachel's enthusiasm. "I won't forget it because you'll be in the shop with me, and you can give the play-by-play description yourself."

"Come on now, walk faster — you have a pregnant lady with a major craving."

Twenty-Five

On Monday, Rachel woke up feeling full of purpose. She looked forward to the testimony of Ethel Schultz, former nurse to Kathryn Dreschler. That afternoon, the moment had come.

Rachel began, "Inquiry Counsel, I call Ethel Schultz to the stand."

Mrs. Schultz walked with grace and composure to the front of the courtroom. Gerhardt Dreschler stared intensely at the fair-skinned woman who still had some remnants of blonde mixed into her white hair. Once she reached the podium, Rachel continued.

"Please state your full name for the presiding counsel."

"I am Ethel Altman Schultz."

"What name did you go by while living in Berlin, Germany?"

"I was called Ethel Altman; Schultz is my married name."

Rachel continued, "Bailiff, kindly swear in this witness." She placed her left hand on the bible.

"Do you, Ethel Altman Schultz, swear to tell the truth, the whole truth and nothing but the truth, so help you God?"

"I do."

"Mrs. Schultz, please be seated," Judge Messenger said.

"Can you kindly explain to the court how you came to be employed by Gerhardt Dreschler?"

"I was working in the Jewish hospital in Berlin. He came there in March of 1942 to find private nursing care for his mother, who was ill."

"Mrs. Schultz, why did a German SS officer come to a Jewish hospital rather than one that was Aryan?"

Showing she had no fear, Ethel made direct eye contact with the Nazi and answered the question. "Herr Dreschler paid a visit to Krankenhaus der Judishen Gemeinder, which was known as the Hospital of the Jewish Community. He came to our facility because German nursing care was costly. I remember that evening; his eyes were only searching out those nurses with blonde hair and blue eyes. Dreschler approached me and asked for my services, and I was not in any position to refuse him. The exact words he said to me were, 'A German nurse will cost me twice as much, so you'll do, Jew. This is my address, come tomorrow morning.'"

Still fixed on him, she continued. "He may look different now, but I'll never forget those dark, cold eyes — they haven't changed over the years."

"You arrived at the Dreschler home the following morning?"

"Yes, and I began caring for Kathryn Dreschler. During the day his wife ignored the ailing old woman and only took care of the child. In Dreschler's presence, she played the dutiful concerned spouse, but her true feelings said otherwise. I remember one day when she was running a fever and whimpering, I went into the bathroom to dampen a cloth to place on her forehead. Frau Dreschler walked in and asked, 'Why all the whining?' and I said, 'Your mother-in-law is running a fever and appears to be in pain.' She looked at me, rolled her eyes and said, 'Keep the old witch quiet. If you don't, I'll tell my husband that you are an incompetent Jew and that will be the end of you.' After uttering those words, she walked out of the bathroom."

It was evident that Ethel was trying to get a rise out of the defendant. He looked at her in disbelief of the testimony she was giving. Suddenly Max Reinhart interjected, "I object! What is the purpose of this witness' statements? Elsa Dreschler's character has no bearing on this case."

Rachel responded, "I disagree with Herr Reinhart's objection, Elsa Dreschler's behavior in the home towards the witness can clearly be construed as a deliberate attempt of verbal intimidation. This, coupled with the known murderous actions of her anti-Semitic partner, proved to be a terrifying work environment."

Reinhart stood again, "I object to the inference of the name being used to describe my client. Prosecuting counsel should address the witness by his rightful title."

"Mrs. Saunders; please refer to the defendant by his correct, known name." Reinhart enjoyed this; the first notch in his belt was made visible. Rachel began again.

"The nerve-wracking situation of caring for Herr Gerhardt Dreschler's mother and dealing with his wife, who clearly had no pity or empathy for the dying woman, showed a strained and unpleasant atmosphere to be employed in. The threat made by Frau Elsa Dreschler outwardly showed Ethel Altman Schultz's safety to be in question. The recollection of this event is pertinent to these proceedings."

Justice Messenger studied the lead prosecuting attorney before ruling, "I will allow the witness' testimony to continue. Mr. Reinhart, your objection is overruled."

His confident stature quickly disappeared.

"Mrs. Schultz, please continue," Rachel said.

"I did my best to see that the ill woman was comfortable."

"Can you further describe the atmosphere in the Dreschler dwelling when her son was present?"

"Yes, Kathryn's bedroom was right next to her son's upstairs office. Every evening, Elsa Dreschler brought dessert and tea to his workplace. I remember hearing him telling her about the rigors of the day; how distasteful it was dealing with the Jewish vermin living in the ghetto. She would ask, 'When you came home, did you wash your hands thoroughly from the dirt and grime of those animals?' I would hear him laugh and say, 'Elsa, don't you know by now that's the first thing I do when I walk into the house? I won't kiss you or Kurt before I do that. You know I don't want any of their disgusting germs near my family.' Dreschler concluded that those cockroaches roam the streets in filth."

Ethel became silent and Rachel spoke. "Mrs. Schultz, Gerhardt Dreschler referred to the Jews of the German ghetto as filth?"

"Yes Mrs. Saunders, he did."

"Were you privy to any other dialogue spoken by him in the home?"

"I was," she said, reciting word-for-word a story about a phone conversation, and the Inquiry Counsel listened ever-so-closely to each syllable spoken.

"One evening I heard commandant Dreschler speaking on the phone in his upstairs office. It sounded like he was talking with another SS soldier. They were joking with one another. Each man was trying to outdo the other with past stories of how they killed and tormented our people. He was telling the other officer a story about his days living in Düsseldorf. He said that two 'Jewish bitches' were walking down the street one day — a mother and daughter. He stopped them and extended the hand he was holding his gun in to the little girl, who was about 11. He said, 'Go ahead, take it and shoot your mother.' The child began to cry and said she wouldn't. Then he said he looked at the woman she was with and said, 'Go ahead and shoot your daughter.' The mother said, 'Please officer, I beg you.' He said, 'Shoot, you Jewish whore, shoot.' He explained that the woman refused. His words to her, as he relayed to the other soldier, were, 'Fine I'll shoot you both.' The commandant was roaring with laughter, and he spoke about how the blood was all over the sidewalk and it poured into the street.

"Dreschler said it took forever to get the stains out. 'Six Jewish scum fucks worked for two hours to remove it from the cobblestones.' He said he learned a valuable lesson that day — whenever he killed 'the vermin,' he walked around the corner into the side alley and did it there because it was less messy and easier to clean. The other officer must have been saying something because Dreschler went silent and then he began to laugh again."

As Ethel spoke, her eyes did not leave Dreschler's. He stared back at her, unaffected by the story she recounted as though the woman was raving mad. Upon the conclusion of the testimony, Rachel looked to the legal panel.

"I have no more questions for this witness." Rachel returned to her seat, Max Reinhart rose from his chair and began to cross-examine the witness.

"Mrs. Schultz; that is quite a tale you just told."

She glared at the defense lawyer. "Sir, it was not a tale — it is a story from the past."

"So you admit it is fiction and not fact?"

"Excuse me, Herr Reinhart, allow me to clarify, it is a fact based on a murder committed by Gerhardt Dreschler that I heard him boast about on the phone while looking after his mother."

Rachel stood, "I object, defense counsel is badgering the witness."

"Objection sustained."

"Pardon me, Mrs. Schultz — with the testimony you just gave, I find it remarkable that you remember such vivid details from so long ago."

"Sir, I remember the facts so vividly because I have been reminded of them every day of my life for the last 56 years," she said, pointing at Dreschler. "Not a day goes by where I don't hear his sinister laughter, not one day."

"Mrs. Schultz, with such a clear sense of recollection, I don't recall hearing you speak about how Herr Dreschler treated his mother."

"He treated her well."

"How well, madam?"

"Very well."

"Is it true that he sat up reading to her in the evenings for hours on end?"

"He did."

"Can you elaborate please?"

"You asked me if he read to her and I replied that he did; how would you like me to elaborate?"

"So what you're telling me is that after he returned home from a long day upholding his duties—"

"Upholding his duties?" Ethel interrupted. "Did that duty include his killing innocent people?"

Reinhart cut her down quickly. "Mrs. Schultz, all you are to do is answer the questions being asked. I object to Mrs. Schultz asking questions rather than answering them directly."

Justice Messenger looked at her. "Mrs. Schultz, please just answer the questions as they are directed to you."

Again, Reinhart felt victorious when the ruling was noted in his favor.

"Mrs. Schultz, please allow me to complete my sentence before answering. What you're telling me is that after Herr Dreschler returned home from a long day upholding his duties, he still found time to stay at his mother's side no matter how tired he may have been. Yes or no please, madam."

"Yes."

"Would you say his devotion to his mother went beyond the basic concern a child feels for a parent?"

"Yes."

"Thank you. I have no more questions for this witness."

During defense counsel cross-examination, she kept her composure and remained unscathed. Rachel admired and respected the way she handled herself on the stand. It was clear that her stalwart demeanor was not well received by the defendant. This courageous nurse left the witness box and focused her eyes on him like a burning laser. Rachel observed the familiar arrogant smirk on his face.

It was 4:45 p.m. — the court session ran over time. Justice Messenger dismissed everyone for the day.

"Ladies and gentleman, we will reconvene tomorrow at exactly 9 a.m., thank you."

Rachel had watched as Alexander Frece sat and listened throughout the day. His face showed that of a man who was in disbelief and distraught about what was being revealed. As the courtroom dispersed and Dreschler was being taken from the area, Alexander tried to get his attention. The SS officer did not stir in the direction of where his son's voice was calling from. She watched and couldn't decide if Dreschler was deliberately ignoring him or if, in fact, he couldn't hear him over the noise in the room.

In the hallway Rachel saw Ethel Schultz.

"Excuse me, Mrs. Schultz; I wanted to say that you did a splendid job today. I commend you for the strength you displayed in Gerhardt Dreschler's presence; well done." The witness smiled after hearing the attorney's esteemed remark.

Danni walked toward Rachel once the witness was out of sight and observed how tired she looked from the day's events.

"Hello pretty lady, again you were brilliant in there."

"Thanks, Hirsch."

"I bet a nice dinner will perk you up."

"I don't think anything will do that, but I'm starving and a burger and fries will certainly help."

"Then a burger and fries it is, let's go," he said, smirking.

After their meal they went to check in on Madam Krieger, who was still experiencing the effects of jet lag and looked very tired when they arrived. Rachel smiled and asked Helena how she was feeling. Madam said it had been a good day, and expressed that she liked her speech therapist very much. They discussed the trial and Rachel didn't mind hearing praise from Helena and Danni.

"Thanks for the vote of confidence; we still have a long way to go." The couple sat with her for about an hour before heading home.

"Danni, I want you to promise me that after court adjourns tomorrow, you will take our girl straight home, she looks exhausted."

"Hello everyone, I'm still in the room."

"Please promise me that you will skip coming here tomorrow." Not wanting to admit it, Rachel felt fatigued and conceded to the request.

"It's a deal; however, we will be back on Wednesday."

"Wonderful, I look forward to seeing you both then."

Twenty-Six

On Tuesday morning, witness testimonies continued. Rachel rose from her seat.

"Inquiry Counsel, I call Mr. Saul Lieberman to the stand. Sir, please state your name to the court."

"My name is Saul Lieberman."

"And by what name were you called by the guards at Treblinka?"

"They called me 467803 — the number on my arm." After he answered the questions Rachel looked at the court officer.

"Bailiff, please swear in the witness." He placed his left hand on the bible and took the oath.

"Mr. Lieberman, please be seated."

Rachel started to question the Holocaust survivor.

"Mr. Lieberman, can you explain to the court how you came to know the defendant Gerhardt Dreschler?"

"He and I attended the same high school in Düsseldorf, Germany. That was the first time I saw him." Dreschler stared at the aged man intensely and Saul returned the gaze, but continued speaking. "Herr Dreschler never knew me personally, I remembered seeing him run on the school track team. I was 28 years old when I was sent to Treblinka and worked outside the camp during the day, leveling the ground at Malkina Railroad Station. Every afternoon the trains would arrive loaded with Jews packaged like cattle. Dreschler was at the train station circling around like a vulture waiting for its prey. As the people were thrown from the freight cars, the commandant sat on a horse and watched with amusement.

"The son of a bitch would laugh with delight as they fell to the ground." With those words, Max Reinhart jumped from his chair and looked at the Inquiry Counsel.

"I object to this witness' crude language," he said, glancing directly at Justice Messenger. "As you said yesterday, sir, the defendant is to be addressed by his rightful name."

"Mr. Reinhart, please do not tell me what I said yesterday. I am well aware of my own thoughts without your help, thank you. Objection sustained, Mr. Lieberman, please address the defendant by his known given name."

Saul Lieberman acknowledged the Judge's request. "Commandant Dreschler laughed with delight as the people were tossed from the train. Then all were assembled in lines. The SS officer would look the lot over as he rode slowly on his horse up and back, studying the group. He took pleasure in taunting those unfortunate souls and played a sadistic game called 'Run and Hide.' Usually he'd pull ten to fifteen people out from the crowd. I remember his words: 'Now you pieces of shit, let's play a game.' He instructed them to start running, he would count to ten, and if he didn't catch them, they would keep running into the forest. 'This is how you can earn your freedom,' he said. Once ten was reached, he rode his horse to each individual who had not been able to escape and shot them dead.

"The train arrived on a particular day; off jumped Ephraim Novak. He attended the same school as Dreschler and I. They were on the track team together. Dreschler was never able to win any race against him. This Jewish athletic champion could outrun a fox."

Rachel examined Dreschler's body language, and finally a nerve had been struck.

"He recognized Ephraim and pulled him from the mob of people to play this sick amusement that brought him pleasure. He ran faster than lightning and made it into the woods. Dreschler commanded two other officers to join the hunt on their horses and they chased after Ephraim, but it was a long while until they found him."

Rachel didn't take her eyes off the defendant, who had become more agitated with each word spoken by Mr. Lieberman.

"The prisoners left the station for the concentration camp. Only I, the other workers and three SS soldiers remained behind. When they found Ephraim, the men brought him to Dreschler. He was tied to the commandant's horse and was dragged back to the station. The German boorish animals who supported this terror reveled in his capture. Barely conscious, he looked Dreschler in the eye and said, 'You are still a dirty player, you Nazi bastard.' I was shocked and couldn't believe what I heard him say. Ephraim, still looking at his tormentor with a smile, recited, 'Gerhardt, tonight when you go to sleep, remember it was a Jew who outran you once again.' Those were his last words before Dreschler spit at him and the bullet went through his skull.

"The commandant glanced in my direction and pointed his gun at me; the expression in his eyes was terrorizing. He began shooting bullets around my feet; Gerhardt Dreschler wanted to let me know he was still in control. In a loathing tone he told me to take Ephraim into the woods. His speech was incessant; 'This Jew scum will fill the belly of a hungry wolf.' I carried his limp, lifeless body to the clearing. I covered him with as many leaves and stones as I could find, trying to hide his flesh from plain sight in the hope of giving this brave man the peace he deserved. After that day, Dreschler never played the game again."

Saul Lieberman's words were powerful. Not a sound was uttered in the courtroom when he concluded his statement. Gerhardt watched Rachel with disgust. The silence was finally broken when she addressed the Inquiry Counsel and spectators. Her eyes were still fixed on the defendant. She stared intensely at Dreschler while walking towards him and spoke in a hateful tone.

"This individual would like us all to believe — how did you put it Herr Reinhart? We should all believe Gerhardt Dreschler was only acting under the sworn duty to his former country. I would like to know, sir; did that duty include humiliation, torture and murder? Please enlighten me, better yet, enlighten everyone who is present here today. I believe you are unable to do so, as is evident by your client's stance. It appears the defendant is about to jump out of his seat. We can conclude he was defeated at his own sick game by those whom he hated most of all in this world, and that who would be a Jew. I have no further questions for this witness."

Reinhart sat silent. Finally Justice Messenger addressed him. "Mr. Reinhart, do you have any questions for the witness?"

The words were caught in his throat as he began to speak. "No, not at this time, however I reserve the right to recall the witness to the stand at a later time."

"Very well. Mr. Lieberman, you may step down." After leaving the stand he walked toward the defense table, stood directly in front of Dreschler and spit in his face.

"That was for Ephraim, you cold-hearted son of a bitch." Two guards ran immediately towards the men and grabbed Saul Lieberman as Dreschler rose to retaliate.

"This is an outrage!" Max Reinhart shouted. "You all observed what just happened; Mr. Lieberman should be held in contempt of court for attacking the defendant." Rachel watched in shock and disbelief as Saul Lieberman was escorted out of the room. A few moments later, Gerhardt Dreschler was also removed. Alexander Frece was astonished by Saul Lieberman's actions and rose from his seat. Before leaving the area, the Nazi quickly glanced at his son and turned his head away from him.

The defense attorney continued. "I demand that Mr. Lieberman be held in contempt of court."

Rachel quickly interjected. "Your Honor Sir, Mr. Lieberman's actions today are wrong, but understandable after the testimony we all heard. He has been cooperative and forthcoming to ensure justice be served at this tribunal by reliving what he observed in the past. Holding him in contempt of today's proceedings would further perpetuate the evil he suffered during his former life."

After Rachel concluded her retort to Max Reinhart's demand, Justice Messenger said, "Let the record show that Mr. Saul Lieberman is held in contempt of today's courtroom proceedings and is hereby sentenced to one day in jail. However, let the record also show that this Inquiry Counsel hereby suspends the sentence and grants Mr. Saul Lieberman probation."

There was pandemonium in the courtroom after the incident. Justice Messenger tried to calm the bedlam.

"Ladies and gentlemen, we will reconvene at exactly 1:00 p.m. with a direct semblance of order." His last gesture was to smash the gavel heavily on its wooden mount.

Rachel made a quick exit into the private chamber room where Saul Lieberman had been taken by the two security guards that steered him away from Dreschler. When entering the space she made her presence known.

"Mr. Lieberman, are you alright?" He was still visibly animated, shaken and breathing heavily. He turned to the direction where he heard the soft spoken voice.

"Mrs. Saunders, forgive me, I was taken over by the powerful bitterness in my heart." While listening to his words, Rachel was fixated on the events that transpired just minutes ago. She was amazed at the old man's tenacity. All the pent up hostility that was hidden for almost sixty years was released in a fleeting moment, and his hate was heard through his actions.

Rachel walked near him.

"Mr. Lieberman; your aggression is understandable." She saw his hand was still shaking.

"Mrs. Saunders don't you see, I let him win today by what I did; it showed that he got the best of me."

"No, Mr. Lieberman, on the contrary, you illustrated that Gerhardt Dreschler had no control and you had no fear. As far as the Inquiry Counsel is concerned, your actions of contempt were noted in the court record; Justice Messenger documented the citation, but has only placed you on probation as opposed to sending you to jail.

God recognized your pain and knows the measures taken were justified. I believe Ephraim is looking down at you with gratitude for your heroism."

Saul clung to her and began to sob uncontrollably. She held him tightly.

"If you must cry; do so for those who perished at the hands of Dreschler all those years ago. Don't shed one tear or feel any remorse for what you did today."

Slowly, he regained his composure. When he was ready, they left the chamber room. Danni was standing in the corridor and watched Rachel grab the elderly man's arm as though he were her escort. The two walked toward the exit at the back of the building. She placed him in a car that took him home.

Danni waited for her and both of them left together trying to avoid the relentless reporters. At that moment all Rachel wanted was to be left alone.

"Ladies and gentleman, I have no comments for you, please let us pass."

He took her to a quiet little café for lunch.

As they ate, the day's events reminded Rachel of the nightmare she had after Saul's deposition, which had taken place around the same time as the bombing in Sacher Park that Mustafa was involved in. Danni noticed that Rachel had been sitting playing with her food, but quickly realized it wasn't simply due to her usual nausea. She looked visibly upset, and when probed, she hesitated, but then relayed the dream to him. Even though it had happened weeks ago, she no longer wanted to keep it to herself. Mustafa had been walking down a Berlin street with Ephraim Novak. Gerhardt Dreschler came toward them; he extended his pistol to Ephraim and said, "Shoot the boy Jew, go ahead shoot him."

Ephraim looked at Mustafa, then at Dreschler. "I will not — he's an innocent child."

Then Dreschler extended the gun to Mustafa and said, "Go ahead, shoot the filthy Jew, shoot him."

Mustafa started to cry and shook his head. "No, I won't."

Dreschler looked Mustafa in the eye and began to laugh. "Very well, I'll just shoot you both." Saul Lieberman and Ethel Schultz's memories of so long ago rang out in Rachel's subconscious and haunted her.

"Now I understand why you didn't tell me about the nightmare, but I'm sorry that you were haunted by it," Danni said. "I saw how kind you were to Mr. Lieberman. Sometimes our emotions take over and surprise us; we may underestimate what we're capable of," Danni continued, eager to change the subject.

"Saul Lieberman received that revelation today and I don't think he was prepared for it. His resilience and inner strength have allowed him to prevail; I'm sure he'll be fine, and so will I."

The atmosphere of the legal forum that afternoon appeared calmer. Both the prosecuting and defense attorneys conducted themselves with a professional demeanor and made no reference to Saul Lieberman.

Rachel stood. "Inquiry Counsel, I call Mrs. Ida Horowitz to the stand. Would you please state your full name for the presiding counsel?"

"I am Ida Posner Horowitz."

"What name did you go by while you resided at the Treblinka concentration camp?"

"They referred to my by the number branded on my arm — 483721." After she responded to the questions, the prosecuting attorney recited the same words that came easily to her. She was then sworn in.

"Madam, can you tell the court about your experience at Treblinka?"

"At the age of 19, I arrived there with my mother, father, two sisters and brother. We entered the camp and walked in an assembly line to the area where we discarded our possessions. That is the place Gerhardt Dreschler stood watching over the barrels filled with jewels and gold. We hid ours in the garments we were wearing and the guards searched each one of us and took everything.

"My father had given my mother an emerald and diamond brooch for their twenty-fifth wedding anniversary. Engraved on the back was an inscription that said *With all my love for you, forever and always, Isaac.* The commandant recognized the quality merchandise that sat within the wooden vessels. He removed the brooch from the rest of the lot and placed it in his pocket. Then he smiled at my mother and said, 'Thanks you Jewish slut, Isaac has very good and expensive taste, I'm humbled by your generous gift.' Then he shrieked with a sadistic sound of laughter, basking in our pain and suffering. It was clearly a sick perversion that gave him pleasure."

Ida Horowitz, unlike the other witnesses that testified, did not make eye contact with Gerhardt Dreschler. She felt uneasy in his presence. Rachel studied her.

"Would you like to take a break, Mrs. Horowitz?"

"No, thank you, Mrs. Saunders." She paused for a moment as her lips started to quiver. "That was the last day I saw my family. Only I survived and have a life sentence of torment. I will never forget the sadness in Mama's eyes after Dreschler took away that gift from my father; he killed any remaining hope she had before being marched to the death showers. My mother died twice that day."

Again, the eerie silence after a testimony fell upon the room.

"I have nothing further." Rachel walked to her seat as Max Reinhart approached the witness box.

"Mrs. Horowitz, you said you saw Gerhardt Dreschler take your mother's brooch."

"Yes, I did."

"Can you please point out Herr Dreschler to the court?"

Rachel rose. "I object — we are all aware of who the defendant is."

"Inquiry Counsel, my request has relevance," Reinhart interjected. "I noticed throughout her testimony that Mrs. Horowitz did not once look at the defendant, and perhaps the reason is because it is not this man who supposedly took her mother's brooch. There were other officers besides Herr Dreschler that held rank at the camp in question."

Before the council could rule, Ida Horowitz looked Max Reinhart directly in the eye as she raised her arm and pointed a finger in the direction of Gerhardt Dreschler. Immediately, her gaze was focused on the alleged criminal.

She began to shake as she spoke in a shaky voice. "It was that man who took my mother's brooch and placed it in his pocket, and those dark grey eyes I saw beaming with joy at what he did."

Max Reinhart stared at her unrelenting and repeated, "Herr Dreschler was not the only officer with dark eyes. It was a long time ago; it could have been someone else you're confusing him with."

"Other SS officers may have had similar eyes; I wonder how many of them had a scar on their left hand shaped like the letter L between the thumb and forefinger? When Gerhardt Dreschler was ogling my mother's brooch, he held it with his left hand. I remembered noticing the old wound."

As Mrs. Horowitz described the mark on the defendant's hand, Rachel's eyes were set on Dreschler's son, and she noticed the acknowledgement on his face. By what the prosecuting attorney read, it was obvious the disfigurement on his father's hand existed.

Rachel quickly interjected, "Members of the Inquiry Counsel, I ask that the defendant show his left hand to the court."

The council members conferred and Justice Messenger said, "Bailiff, please walk to where the defendant is seated."

When the bailiff reached Dreschler, Justice Messenger continued his verbalization.

"Mr. Dreschler, kindly hold out your left hand. Bailiff, can you tell us if there is any visible disfigurement on Mr. Dreschler's hand?"

"Yes, Your Honor, there is a small scar shaped like the letter 'L' on his left hand."

"Mr. Dreschler, you can sit down." With every attempt to

discredit a witness, Max Reinhart had only opened up new damning information.

He looked at Ida Horowitz. "I have no other questions for this witness."

"Mrs. Horowitz, you may step down."

Again Rachel carefully viewed Alexander Frece, and she saw he was visibly disturbed by all the witness testimonies he heard over the last week-and-a-half. Her focus was on winning this case, however she felt sorry for the middle-aged man who stood by a person unworthy of his loyalty. Max Reinhart was becoming desperate and grasping at straws. From her professional legal per-spective, he most likely would try and pull some magic trick out of his hat and continue to raise questions about the witness accounts of Dreschler's evil past.

Once Mrs. Horowitz was seated, Justice Messenger spoke into his microphone. "Ladies and gentlemen, it is 3 p.m., I call a 15-minute recess." The sound of the gavel echoed throughout the room.

Max Reinhart took his client into a private chamber. Dreschler began to speak with him in an aggravated tone.

"Max, what are you doing?"

"What do you mean, Werner?"

"Whenever you pose additional questions to these witnesses it places me in a worse position."

"I'm trying to discredit their testimonies; it's difficult if I don't know what additional information they have to say when it has not been documented in their transcripts."

"Is that allowed?"

"Yes, it is if the statements are true. You saw that I didn't cross-examine Saul Lieberman this morning because I felt and saw the reaction from the room after they heard his words. I'm trying to use my judgment regarding when and where not to question the prosecuting witnesses."

"Then try harder," Dreschler said in a condescending tone.

"Werner, I wanted to give you fair warning. I need to call

Alexander to the stand today; with what just happened the timing is right."

Gerhardt stared intensely at his lawyer. "If you do this, Max, I warn again, be prepared to refute that woman. Do I make myself clear?"

"I told you, leave it to me."

"Do I make myself clear?"

"Yes, Werner."

At 3:15 p.m. the hearing continued. Max Reinhart motioned to the bailiff and handed him a paper that he requested be given to Justice Messenger. After the judge reviewed the document, he looked in the defense lawyer's direction.

"Mr. Reinhart, please proceed with your witness." Rachel's greatest fear was about to come to fruition.

"Inquiry Counsel; I call Mr. Alexander Frece to the stand."

Twenty-Seven

Alexander walked to the box and stood in front of the seat within. Herr Reinhart spoke loudly.

"Sir, would you please state your name to the presiding counsel?"

"My name is Alexander Frece."

"What is your relationship to the defendant seated in this room today?"

"I am his son."

"Please place your left hand on this bible, Alexander Frece, do you swear to tell the truth the whole truth and nothing but the truth so help you God?"

"I do."

Max Reinhart proceeded to question his witness.

"Mr. Frece, how would you describe your father's character and the relationship you have with him?"

"He is a wonderful parent who has always been a warm, devoted, nurturing and caring man. My father always took me to school and found time to coach my athletic endeavors. He helped me excel in swimming, running and pole vault. As a result of his hard work and efforts, I became a champion. On weekends we went fishing and to the cinema. My father was a very good fisherman, and I was excited the first time we went out on his boat and I learned how to fish. We sat for hours and waited; the frustration I felt as a child wanting to experience the tug on my rod was unbearable. Many hours passed, yet he sat patiently with me until it happened, and then it did. I will never forget the look of relief on Papa's face when the shank began to move. His support was not so much that I caught the fish, but the pain he felt from seeing my disappointment was alleviated. The delighted expression he displayed is something I won't ever forget.

"And when it comes to my son, Erik, he is definitely a doting grandfather and has embraced my wife as a daughter. My boy always enjoys being with my father. I'm sure you've heard the expression, 'Children are the greatest judges of a person's character.' They have an innate sense of their nature; if a youngster gravitates towards someone, it shows the individual to have a strong moral fiber." Alexander smiled and stared at his father. "Erik's disposition while in the presence of the man seated over there has always been happy; I see how secure he feels with him. If everyone here witnessed this, you would all know that no evil could emanate from my father. Also, over the years, I've seen his many acts of charitable generosity."

"Would you kindly elaborate?"

"He created a foundation called *The Frece Endowment Fund for Lung and Liver Dysfunctions.* This organization has made several strides in finding cures for many lung and liver diseases. Papa has been recognized and honored for all the money he has contributed and raised for this worthy cause. Through his crude oil refinery, he hosts a yearly event called 'W. A. Frece for the Impoverished Community.' Money raised at this yearly gala is matched dollar for dollar, and all the proceeds are given to an Austrian governmental agency that provides food and shelter to displaced families."

Even though Gerhardt Dreschler showed himself to be emotionally removed at the trial, tears welled up in his eyes when he heard Alexander speak. Rachel sensed and saw the pain of a parent. As one herself, she wouldn't want David to be subjected as a witness defending her honor under such circumstances. It was as though two men were present in the legal forum; first was the sociopath that existed during — and prior to — World War II. Then a warm caring man emerged, disconnecting himself from the events that took place years before his life began in Vienna. Rachel continued listening to the testimony of a human being blinded by love, and was dreading her cross-examination of him.

After Alexander gave his testimony, Max Reinhart concluded his cross-examination, and Justice Messenger interjected.

"Ladies and gentlemen, it's just about 4:30. Tomorrow is *Tu BiShvat,* therefore no courtroom proceedings will take place. On Thursday, Friday and Sunday the yearly Israeli Delegation Meetings are being held to vote on homeland security laws, and my presence is required at these summits, so we reconvene on Monday at 9:00 a.m."

Between *Tu BiShvat* — the Jewish Arbor Day — and Justice Messenger's necessary absence, Rachel was happy to have the reprieve a little while longer. Danni met her in the lobby and noticed the pre-occupied look on her face.

"Hello beautiful, what's wrong?"

"I think you know the answer, I'm not looking forward to my cross-examination of Alexander Frece on Monday." She wondered, *Will I be able to do what's needed, or will my sentiment as a human being prevent me from doing so?*

"You were right; Max Reinhart called Alexander Frece to the stand, just as you predicted he would," Danni said.

"In my heart, I knew it all along, even though I hoped it wouldn't happen," Rachel replied.

He continued to observe the anguish she was feeling. Still, he wondered why the son of this mass murderer had such a hold on her. He dare not speak it aloud, especially now. The last thing he wanted to do was antagonize Rachel.

"I know you'll do what needs to be done," he answered.

Once more she questioned herself inwardly.

Will I?

Twenty-Eight

Danni was doing everything he could to get Rachel out of the courtroom mindset so she could relax. He took her by the hand.

"Right this way, beautiful, I have a surprise for you."

"What surprise?"

Danni led Rachel into the den and pulled an envelope out of the top drawer of his desk, then handed it to her. She opened it and stared at him.

"I bought tickets to the Israeli Philharmonic Orchestra for Saturday night; the concert will have featured works of Chopin." Danni paused. "I know how much you love the Philharmonic, you've often told me about the wonderful performances at Lincoln Center in New York that you have gone to. I specifically remembered you mentioned a concert featuring Chopin, and I thought this would make you happy."

She showed him a faint smile. "Thanks; it sounds wonderful, and that was very sweet of you," Rachel replied. But she was barely convincing. At that moment, the last thing she wanted to do was go someplace that gave her pleasure.

Later that night, Rachel tossed and turned endlessly, and her stirring kept Danni awake. He pulled her close to him and whispered in her ear, asking if she wanted to talk. Rachel hesitated and explained that she was still feeling anxious about the upcoming cross-examination of Alexander Frece. The thought of questioning him wouldn't leave her mind, even though all she wanted to do was stop focusing on it. He wrapped his arms around her tighter, and a peace came over her. She finally settled and slept.

Alexander Frece was not mentioned at all on Saturday. That evening they dressed for dinner and the Philharmonic. Danni made a reservation at an upscale French restaurant in Jerusalem called Cavalier; Rachel loved French cuisine. Danni wore a stunning charcoal gray suit with a light blue shirt, and an elegant tie with different shades of grays and blues embedded in its pattern. Rachel wore a gorgeous Donna Karan royal blue cocktail dress with perfectly matching shoes. Her attire magnificently offset his ensemble. Rachel showed no visible signs of her pregnancy; she appeared trim in the form-fitting frock.

They could have been recognized as Hollywood stars when arriving at the elegant bistro. The Maître de warmly greeted and seated them at one of the finest tables in the establishment. Danni handed him twenty American dollars, and he tried to refuse, but Danni insisted.

Rachel read the menu. "Let's get the five course meal."

"Only the five course, why not the one with seven?"

"Have you seen the dress I'm wearing? I'll be happy if I can breathe after a five course meal."

He smiled and grabbed her hand. "I can't see anything past the dress you're wearing."

She began to blush again. "Why is it that only you can give me flutters in the pit of my stomach like a lovesick teenager?"

"Maybe it's the baby you're feeling."

"Good try, it's too soon, nope, the flutters are all you."

"In my eyes you are — and will always be — that teenage girl I fell in love with on the soccer field in Tel Aviv."

After a wonderful dinner, they went to the Philharmonic. Danni had gotten box seats — the best in the house. It was a first-class evening through and through. Once escorted to their seats, Rachel saw, sitting below in the orchestra, Lieutenant Yoel Agassi. Beside him was a beautifully dressed woman.

"Look, there's Yoel Agassi, the classy gent who called me a 'nice piece of ass,'" Rachel said, turning to Danni.

The lieutenant was looking around the music hall and noticed them. He immediately acknowledged their presence and waved. Rachel and Danni returned the gesture, then looked at each other and chuckled.

"Good evening, distinguished guests, we are honored to have a very special person with us tonight. Sitting in the audience tonight we have Lieutenant Yoel Agassi, who has served our country with valor. Lieutenant, would you please stand?" the conductor said into the microphone.

As the military man rose, everyone applauded him. Desperately trying to quiet the crowd, he attempted to speak. Due to the size of the performance hall, it was difficult to hear him.

The conductor invited the lieutenant on stage where he could address the audience. Agassi walked with a charismatic stance as he made his way to the podium.

"Ladies and gentleman, I want to thank you all for the homage you have paid me this evening, it is greatly appreciated and entirely unnecessary. Tonight we all should give that reverence to another, as reported in the media, one who, over the past weeks has proven to be a true conqueror in our region." He pointed his finger in the direction of where Rachel and Danni were sitting. "It is our honor to have Rachel Saunders present with us here this evening. Her unwavering hard work during a world-renowned tribunal has well exceeded all of our expectations."

Danni looked at Rachel in awe as the lieutenant praised her accomplishments and a spotlight appeared on her. Showing his support, he stood beside her and began to applaud. All others in the music hall followed his lead and did the same. Rachel was humbled and self-conscious of the acclaim. She looked to the lieutenant and expressed her gratitude as he commended her. Then the lawyer waved her hand in response to the crowd above, below and alongside her. Rachel hoped the room would become silent and return to the usual decorum befitting a theater.

Yoel left the stage and went back to his seat. The conductor began to prepare the orchestra for the performance. Danni held her hand firmly.

"You are a superstar, my girl. The country is in love with you."

Rachel was overwhelmed with the attention she received and hadn't really thought about the impact the trial had within Israel or around the world. But her shock was interrupted by the start of the concert, and the beautiful music of Chopin filled her ears and quieted her anxiety.

The performance was wonderful. After the show, while exiting the theater, people in the lobby greeted her with handshakes and words of praise. It was a surreal experience; one she would never forget. Outside, none other than Yoel Agassi was waiting to speak with them. The lieutenant walked toward the couple with the woman he escorted to the show. When all were together, Rachel immediately extended her hand to him. "It is a pleasure to see you again, Lieutenant."

"Likewise, Mrs. Saunders. Danni, it's good to see you too." He shook Agassi's hand. "This is my sister, Maya." They greeted the woman warmly.

"Lieutenant, I want to thank you for the kind words this evening, it was totally unnecessary," Rachel said.

"The hell it was, this country is indebted to you. I have observed your expertise in the courtroom on a few occasions during this trial and have to say you are a gifted attorney," Agassi replied. He hesitated. "Mrs. Saunders, may I speak with you privately?" Rachel looked at Danni, then at Maya.

"Certainly, would you both excuse us for a moment?" They walked to a quieter area. "Lieutenant, is there something I can help you with?"

"Yes, Mrs. Saunders, actually there is. I never properly apologized to you the evening we met at the Israeli Consulate and I made that crass remark. It has been bothering me ever since."

"I believe you just have, and earlier this evening as well with your grand acknowledgement in the auditorium. I accept your apology, what happened is forgotten."

"Thank you. I wish you the best of luck with the rest of the trial," Agassi said.

When they returned to where Danni and Maya were, everyone bid each other a good evening. On the way to the car, Rachel told Danni about Agassi's apology, and he remarked that it was a positive end to a wonderful evening.

Twenty-Nine

On Monday morning, court was back in session. Rachel stood in front of the prosecution table and addressed the committee. The moment of truth had finally arrived, and she had to stop her hands from shaking as she called Alexander Frece to the stand.

"Inquiry Counsel, I recall Mr. Alexander Frece to the stand." When he was seated she started her cross-examination.

"Mr. Frece, last Tuesday I heard you, rather — we all — heard you say, 'No evil could emanate from the defendant here today.'"

"Yes Mrs. Saunders, that is what I said and I stand by my words."

"How can you be so sure?"

"I know the man; I lived with him and saw his kindness."

"Mr. Frece, for two weeks you have been sitting in this courtroom listening to depositions and verbal testimonies given by many people who say that your father — the accused — is and was anything but kind. Isn't that true?"

Alexander paused for a moment. "Yes, but—"

"So, you see, there is a strong contradiction here, your voice is one and theirs are many."

Max Reinhart stood. "I object, Mr. Frece had not finished speaking. Prosecuting counsel interrupted him before he could complete his thought."

Rachel looked at Reinhart. "I asked Mr. Frece a question that only

197

required a yes or no answer, just as you had done to Ethel Schultz. Herr Reinhart, I believe your exact words to her were, 'Yes or no please, madam.'"

"Objection overruled." Alexander was clearly flustered by the decision. He merely acknowledged what the other witnesses had said in the courtroom. Rachel saw his loss of composure and discomfort; he was not the only one feeling uneasy with this line of questioning. If there was any moment during her career where Rachel felt like the cliché of the sleazy attorney, it was now. She tried to hide it while standing center stage.

No longer able to watch the witness, she became focused on Gerhardt Dreschler. The defendant looked intently through her. She read a father's trepidation to ensure no harm come to his child. The Nazi's eyes showed a warning that Rachel not go too far with questions posed to his son. She remained fixed on Dreschler.

"Mr. Frece, I noticed when Ida Horowitz mentioned the scar on the defendant's hand you didn't look surprised. Can you please tell us more about the mark? How did he get his wound?"

"My father told me he was sawing lumber while working and the blade hit his hand."

"Thank you, sir." Rachel looked toward the woman transcribing all vocalized courtroom testimony. "I ask that Mrs. Horowitz's transcription be read aloud at the point where she mentioned the scar on the defendant's hand."

The stenographer began to search for the documentation, and when it was located she stood and read the page. "'Sir, other SS officers may have had similar eyes, but I wonder how many of them had a scar on their left hand shaped like the letter 'L' between the thumb and forefinger?'"

When she finished speaking Rachel paused for a moment and then continued. "Mr. Frece, you, I and all the others seated here heard those words."

Rachel saw him slowly becoming defensive.

"Mrs. Saunders, you referred to Ida Horowitz's testimony last week, so why not recall my own? You heard me state to the court that my father was a loving parent, grandfather and a charitable man."

She turned toward Max Reinhart, who looked pleased at how the witness led her. Danni became uneasy and wondered why she hadn't interrupted him. Though she didn't want to challenge or antagonize, Rachel had no choice; her reputation was on the line.

"Yes, Mr. Frece, I heard your statements and recollections of your father, specifically how he worked with you and taught you to run like a champion. I wonder if thoughts of Ephraim Novak crossed his mind while passing his wisdom onto you? Or perhaps from Ethel Schultz's testimony about the defendant's phone conversation with a fellow SS officer — how Dreschler told the other soldier about a murder he committed on a Düsseldorf street, I wonder if it is that eleven-year-old little girl's face he sees while playing with your son?"

Max Reinhart rose immediately. "I object! The prosecution is trying to provoke the witness."

"Objection sustained."

Rachel turned and looked Alexander Frece in the eye. "I'll keep saying it, your voice is one, and the other witnesses who testified cited multiple incidents of torment and suffering under your father's rule."

"You and them know nothing, Mrs. Saunders; my father was thoughtful and caring. I remember once when I was a child, it was a warm summer night, and the coolest spot in our home during those months was in the wine cellar. I used to love playing with my toys there under the steps. Papa came down and didn't know I was around, but there was a place where he kept all his legal and important papers. Once, I saw him take a necklace from there that he placed in a box and wrapped for my mother. He gave it to her for their tenth wedding anniversary," Frece said. "It wasn't an uncommon occurrence. Throughout the years he always showed himself to be a loving husband. It was a very positive and happy atmosphere to grow up in."

Immediately, Rachel's eyes turned to Dreschler for his reaction. He stared at her, stone-faced. Danni began visualizing the wine cellar

Alexander Frece mentioned. Thinking carefully about the area where the stairs were located, he realized that underneath them was an open spot where one could stand. Across from this section was the wall, which housed a huge wine rack, and next to that was the picture of Dreschler at his refinery gala. In front of those places toward the middle of the room was a rectangular table about six feet long, which stood with six chairs.

Quickly he got up and appeared visibly anxious. The prime minister and Liam Vuturi looked at him. Danni motioned to his superior officer to stand and the two men left the legal forum.

"What's wrong?"

"I need to go with my team back to Dreschler's home in Vienna. It's in the wine cellar."

"What's in the wine cellar?"

"How quickly can we be flown on a private charter to Vienna?"

"You still haven't answered me, what's in the wine cellar?"

"I'm not sure, but my gut tells me something is down there that we missed." His superior nodded and walked away to call headquarters to make the arrangements.

"A plane has been reserved at a private air strip at Ben Gurion for you and your crew to depart from in two hours. The aircraft will land at a non-commercialized field at Vienna International. A minivan will be there waiting for you and your men." Danni contacted each team member, and they were all instructed to pick him up immediately outside the Knesset building, and from there, all would drive to the airport.

"Liam, when the court session is in recess, ask Rachel to get a postponement for a couple of days. She needs to tell Messenger that additional evidence is being pursued. Explain to her that I have a hunch there is something in the wine cellar and I will be in touch with her as soon as I can."

"Sure, Danni."

Liam returned to the courtroom and listened as Rachel continued her cross-examination of Alexander Frece. She was intensely focusing on the witness.

"Mr. Frece, certainly you must have doubts about your father's character after listening to what has been said about him. Perhaps deep down in your soul you know everything that was told here is true. Do you hear the cries of the guiltless begging for their lives while Gerhardt Dreschler watched as they fell to the ground, one by one from the bullets in his pistol?"

Max Reinhart rose. "I object, again, the prosecution is intentionally goading the witness."

"Objection sustained. Mrs. Saunders, be careful, this is your second warning."

Alexander was vividly distraught as he looked at her with a sense of appeal.

"I ask why you continue to support this man who knowingly and deliberately wreaked havoc on innocent lives?" Rachel continued.

His voice was broken. "Because he's my flesh and blood, and I won't desert him. If it were your father—"

"Mr. Frece, my father isn't on trial. I will allow you to consider this: if it were my father, whom I loved very much, his fate at Treblinka would have been held in the hands of a twisted, demented killer." Before making her final statement, Rachel did not remove herself from Gerhardt Dreschler's sight as he glared back at her with unrelenting contempt. "Sir, it wouldn't be the first time that truth was blinded by loyalty or love." Rachel had broken this fragile man and hated herself for it.

Walking to her chair she said, "I have no further questions for this witness."

"Mr. Reinhart, do you have any more questions for your witness?"

"No sir, I don't," he replied solemnly.

"Mr. Frece, you may step down." When Alexander walked away from the podium he looked straight ahead, making no eye contact with anyone at all as he left the courtroom. People began to clamor amongst themselves. The clashing of the gavel was heard as Justice Messenger attempted to regain order.

"We will reconvene at 1 p.m."

It had been a grueling morning and it clearly showed on Rachel's face. She walked out of the legal forum with her co-counsel. She searched for Danni in the hallway.

"I'll see you after lunch," she said to Chayim. Liam made his way toward her.

"Liam, have you seen Danni?"

"He's on his way to Vienna."

"Vienna, why?"

"He's convinced there's something in Dreschler's villa that was missed. Rachel, Danni told me to tell you to ask the judge for a postponement, convey to the Inquiry Counsel that additional evidence has come to light and they need a few days to pursue it."

She was puzzled. "Liam, did he give you any details?"

"All he said was it's in the wine cellar. I know as much as you do. Danni said he'd call."

During lunch, Dreschler met in a private chamber room with his lawyer.

He glared at him. "What the hell was that, Max? I told you not to put Alexander on the stand, and you were so sure that bitch wouldn't do anything to him. You sat while she tore my boy apart."

"That isn't true, I objected whenever I could. Messenger warned her to be careful with the way she was posing questions to him. He was your only real hope. The nurse only helped ever-so-slightly; the strength lies within your son's testimony. I had no choice but to have him testify, and you know it."

After lunch ended and court was back in session, Rachel asked to meet with Justice Messenger, the other panel members, Chayim Rabinowitz and Max Reinhart privately. She requested a two-day trial adjournment, and explained that additional evidence had been unearthed by Israeli Intelligence. Justice Messenger conferred with the other committee members and concluded that the trial would resume on Thursday morning.

Court was dismissed. Dreschler's lawyer met with him to explain the delay.

"Werner, is there anything you aren't telling me?"

"What do you mean?"

"I mean, is Israeli Intelligence going to find anything in Vienna that I need to know about?"

"Relax Max, you worry too much."

Thirty

Meanwhile, Liam notified the Austrian government of his group's arrival. Gaining access to the property would be easy due to the Israeli government having jurisdiction over this trial. Mossad still held the keys to Dreschler's home. At 5:00, the seven men from the original trip arrived in Vienna. They drove to the villa and immediately proceeded to the wine cellar. They each wore a knapsack containing a variety of tools and other equipment.

Danni stood underneath the steps and tried to re-enact what Alexander Frece witnessed as a child. He slowly walked across the room to the wall where the wine rack and picture stood, carefully studying everything around him. His eyes became fixed on the photograph frame.

"There it is, don't you see it?" The agents looked at him and then at each other. They shrugged.

"See what?" one of the agents asked.

"This," Danni said, lifting a small concealed flap from the mounted octagon picture frame and turning it clockwise. The image that was laminated into the casing turned and presented itself to be a door that was now resting against the outer wooden panel. Many documents were clearly visible — the deed to the home, legal refinery papers and a last will and testament. The storage space was dark; it was difficult to see what else lie within. Danni reached into his backpack and pulled out a flashlight, returned to the hidden vault and turned it on. Low and behold, within the wall laid a long metal box which was approximately two feet deep and ten inches wide.

"Quick, help me," he said. The container was heavy and sealed by a padlock. They placed it on the long table which, no doubt, was down there for the purpose of this concealed safety container. Another agent opened a different sack and pulled out a power drill, positioning the bit on the nose of the tool and placing it into the keyhole of the deadbolt. The sound was deafening, and finally it opened. Danni lifted the top of the metal structure. The radiance from many gemstones glistened throughout the dark room.

Danni placed his hand over his mouth and ran his fingers through his hair in disbelief.

"My God, my God; the clever bastard hid it in the wall." The storage bin housed diamonds, gold and other precious stones of all sizes, golden necklaces, bracelets, watches, rings, and even fillings in the shape that would be on the outer layer of teeth. They continued to stare at the commandant's trophies of war and looked toward Danni with expressions of admiration at his findings. He continued to shuffle his hands through the treasure and pulled out a cardboard envelope from the bottom.

Inside of it were many different photos of Dreschler dressed as an SS officer. Most of the photos showed the smug look of accomplishment as he documented the torturous acts he committed against Jewish people.

Danni looked at his guys. "Let's go to the vehicle, get all the fanny packs and start loading the evidence into them. We'll hide everything underneath our garments; the jackets we're wearing will mask the bulkiness. If anyone is watching, none will be the wiser when we leave; between the seven of us it will all be concealed."

Prior to leaving Dreschler's villa, Danni took special care safeguarding the photos he found. His placed the pictures — which would guarantee a conviction without question — close to his chest. From years of rigorous training, Danni used a special tape that affixed the photos to his body, ensuring they would not be damaged and kept in perfect condition. Additionally, he placed some of the jewels in one of the small sack belts, which he attached to his lower back. They drove directly to the private airstrip at Vienna International Airport. Before boarding the plane, he called Rachel.

"It's over for Commandant Dreschler; I have everything you need to make sure he rots in hell. We're on the way back to Israel. I'll explain it all to you when I get home, see you soon my love."

Danni hung up immediately because he needed to board the plane, and Rachel was left wondering what damning evidence they had found.

It was almost 3 o'clock in the morning on Tuesday when the private charter returned to Ben Gurion Airport. All jewels and photos were taken directly to Mossad headquarters. Everything needed to be thoroughly documented and disclosed as discovery for all legal parties to have access to.

Liam watched while the findings were safely locked away and methodically inventoried — at the conclusion of the trial, the Parliamentary Inquiry Committee for the Location and Restitution of Property of Holocaust Victims would notify the injured parties' families of the items found in Dreschler's basement. He commended each agent. The team humbly credited their superior officer who detected the proof.

Danni was holding a mug of coffee as he looked at the group. "Go home and get some well-deserved rest; I'm sure Dreschler would want you to."

He remained with Liam as the others exited the evidence room. His director stood and stared at him. "How did you figure it out and know where to look?"

"It was all because of Herr Friederike Grunwald, the son of the builder Dreschler worked for before the Nazi movement. He illustrated to Rachel and me the unique carpentry designs created by Dreschler. If this man hadn't shown us the octagon-shaped passageways Dreschler built into walls, we never would have found this.

When I heard Alexander Frece's testimony yesterday about a place where his father kept documents in the cellar, I knew there was something we overlooked."

"Superb job. Go home and get as you said some well-deserved rest, that's an order!"

Danni returned home after a grueling journey and was looking forward to seeing Rachel and finally getting some sleep. But when he arrived, Rachel did not match his excitement — she was visibly upset, and he couldn't understand why. After several minutes she finally spoke.

"You heard my cross-examination of Alexander Frece, right? Up to the part where he mentioned being in the wine cellar as a child? Hirsch, I went too far and I was awful to him."

"You did what was necessary."

"No; I destroyed an innocent man on the stand yesterday, and that most definitely wasn't necessary. Damn that Reinhart!"

"Racheli, he had no choice. The only real credible character witness he had was Alexander Frece. If the tables were turned, you would have done the same." His observation was true and she recognized it. Still, Rachel was troubled by what had transpired, and Danni couldn't understand why. Instead of feeling victorious following Danni's breakthrough in Vienna, her mind was focused on the son of a Nazi. He said nothing else, and decided to let it be. Perhaps she needed to undergo the discomfort in order to heal.

She went to the phone and immediately called Chayim. He placed a conference call to Justice Messenger, and Max Reinhart was notified as well. The following morning, a meeting was scheduled for the defense, prosecution and Inquiry Counsel to gather in Messenger's chambers to discuss the findings.

Rachel hung up the phone. She returned to Danni's lap and rested her head on his shoulder.

"You should get some sleep."

"Will you come to bed with me?"

"I couldn't sleep right now if I tried."

"Did you hear me mention anything about sleep?"

"You, my prince, look like you're about to fall away."

"Looks can be deceiving, there's a lot of life left in this old boy, and I can prove it to you for the next couple of hours."

"The next couple of hours?"

"Yes, after all, I've been awake for more than a day, so under the circumstances my stamina is a bit off."

She laughed. "You're incorrigible." Rachel felt fragile and emotional, and though her priority was the legal task at hand, being held and caressed at that moment gave her a sense of comfort that she needed from him then and there. "Very well, Hirsch, let's see what you've got." With that, he carried her upstairs.

Thirty-One

On Wednesday, all legal parties were assembled. The evening before, six copies of the Israeli Intelligence inventory docket were delivered to Danni's home. At the summit, Rachel handed one to each individual in attendance. The records methodically listed every item found in the concealed vault in Dreschler's villa. Max Reinhart turned pale while reviewing each page.

After several speechless minutes passed, he addressed Justice Messenger. "Sir, in light of the new discovery disclosure, I request to see the evidence in person and ask that our next court session not reconvene until this Monday. I need ample time to confer with my client." He was visibly affected by these new findings and humble in his approach to the committee.

"Very well, Mr. Reinhart, I will see everyone on Monday at 9."

When the meeting adjourned, the defense attorney proceeded to Rimonim Prison. Gerhardt Dreschler noticed the despondent, lost expression on his lawyer's face.

"Max, what's wrong?"

Dreschler heard no response. "Max, look at me, what happened?"

"I asked you on Monday if there was anything you weren't telling me. Guess what Israeli Intelligence found hidden inside the wall of your wine cellar. Go ahead Gerhardt, try and speculate."

It was the first time Reinhart had addressed him as 'Gerhardt' instead of 'Werner.' The lawyer's candor was somewhat surprising to Dreschler. Every memory the former SS officer had suppressed for fifty-six years was about to spill forth from his mouth like an erupting volcano. With an air of self-importance in his voice, the defendant stared directly into Reinhart's eyes.

"I took the jewelry from the vermin when they arrived at the camp. There are pictures of myself and fellow colleagues; the snapshots showed what was done to the weak-willed pests."

The only remorse he felt was seeing his son's mental anguish and for Mossad's discovery. Max Reinhart finally witnessed his hatred for Jews firsthand. He listened to him proudly admit to the complicit acts against innocent lives. A look of disgust appeared on the lawyer's face when he heard Dreschler professing those actions with self-gratification. This man, a seemingly respected citizen in Vienna, had exposed his true self then and there. It sickened Max Reinhart as his client revealed the truth.

The defendant stared smugly at his attorney.

"Max why do you look so surprised? Admit it, you knew deep down who and what I was before hearing everything over the past weeks. Perhaps you are the one who has been in denial all these months. You've been too distracted by all the notoriety to realize who I really am. The bottom line is that you knew this trial would make your career, so you turned a blind eye."

"Gerhardt, you sat in that courtroom and listened to all of them relive the horror and terror you were responsible for. I knew about your being an SS officer; members of my family had been and were convicted of war crimes. I was raised on the notion that they were only doing their duty working under the direction of the government," Reinhart replied. "You became a righteous, respected civilian of Austria, and in my mind you portrayed yourself as a caring, charitable man. Such a person could only have acted out of benevolence to the establishment during the war. You enjoyed what you did, and perhaps my family did as well. Maybe in my parents' disgrace of knowing the truth, they wanted to shield me from it and invented the noble facade of obligation."

"Cheer up, Max. There are sympathizers who live and applaud what you are doing for me; in their eyes Max Reinhart is a true hero and leader. You will be looked upon as an honorable man, one who continues to fight for our cause to support Aryan dominance in the world."

"Shut up, Gerhardt. Your interpretation of me is repulsive. I will finish what I started because it is my legal obligation to uphold my duty. But don't you dare put me on a pedestal as being a champion among men, because it nauseates me. Have we hit on everything, Commandant?"

"Yes, you know about all of it."

"We're back in court on Monday. Alexander was supposed to be the substance of your character and the Jewish nurse was merely my attempt at icing the cake. Gerhardt, we're in trouble. As I took my oath, I will do my best to defend you. But it looks grim."

"Wait, the Jew nurse." He smirked at Max.

"Why the cynical smile?"

Since the true beast had materialized, his attitude was domineering. Reinhart hated his new outwardly apparent arrogance and righteousness.

"I ask you again, Gerhardt, why so cynical?"

"I always covered my tracks. When I hired the Jew nurse, I had falsified papers stating she was of Aryan descent in the event that she was ever questioned. You've seen her features; she could easily pass for a true German citizen."

"I know you gave her phony identification documents. It's in her deposition transcript."

"Fool, why didn't you bring it up when you cross-examined her? If I had a Jew lawyer, despite the filth that they are, their innate conniving nature would have come to the surface immediately. Look at Rachel Saunders, she hasn't missed a beat and has left no stone unturned," Dreschler paused. "Besides, her German is flawless. Just imagine if I hired one of them." His laughter shattered across the room with a reverberation possessing a sense of evil that tore right into Reinhart's soul.

It took every ounce of control for him not to punch his client. After the shock left him, he continued to glare into Dreschler's dark evil eyes.

"You superior egotistical bastard, I have tried to portray you as a good and decent German soldier who was simply following orders to serve his country. My deliberate omission of the doctored identity documents was to your advantage. If I had done so, it would have shown you to be a hypocrite; someone that was fearful of unlawful wrongdoing, trying to pass her off as one of your own to the Reich," Reinhart said. "It also may have reinforced Mrs. Schultz's own statements that she was your employee because Jewish nursing services were less costly than German professional care. By saying you gave her the fabricated credentials, three questions would come into play, that being truth, justice and shame. What makes you think any Jewish attorney would have ever pled a case on your behalf, you Nazi son of a bitch?"

"Very good, Max. I see your point. All you need to do is bring some of that rage into the courtroom."

"Gerhardt, I strongly urge you not to testify."

"Don't be ridiculous, it's all going to come out. If I don't testify, it will clearly show me as afraid and guilty. I am not, and they need to hear from my lips what we did and how it was better for the world. Everyone should know the truth."

"What truth?"

Dreschler stared him down. "The truth about our pre-eminence and ascendancy. The facts of what we did because Jews were a poison, destroying mankind."

Reinhart glared at Dreschler as he walked to the door. He knocked and the guard reappeared. "We're done here, you can take him."

Before Gerhardt left the room he smiled like a Cheshire cat that had just swallowed a mouse.

"Thank you, Max."

Thirty-Two

On Sunday afternoon, Rachel went alone to visit Madam Krieger. She entered her bedroom and was greeted with a warm smile.

"Hello, dear heart."

Even though the empathetic attorney had developed an understanding of Helena's words, her speech was still lacking the clarity that needed to be heard in a court of law. But still, Rachel was always able to sound encouraging to the fearless woman she adored.

Rachel was still struggling with her demons, but now needed to focus on the task ahead. It would be the most critical moment of the trial: her one-on-one with Gerhardt Dreschler.

"When will Dreschler be testifying?" Helena asked.

"He will be brought to the stand tomorrow. But we need to talk — there are going to be some things you'll hear and see when I question him, and it might be hard for you to witness them. I don't want to subject you to any additional pain."

"There is no greater pain than what I endured at Treblinka. Nothing I see or hear will ever compare to what I suffered, so do not worry about what I can handle," Helena said. "Several months ago I told you that for years I've prayed to see the day when I can watch that devil be ripped apart. All you need to focus on is breaking and destroying his spirit, and I will overcome everything else once that is done."

Madam Krieger's strength and resolve were unwavering.

"Then I believe we are both ready for Gerhardt Dreschler."

That evening, Rachel called Chayim Rabinowitz at home.

"Chayim, tomorrow I am planning on calling Gerhardt Dreschler to the stand."

"Yes, I know."

"I'm going to be arriving to the courthouse a few minutes late and I need you to stall for time. I want to enter the courtroom after Dreschler has been seated already."

"Rachel, I don't follow."

"The usual protocol is he always comes into the courtroom once we are all accounted for. But tomorrow, I want it to play out differently," Rachel said. "Please tell the Inquiry Counsel that I contacted you and I am running a few minutes late, and that I extend my apologies. Tell them that I asked you start the proceedings on my behalf. When Dreschler arrives, give me one ring on my cell. I'll be nearby."

"OK, whatever you say."

"Thank you, Chayim. Goodnight, I'll see you tomorrow."

When she hung up the phone, Danni studied her.

"Don't look at me like that, Hirsch; there is a method to my madness."

"Oh, I have no doubt, care to share?"

"Let's just say, I want to catch the defendant by surprise when I walk into the courtroom."

On Monday morning, all but one key player were assembled in the legal forum. Danni wheeled Helena Krieger inside and situated her in the back of the courtroom. Alexander Frece was seated in his usual chair. Over the long weekend, he made no attempt to visit his father at the prison. This trial had taken its toll on him, especially the finale of the last court session. There was nothing he could say to Dreschler. Alexander continued to show his support, displaying the loyalty of a dutiful son despite all that he had heard.

The Inquiry Counsel was gathered and ready to start. Chayim Rabinowitz made his way to the podium where they were seated.

"Excuse me, might I have a word with you for a moment?" Chayim said, looking directly in the direction of Justice Messenger.

"Yes, Mr. Rabinowitz?"

"It's Mrs. Saunders, sir. She's been delayed this morning and wanted to extend her apologies to you."

"Is something wrong?"

"No, she asked that I begin on her behalf. Mrs. Saunders should arrive momentarily."

"We can wait," Messenger said.

"Well, sir, in the event that she is delayed longer than expected, her preference is for us to start without her."

"Very well, Mr. Rabinowitz."

With the familiar crash of the gavel, Justice Messenger called the proceedings to order.

"Bailiff, please bring in the defendant."

Gerhardt Dreschler was seated beside Max Reinhart, and underneath the prosecuting counsel's table, Chayim Rabinowitz discreetly pulled out his cell phone and hit one button to speed-dial her. Rachel was standing outside the courtroom near the back doors on the left hand side. Normally she came through the back middle portion of the room. Today her arrival would present itself differently. Within two minutes of Chayim's call, she opened the door. As the door swung open, everyone in the courtroom turned to see who it was.

She stood for a moment then spoke in a loud voice.

"Inquiry counsel, I apologize for my tardiness this morning."

Justice Messenger nodded his head. "Mrs. Saunders, please join us."

All eyes were upon her. Helena Krieger watched Rachel with

pride. The usual routine would be to amble down the middle aisle of the courtroom, which usually placed her in close proximity of the prosecution table. Today, entering from the back left hand side meant Rachel would stroll down the aisle near the defense table where Gerhardt Dreschler was sitting. Her saunter was slow and deliberate. She wore Helena Krieger's one-of-a-kind superb chocolate brown woolen suit, which was trimmed with a mink collar, matching mink wrist cuffs and a pair of Jimmy Choo snakeskin shoes that offset the outfit perfectly. Rachel looked confident and powerful. Here it was — the moment that played again and again in her mind. Walking past the defense table, she made sure to make direct eye contact with the Nazi. It was a triumphant occurrence. Dreschler was seething.

Rachel's ensemble represented every fiber of Jewish existence he hated. His expression was priceless. Her late arrival had been perfectly orchestrated. Rachel achieved the reaction she sought. Helena's eyes did not leave Dreschler as she felt victorious with his response. Danni, still puzzled by her grand entrance, sat and watched with anticipation. The prime minister was sitting next to him just as he had during the critical witness testimonies. Chayim Rabinowitz was also unclear of her reasoning, but did as she requested.

Justice Messenger looked at her. "Please proceed."

Rachel stood. "Inquiry counsel, I call Herr Gerhardt Dreschler to the stand."

A chorus of gasps was heard throughout the courtroom as he stood and made his way to the stand. She did not take her eyes off the Nazi as she spoke.

"Please state your name to the court."

Before answering, Dreschler studied her intensely. "To many, I am known as Werner Frece."

Looking him directly in the eye, Rachel replied in German. "That is all well and good, sir. However, I ask you to state your name as you are legally known."

He smiled at her swift response. "My name is Gerhardt Dreschler, Mrs. Saunders."

"Let the record show that the defendant has identified himself as being Gerhardt Dreschler."

"Bailiff, please swear in the witness."

He stood in front of Dreschler and began, "Sir, please place your left hand on this bible and raise your right. Gerhardt Dreschler, do you swear to tell the truth, the whole truth and nothing but the truth, so help you God?"

"I do."

As Dreschler sat, he did not take his eyes off of Rachel and she returned his glare. Speaking in English, the petite prosecutor continued in a calm, confident tone. He adjusted his earpiece as she spoke to ensure that he didn't miss a beat.

"Herr Dreschler, over the past several weeks, we in this legal forum have heard testimonies given by several civilians who survived World War II. A group of courageous people who endured a terrible time in our world's history came forward to speak about many horrible atrocities against humanity committed by you. Reliving stories about your complicit, vile, unthinkable acts of carnage, which no man or woman should ever be subjected to. Yet, they say you committed them anyway," Rachel paused. "From the testimonies we've heard, it appears that you are responsible for these heinous crimes. Did you do this, and why?"

Dreschler still looked into Rachel's eyes and did not answer her.

"Herr Dreschler, did you kill a particular group of innocent people — perhaps out of your own hatred and feelings of superiority?"

Max Reinhart stood. "I object! The prosecution is summarizing the defendant on her own interpretation of what she believes he did."

Though he outwardly objected, he inwardly applauded Rachel.

"Objection sustained. Mrs. Saunders, please rephrase your question to the defendant."

"Herr Dreschler, would you be so kind and answer the court, did you kill a particular group of innocent people?"

Her polite demeanor made him boil inside. He decided to play her game, reciprocated the civil dialogue and smiled. "Mrs. Saunders, would you be kind enough to define 'a particular group of innocent people?'"

Rachel kept her composure, returned his grin and spoke in German. "Certainly, Commandant Dreschler, when I refer to a particular group of innocent people, I mean a select group of Jewish individuals."

"No, madam, I did not."

Reverting back to English, she went further. "Sir, how do you explain the witness testimonies we've heard in this courtroom?"

His steadfast equanimity remained while he answered her question. "They must be mistaken; I did not commit these acts."

"Forgive me; I am just trying to understand how all these people can be mistaken about this mass slaughter you orchestrated and carried out. Your attorney would like us to believe that your actions were based on legal obedience and duty to your country, but I find that defense mechanism to be farfetched. Your despicable behavior went above and beyond any official obligation of enforcing orders. One thing puzzles me, though — why in the past have you gravitated toward Jewish people?"

Dreschler swallowed hard as Rachel spoke. Elated by his discomfort, her words kept flowing.

"Commandant, do you like what I'm wearing?"

Reinhart rose again. "I object, this line of questioning is very inappropriate and irrelevant. I don't see how Mrs. Saunders' attire is pertinent to the trial. Asking Mr. Dreschler if he likes your attire can be misconstrued as you looking for flattery from the witness."

Before Messenger could rule, Rachel quickly jumped in. "I will show the court that my question is extremely relevant to this trial, and I would also like to address Mr. Reinhart's remark of this line of questioning being inappropriate. Let the record show, I have no personal interest in the defendant; he is most definitely not my type."

The spectators began to giggle, which allowed for a moment of levity when she made her last statement. Gerhardt Dreschler was not amused; his self-control began to unravel. In a loud, firm tone, Justice Messenger responded, "I'll allow it. Objection overruled."

"Herr Dreschler, please let me repeat the question for you. Do you like what I'm wearing?"

His dark grey eyes were filled with poison. He took a long pause before answering. "Mrs. Saunders, I am no fashion expert."

"The reason I ask is because it has come to my attention that you are not fond of the color brown. Perhaps over the years this has changed; I was just curious. Going back to my observation of you having gravitated toward Jewish people in the past, it's true, sir, isn't it?"

His nasty character was becoming more outwardly apparent. "I don't know what you mean."

"When you lived in Düsseldorf. Elsa; I'm referring to your wife."

In a defiant tone Dreschler interjected, "Do not refer to my wife by her first name."

"Forgive me, sir. Your wife — Frau Dreschler — isn't it true that there was a dress shop in Düsseldorf she would frequent, which was owned by Jews?"

"It was a long time ago, I don't remember."

"Let me help jog your memory. Back in the 1930s there was a Jewish shop in Düsseldorf called *In Der Art* owned by Helena Krieger's family. Even though you claim not to be a fashion expert, in recent years you have paraded yourself in the most affluent circles of Vienna. I have no doubt that you've heard the name 'Helena Krieger,' the world-famous fashion designer. She is a respected citizen who owns a villa in Austria."

"Please get to your point, Mrs. Saunders."

"My apologies, sir, am I going too slow? Is there another pressing engagement that my line of questioning is keeping you from?" Again the room clamored with laughter as Rachel belittled the former SS officer.

"Back in 1939, The Furor, Adolph Hitler, was throwing a party that you and Frau Dreschler were invited to. For this particular occasion, Frau Dreschler brought you to this clothing store to buy a special gown for the Furor's celebration. It was Anna Krieger, Helena's sister, who helped your wife. She went in the back of the shop and came out with a beautiful brown velvet gown she designed."

Rachel walked to her table, and on it was Helena Krieger's deposition. Chayim had it laid out for his colleague. She searched through the pages. "Here it is, I repeat: Anna Krieger went in the back of the shop and came out with a beautiful brown velvet gown she designed. You sir, looked at it, snickered and said, 'No, it can't be brown, I hate that shade, it's the color of garments worn by money-grubbing haughty Jews. All of you love to wear brown and strut around the streets in mink coats thinking the world should bow down in your presence.' Herr Dreschler, do you think I'm haughty?"

Max Reinhart quickly stood. "I object, the prosecution is deliberately provoking the witness."

"I am doing no such thing Mr. Reinhart; I am merely reading Helena Krieger's testimony to the court and it states that Herr Gerhardt Dreschler said that brown is the color of garments worn by money-grubbing haughty Jews. Inquiry Counsel, the prosecution simply asks the defendant to respond to his words. I am a Jew who's wearing brown, and I would like an answer."

In a very loud voice Max Reinhart continued, "Again, I object to you bringing your religion into play, it is an anti-Semitic remark."

Rachel came back strong. "Sir, object as much as you like, I merely acknowledged the facts about myself. It hardly qualifies as an anti-Semitic remark, furthermore, I am the only one who could object on this point and proceed with a lawsuit about these statements. Therefore, I strongly suggest we move on because, Herr Reinhart, I have no intention of filing legal action against myself."

Danni and Chayim were no longer confused or curious. It's been proven that Rachel is gifted at her craft. The grand entrance into the courtroom today was one of the most shining and recognizable moments of this attorney's career. Her facilitation of events was carefully planned and could only be described as pure genius. The crowd roared with screams and applauded after she rebutted Max Reinhart.

At that very moment, Gerhardt Dreschler's blood pressure must have skyrocketed. Justice Messenger banged the gavel as hard as he could to regain order in the courtroom. The arena became silent.

"Mr. Reinhart, I overrule your objection on Mrs. Saunders provoking the witness, and I also overrule your objection of Mrs. Saunders' admission of her own religion as being an anti-Semitic statement."

Once again Max Reinhart had no impact on the proceedings. Rachel stared intensely at the Nazi. "Herr Dreschler, you heard me read aloud the testimony given by Helena Krieger."

Max Reinhardt interrupted, "Mrs. Saunders, you mean the alleged accusation given in a deposition by Helena Krieger. I am asking that the defendant respond to the specific information in Helena Krieger's sworn-under-oath affidavit."

"Herr Dreschler, answer me, sir, do you think I'm haughty?"

"Yes, madam, I most certainly do."

"In my opinion, that is the first honest answer we have heard from you today. Do you also think I am money-grubbing?"

"That I can't answer, I don't know how much you charge by the hour for your legal services." The audience laughed at his sharp retort.

She returned his serve. "Herr Dreschler; my fee structure is nothing you need to familiarize yourself with, because we will never be working together." The audience was clamoring again.

"Isn't it true that you saw Anna Krieger a few years after your departure from Düsseldorf?"

He sat silently.

"I'll repeat the question, Herr Dreschler, didn't you see Anna Krieger a few years after your departure from Düsseldorf?"

"I don't remember," he said with arrogance.

"Please, let me help you remember." Rachel walked to the prosecution table and reached for a manila envelope. She quickly strode to the witness stand and stood close enough to hear the defendant breathing. Before revealing what was inside the packet, he already knew and his heart began to race.

Rachel opened it and took out the photos, which were evidence that depicted the evil crimes he committed. "Here sir, now do you remember Anna Krieger? You are stepping on and digging your heel so hard into the shoulder of her motionless body, it appears obvious that her arm was breaking off. You shot Anna Krieger before Sergeant Lennart Bergmann fetched the camera that took snapshots of this unmentionable act of violence," Rachel placed the photos right in front of him. When the photos were exposed, Helena was visibly affected but would not allow herself to lose control. Rachel was unrelenting in her questioning. "Do you remember the day you killed Anna Krieger? Do you recall what you said to her moments before you took her life? Allow me again to bring you back to the past." Rachel went back to the prosecution table and grabbed Madam Krieger's transcript again. Then she quickly walked to the witness stand and stood close to the podium.

She looked him straight in the eye.

"Listen as I read you Helena Krieger's words. It was a cold rainy day when the sirens summoned us to the yard. The commandant noticed Anna as if he were a rabies-infected dog sniffing out his prey and said to her, 'Hey, brown-dress Jew.' She began to shake as he continued, 'Haughty whore, not so high and mighty now?' With that, Gerhardt Dreschler raised his pistol, pointed it at her, and the next thing I saw was my sweet, sweet Anna fall to the ground. Do you now remember taking Anna Krieger's life at Treblinka?" Rachel said loudly. She began breathing heavily. Danni became uneasy.

"I demand you answer the question."

The only words he spoke were, "You demand?"

"Yes, not request, I demand that you answer the question."

In English his response was, "Well, you know what they say Mrs. Saunders, a picture's worth a thousand words." Helena began to cry at the condescending response. His coldness penetrated throughout the room. Rachel was taken aback by the answer she heard; it was unexpected, and not one person uttered a sound after he spoke.

She slowly turned and looked around the court while moving

away from the witness box. Dreschler knew he got a rise out of her and was pleased. Her eyes wandered and she saw Ida Horowitz, Ethel Schultz and Saul Lieberman seated together in the crowd. Each day the three appeared at the trial, but they usually sat separately. Today, they united as one to hear what Gerhardt Dreschler had to say. Rachel noticed Alexander Frece and the devastation that was written on his face while he watched his father. For that moment, no one else existed in the room but the two men. Alexander seemed to be entranced. Why was this man, whom he loved so dearly, acting and speaking the way he was? Frece had never seen this side of his father and it appalled him.

Rachel walked slowly back toward the witness stand. Looking the defendant directly in the eye, the confident enraged lawyer continued.

"Sir, I demand a direct yes or no answer to my question and I will repeat it again."

He interrupted her. "A Jew demands something from me?" The sting of his words penetrated the room. Max Reinhart knew it was the beginning of the end for his client, and in his mind he was relieved. After all, Dreschler admitted that he was nothing more than an infectious disease that needed to be annihilated.

"Yes, I, a Jew, demand a direct answer to my question. Do you remember taking Anna Krieger's life at Treblinka?" The room was thick and silent. She felt her adrenaline soaring as she reiterated the question.

Dreschler broke the stillness. "Yes, I remember killing the weak, cowardly Jew girl." Glaring with his demon eyes, he was focused and unable to remove his sight from Rachel.

"All of you are so meek and spineless; not one of you ever fought back. Men, women and children went so willingly. Everything happened as it did because we Aryans were superior; our race was born to lead and rule. You and yours, Mrs. Saunders, were programmed to conform and obey while we took control."

She had done it. He came apart; the perfectly crafted facade created in Vienna disintegrated in front of her. It was unbelievable;

Gerhardt Dreschler spoke with pride about what he and his fellow officers did. Rachel remained silent while his unremitting speech persisted.

"It was easy," he rambled, "the Jew is not a complex creature. Your mentality is geared to make money, always make money. Jew doctors, lawyers — and let's not forget accountants. We are made differently, our common sense far outweighs your scholarly knowledge, and this is what's needed to survive in the world. You Jews grabbed everything, so we took back what was rightfully ours. It was all going well; going as planned. Then your country, Mrs. Saunders, intervened." He stopped and continued to stare at her. "What's wrong, Mrs. Saunders, at a loss for words? You don't have anything to say?"

Rachel was filled with emotion, but she would not permit herself to shed one tear as she began her monologue.

"Commandant, I suppose it's easy to be viewed as cowardly or meek when a gun is being pointed at your head, which is reinforced by guards who are also ready to kill, making you defenseless." She walked to the prosecution table, opened her briefcase and took from it a small velvet pouch, then quickly made her way back to the witness box. When she was within arm's length of the defendant, Rachel attempted to hand the small sack to him. "Commandant, please remove the contents of this bag."

He looked at her without the slightest bit of apprehension and extended his hand to take it. She placed the item in his palm. Dreschler removed the diamond and emerald brooch that Ida Horowitz described. Everyone in the courtroom held their breath when the contents were shown.

"Would you please describe to the court what you are holding in your hand?"

"It's a diamond and emerald brooch."

"Is there an inscription on the back of this brooch?"

He turned it over. "Yes."

"Kindly read aloud what you see written."

He read, "'With all my love for you, forever and always, Isaac.'" The spectators sat in silence as he spoke the words.

Rachel's eyes were fixed on him and he was breathing heavily as she became more enraged. Max Reinhart sat and said nothing.

"I will recall again what the defendant's attorney stated when this trial began: 'commandant Gerhardt Dreschler was only acting under the sworn duty to his former country.' I ask, did this sworn duty include murder and theft?"

Rachel received no answer to her question.

"Bailiff, would you please."

The bailiff left the courtroom, and returned wheeling a cart with a metal box on top of it. He placed it next to Rachel in plain sight of the former SS officer; and she opened it in front of Dreschler. All of the stolen jewels were in the lockbox, and Rachel showcased the countless treasures that once belonged to those who were slain by the Third Reich. The shock from the audience was heard in loud gasps and whispers.

Her presentation was grand. After displaying the showcase to him, Rachel walked the cart toward the Inquiry Counsel. Dreschler, clearly outraged, sat in silence while the legal panel observed the container.

It was a surreal moment for Alexander Frece. All he had ever known was built on false pretenses. He feared that there was truth to the accusations, and it paralyzed him. His wish for this all to be just a horrible dream had been destroyed. Rachel made her way back to where Dreschler was positioned, and she studied him carefully. She continued to read from her memorized script.

"I suppose you've been dying inside wondering how this evidence was found. Your masterful craftsmanship of inlaid woodwork is still admired and remembered. I saw firsthand when I went to Düsseldorf how talented you were. Prior to the war, you worked for Hendrik Grunwald who had a son, Friederike. In speaking with Friederike, he recalled his father telling him with great reverence about your innovative ability to design and build compartments and storage places that were undetectable and hidden within walls. From what I've learned, this ability was brilliant; the inner vault you assembled was masterful." She touched the jewels. "You even took gold from teeth. Look inside, commandant. Take a good long stare and see what you will never have access to again."

Dreschler became enraged.

"Oh, Commandant, am I upsetting you? Are you angry that I am handling your special souvenirs from the war? Are you feeling unnerved, Gerhardt?"

He quickly interrupted her. "Jew, do not call me by my first name. It is *Sir, Herr* or *Commandant*."

Rachel smiled, closed the metal box and asked the bailiff to remove it from the courtroom. Then she turned her attention back to Dreschler. "Did you or did you not state today that Jews never fought back? You were referring to all Jews?"

"Yes, I was."

"You know that isn't true; there was someone who fought back. I noticed when I looked through all these photos you've kept as tokens of your finest moments; there is not one picture of Ephraim Novak, is there? Do you know why?"

Dreschler turned his head and would not answer the question. Rachel continued, "According to Saul Lieberman's testimony, that's because Ephraim Novak proved again that he triumphed over you. He battled and defied your presumption; he chose his own destiny and you couldn't stand it. Ephraim Novak did not go quietly without a struggle. Admit it, for all these years, he has been a reminder of a spirit you couldn't break."

Dreschler sat silently. Rachel continued, "He represents someone who not only defeated you in life on the track field back in high school, but also in death at the Malkina Railroad Station. His last words to you were, 'Gerhardt, tonight when you go to sleep, remember it was a Jew who outran you once again.'"

In German, Rachel added her final thought. "Well, *sir*, you are a lucky man and have been twice blessed with a special memory by a

Jew. Tonight when you go to sleep, remember it was a Jewish lawyer who brought your true crimes to the world today. Would you like to comment on any of the statements I have just made?" His demeanor was that of a lifeless wax figure, frozen in its place without sound, as if he were on display in a museum.

In English she said, "I have no more questions for the defendant."

"Mr. Reinhart; do you have any questions for the defendant?" Justice Messenger asked. Max Reinhardt shook his head and said no.

Justice Messenger concluded, "Mr. Dreschler, you may step down." He didn't move from the chair. Rachel began to return to her seat. Dreschler did not take his eyes off her.

Justice Messenger repeated, "Mr. Dreschler, you may step down." The Nazi started to exit the witness stand and remained focused on Rachel. Within seconds it ended — whatever little bit of self-control he had left was gone. His mind snapped when he lunged and ran toward her, yelling in German, "I'll kill you, Jewish whore."

Danni leaped from his chair. "Racheli, look out!" he shouted.

She turned, but it was too late. Gerhardt Dreschler's hands were around her neck. He slammed Rachel's head down on the prosecution table as he choked her. Danni raced toward them.

"Get him off her!" Danni screamed. It took three guards to restrain the Nazi. Even though he was older in years, his body exhibited the strength of a youthful boy. She was breathing, but unconscious, and Dreschler's fingerprints were visible on her neck. Danni lifted Rachel and frantically rushed toward the exit.

"There's no time to wait for an ambulance; I need a police car now!"

Thirty-Three

As Danni raced out of the courtroom, an officer followed quickly behind and called for assistance. A police car was waiting when they exited the building.

"Hurry, go to Hadassah Medical Center," Danni shouted as he carried Rachel into the car. The sirens roared. Danni saw his sleeve covered in Rachel's blood, and a swollen gash on her head was pressing on his inner arm.

"Racheli, wake up! Please, *motek*, my love, wake up." He looked at the officer. "Can't you go any faster?"

"I'm going as fast as I can, Mr. Hirsch, try and calm down."

"Calm down? She won't open her eyes."

When they arrived, Danni jumped out with Rachel still in his arms and ran inside the emergency room. She remained comatose, and he was shaking with worry.

He stood in the middle of the emergency room screaming for a doctor. His tone was loud and commanding. He was desperate for someone to come and help them.

Dr. Sammi Amar came running.

"What's wrong? Bring her here," he said, not realizing who Rachel was. Danni placed her gently on the gurney.

"My fiancee was brutally attacked and she's pregnant. There is a gash on the back of her head that's bleeding."

The doctor picked up the phone and called for two nurses to assist him. They came immediately running down the hall. They helped him remove Rachel's clothing so he was able to do a thorough exam. The doctor ordered Danni to leave the room, but he refused and pulled out his badge.

Suddenly Rachel began to stir and whimper. Danni reached for her hand.

"Racheli, wake up."

"Hirsch?" she asked in a raspy tone.

"Yes, it's me. Please open your eyes." Her amber-brown eyes looked directly at him and he sighed with relief. "Are you OK?"

It was hard for her to speak.

"My throat hurts me."

The doctor was on the other side and gently felt Rachel's stomach. "Miss, do you have any pain where I'm touching you?" She shook her head. Dr. Amar looked at Danni.

"The baby seems to be fine, but I'm going to do a sonogram just to be sure. How many fingers am I holding up?"

"Three," Rachel responded in a raspy voice.

"What is your full name?"

"Rachel Saunders." He was shocked when hearing her reply and glanced at Danni.

"Mrs. Saunders, are you dizzy?"

"No, but I do have a headache."

"We're going to try and alleviate the pain, try not to move. I'll be back in a moment to do the sonogram."

He motioned for Danni to join him in the hallway. "Is that Rachel Saunders, the lawyer?"

"Yes, it is. She was in court today and Gerhardt Dreschler went mad. He ran toward her and choked her, then smashed her head into a table. Did you check the bump?"

"I did. She may have a concussion, but it's hard to say without a CT scan, and due to her pregnancy, I won't order one. Mrs. Saunders received a significant amount of trauma to the back of her head. The next twenty-four hours will reveal the effects of her injury," the doctor said, scribbling on his clipboard. "I'll see that she is given a private room and we'll monitor her carefully. There is obvious bruising, but it doesn't look like as though she has a broken larynx. Considering what happened, she was speaking pretty well and a sore throat is normal."

Just as Danni was about to go back inside with the doctor he saw Max Reinhart walking toward him.

"Doctor, tell Mrs. Saunders I'll be in shortly, please." Reinhart stood in front of Danni.

"Mr. Hirsch, how is Mrs. Saunders?" Danni didn't answer. "Please, Mr. Hirsch, tell me how she is."

"Why don't you ask that animal you're representing? Better yet, how about I go to Rimonim Prison and smash *his* head into a table and keep doing it until he stops moving." Danni turned and walked away.

When Danni re-entered the room, Dr. Amar was in there examining Rachel. She was happy when he returned. She told Dr. Amar that her head was still aching, but even though she had a deep cut, he assured her that she wouldn't need stitches. He ordered the nurse to get her some Tylenol and to start a glucose IV because it hurt for her to swallow. Dr. Amar was concerned that Rachel had a concussion, even though she said she wasn't nauseous. As he began the sonogram, he reassured Rachel that he baby seemed to be OK.

When Dr. Amar left she looked at Danni.

"What did the doctor say when you were outside in the hallway?"

"You may have a concussion."

"What else?"

"He doesn't think you broke your larynx, even though you have pain in your throat. The soreness you're feeling is normal after what happened," Danni said. He paused. "Racheli, do you remember what happened?"

"Yes," she said, and she began to cry. "I'm sorry."

"Sorry for what, my love?"

"I promised not to jeopardize the wellbeing of the baby, and today I did. Please forgive me."

Danni wiped the tears from her eyes. "There is nothing to forgive." He held her hand firmly. "I got scared when you wouldn't wake up."

Rachel paused. "I really broke him today." Danni didn't respond.

"Did you hear what I said? I broke him."

"He almost broke you in return."

The nurse came in to bring Rachel an extra blanket and a pair of socks.

"Remember when Zvi Artandi's crew didn't give the beast a blanket shoes and socks? Why did I fight to get them for him when all he said to me was, 'I will kill you, Jewish whore?'"

"Look at me, Racheli; he will never get close enough to hurt you ever again. I promise, if he ever tries to come near you, I'll kill him myself."

"How could I insist they give him those things? Nothing could warm the coldness in his heart."

"You are a decent person and you always do the right thing."

"Not always, Hirsch, look what I did to Alexander Frece. That poor man. Today I saw his face, the hurt and disbelief of what he witnessed in the courtroom. Max Reinhart could have opposed me more and he didn't."

"Reinhart was here."

"What do you mean?"

"He had the nerve to come to the hospital to see how you were. The bastard he's representing almost killed you."

"What did you tell him?"

"Let's just say I made him aware that his presence wasn't welcome."

An orderly came in to transport Rachel to her permanent room on the sixth floor, where she would have her own space and be treated like a celebrity. Danni stayed by Rachel's side as the medical team settled her in.

As she was getting comfortable, the prime minister called Danni. He briefed him on Rachel's condition, and he offered to get her anything she needed. When he hung up the phone, Rachel was dozing and the nurse came in to remind him to wake up her up every two hours in case she had a concussion — if she fell asleep for too long, she could possibly fall into a coma. He didn't like the way it sounded when the nurse gave the explanation.

Meanwhile, it was 10:30 a.m. in Hartford, Connecticut. David had just finished a class at Yale Medical School and was headed to the student lounge to grab a quick bite. As he was about to enter the dining hall, a friend of his stopped him.

"Hey Saunders, how is your mother?"

David looked at him, puzzled. "What do you mean?" His friend was silent. "Come on, tell me, what you are talking about?"

"It's all over the news, that German war criminal attacked your mother in open court today in Israel."

David ran inside the lounge. On the wide screen television hanging above him he heard a newscaster giving a report. David was in shock as he listened to the story of what had happened to Rachel. He immediately called the hospital in Jerusalem and demanded that they connect him to Danni. He finally got through to him and Danni explained everything that happened, then assured him she was being well-cared for. David said he would get on the next flight there.

David called several airlines to try to find the earliest flight to Israel, then called his uncle Michael to tell him what had happened. Michael's assistant said he was in a meeting, and David said it was urgent and that he should be pulled out of the meeting. When he finally got on the phone, David relayed all the information he had and Michael also agreed to get on the next flight to Israel.

Rachel slowly opened her eyes, and Danni sat watching her. The covering doctor on call came in to check on her. She was feeling nauseated — another sign of a concussion, not morning sickness. She was in a cold sweat.

"The swelling hasn't gotten any worse, but you clearly do have a concussion. Try to lie back and move as little as possible," the doctor said. "Under the circumstances, these symptoms aren't unusual."

The nurse re-entered the room. "Excuse me, there is a Mr. Chayim Rabinowitz outside Mrs. Saunders' room."

Danni met him in the hallway. Chayim extended his hand to him. "How is Rachel?"

"She's sleeping right now. They think she has a concussion."

"Is there anything you need; anything I can do?"

"No, thank you." He handed over Rachel's purse and briefcase.

"We're all in turmoil from what happened today, and the reporters are having a field day with it. I heard it's all over the news here, in Europe and in the states."

"You won't believe this; Max Reinhart was at the hospital earlier. He wanted to know how Rachel was."

"I'll be damned, please send her my best."

Danni realized he should probably call Ariella and Ronni to let them know what was going on. He asked Ariella to pack a back of Rachel's things to bring over to the hospital. Finally, the last phone call he made was to Helena Krieger. He explained that was Rachel was OK, and that they were monitoring her closely.

Danni didn't want to speak to anyone else. He just wanted to sit with Rachel and make sure that she was OK.

Thirty-Four

The next morning, Dr. Kashan, her OB/GYN, came to check on Rachel and to perform a second sonogram and amniocentesis.

"Wow, the lengths people will go to get some attention," he said. Rachel laughed and felt comfortable in his presence.

He performed the tests and assured her that everything with the baby was fine.

"Your little girl is thriving," he said. Rachel and Danni were overjoyed, even in the midst of the crisis.

That afternoon, Ariella and Ronni arrived to the hospital with Rachel's things. After the nurse help her put on the pajamas Ariella brought, Rachel stood in front of the mirror to brush her hair and noticed the purple bruise on her neck in the reflection.

"Mrs. Saunders, may I help you?" the nurse asked.

"Yes, I'd appreciate that; thank you." Rachel still felt a bit unsteady and didn't want to overdo it.

"There, you look lovely. I would like to say something; Mr. Hirsch's devotion to you is unrelenting. The man wanted to care for you by himself and would not leave your side last night. He is a rare find — one I would hold onto."

Rachel smiled. "Yes; I'm a very lucky woman and I have no intention of letting him go."

She was wearing a lovely set of periwinkle silk pajamas that had a matching robe. She sat in bed and had the deportment of a debutant, despite her injuries and the trauma she had suffered the day before. The others returned.

Ariella stood beside her. "You look like a princess," she said. Ronni agreed and Danni couldn't take his eyes off her.

"I thought this ensemble would offset the color of my purple neck," she said in a raspy voice. None of them laughed or responded. "Come on guys, lighten up."

A few minutes later, David and Michael arrived. Rachel was relieved to see them.

"Shelly, even after everything, you look great.," Michael said, giving her a kiss.

"Thanks, do you like how I coordinated my bedroom wear with my eggplant-colored neck?"

"Yes, it blends nicely." Rachel looked at Danni, Ronni and Ariella. "At least we Landaus have a good sense of humor."

"So, what's new?" Michael asked in an attempt to distract her.

"Hirsch, Michael wants to know what's new; can you think of anything we can tell him?" she said, smirking.

"Hmm, let's see, as a matter a fact something does come to mind. Racheli, shall you or I do the honor?"

With that, loud as her croaky voice would allow, "I'm going to have a baby in late September."

The group seemed to be in shock; not one of them uttered a word right away. David studied his mother carefully.

"That's wonderful," David said with a smile, breaking the silence. "Do you know if it's a boy or a girl?" Rachel nodded yes to her son.

"Will I have another brother, or finally a sister?" Ariella asked. "I think we're going to have a sister."

Ronni added, "A sister would make sense; it would even out the sides — two and two."

Michael smiled, "Come on Shell, am I going to have a niece or another nephew?"

"Hirsch, don't keep them in suspense," Rachel said.

"I am happy to announce we're all going to have a little girl." The room roared with happy excitement. Everyone embraced Danni and Rachel; it was a warm, well-received family moment.

Once the group left for the evening, Danni and Rachel were alone in the room.

"Racheli, this time things will be different. When Ronni and Ariella were little, I worked long hours and missed a lot. I regret that," Danni said. "Once the trial ends, I'm going to let Liam know I'm retiring."

"And I'm going to stop practicing law," Rachel added. "I left the DA's office because I hated the horrible things I witnessed day after day. Everything I learned as a prosecutor helped me nail that cold-hearted animal, and this trial has proven to be the highlight of my career. I couldn't have hoped for a more perfect culmination. I'm ready to call it a day; there's nothing more for me to prove."

"God gave us a very precious gift — our own little girl to love and nurture. It's our new beginning," Danni said.

A few minutes later, David came back to the hospital to take Danni home. He kissed Rachel goodnight and assured he would be back in the morning.

When Rachel was finally alone, her mind wandered back to Alexander Frece. What could he be thinking? Watching the man that raised him transform into a different person before his eyes must have been overwhelming and hard to see. On that horrible day, he was hounded by reporters when leaving the court building and again at his hotel. After all that happened, Alexander continued to be faithful to the trial. Each day his wife called and begged him to return to Austria, but the dutiful son wouldn't give up his determination to see the trial through to its very end. Yet, he had no desire to speak with his father. No words could justify the evil acts of aggression committed by the Nazi's own hand. Alexander's only motivation to prevail was to focus on the goodness in the person who reared him. It still had to exist somewhere in the soul taken over by malevolence; he had to believe it.

Two days had passed since the awful attack played out in the courtroom. Ethel Schultz paid an early morning impromptu visit to Chayim Rabinowitz at the Knesset.

"Mr. Rabinowitz ..." the elderly woman had trouble expressing herself and Chayim saw she was visibly bothered.

"Mrs. Schultz, is something wrong?" She hesitated before answering.

"Sir, there is. I would like you to arrange a visit for me to Rimonim Prison. I have something to say to Gerhardt Dreschler that I can't hold back any longer, and I would also appreciate if you and Mr. Reinhart were present with me at this meeting."

He looked puzzled. "What is it that you have to say to him?"

"Please, do not to make this any harder for me than it already is. You will hear what I have to say when I speak directly to him."

"The reason I ask is because if I am able to facilitate a meeting, I'm sure Dreschler will want to know the nature of the appointment."

"Just tell him not everything is as it seems. I'm sure those words will spark his interest," Ethel paused. "I would greatly appreciate if you could do me this service; you know how to reach me."

When Ethel left, Chayim arranged to meet with Reinhart. The two men were cordial to one another. Before they began Max asked with the greatest sincerity, "Mr. Rabinowitz, how is Mrs. Saunders' recovery coming along?"

"Mrs. Saunders is a strong woman, she's doing well."

"When you speak to her, please send my sincerest regards and that I hope she recuperates quickly."

Chayim was floored by his genuine words. "I will relay your sentiments to her."

"Thank you."

"I'm sure you're wondering why I've asked you to come here today. This morning Ethel Schultz was here, and she asked that I set up a meeting with Gerhardt Dreschler at the prison and claims to have something to say to your client. Her exact words were, 'Tell him not everything is as it seems,'" Chayim said. "Mrs. Schultz was very cryptic; that was all she would reveal. If he agrees to proceed with this discussion, I am ready to go forward and have the arrangements made. Dreschler would be in a room with a glass partition and the three of us will be on the other side of the panel."

Reinhart agreed, and was also curious to know what Ethel had to say.

The defense attorney left the Knesset and headed to Rimonim Prison. Upon his arrival, he was escorted into a private meeting room and waited for his client. Gerhardt Dreschler's hands were cuffed and he had shackles on his legs. Usually they were removed, however after what had played out in the last court session, the iron restraints remained. Today a guard stood inside the space rather than his usual outside post.

Dreschler looked at his attorney. "Have you come to tell me the Jew is dead?"

"Mrs. Saunders is recovering nicely, no thanks to you. I've come about another matter. Ethel Schultz, your mother's nurse, wants to come here. She has something to say to you."

Dreschler smiled. "So, the old woman wants to thank me?"

"*Thank* you?"

"Yes, for the papers I gave her."

"Gerhardt, I don't know what it's about. She spoke to Rabinowitz and said to tell you that not everything is as it seems."

Dreschler's cocky smile became a sullen look of curiosity. "Is that all she said?"

"Yes, that was it. Will you see her?"

"Fine, when is she coming?"

Reinhart exited without responding, and immediately called

Chayim to arrange the visit for the next morning. He went back into the room and told Dreschler the plan.

"Max, you didn't even ask me how I'm feeling after my ordeal the other day."

"What do you mean, 'your ordeal?'"

"When I grabbed her, I hurt my wrist and think it's sprained." He looked at Dreschler then to the guard.

"We're done here."

Thirty-Five

The next morning Chayim Rabinowitz arrived at Ethel Shultz's home. His curiosity about the meeting with Dreschler was intensified as they made their way to the penitentiary. When they arrived, Reinhart was already waiting inside. He was cordial and polite to the nurse as they made their way to the elevator. The three were escorted to the meeting room. After they were situated, a guard appeared. There was a glass partition separating Dreschler from his visitors. Dreschler smiled at Ethel in his usual conceited style. She nodded her head to him and acknowledged his presence.

"I hear your partner is recovering well, be sure to give her my very best regards," Dreschler said, breaking the silence. Rabinowitz did not acknowledge the remark. "So, have you come to thank me?"

"*Thank* you? Thank you for what?" Ethel replied.

Gerhardt focused his attention again on Chayim Rabinowitz. "Listen to what she has to say, Mr. Assistant Prosecutor. The old woman has come to thank me for the freedom papers I gave her. You read about them in her deposition."

"That's the reason you think I'm here? You didn't give me those documents to help me; they were provided to cover you," Ethel said. "If the Reich found out a Jew was in your employ, it would have been a reprimand or a possible demotion. It was definitely in your best interest to secure my freedom out of Germany, you sick, twisted pig. What I'm about to say I've held in my heart for over fifty-six years."

"Stop talking in riddles; why did you come?"

"I came because not everything is as it seems."

"What the hell is that supposed to mean?" Dreschler was becoming visibly frustrated.

"Did you tell your lawyer that March of 1942 was not the first time we met, or don't you remember?" Ethel began. "Perhaps you can't recall our original encounter with one another because I was wearing a surgical mask."

Dreschler looked puzzled.

"No, gentlemen, the first time I met Herr Dreschler was on January 25, 1942 — the night he brought his wife to the Hospital of the Jewish Community. Is it coming back to you, Gerhardt?" The Nazi was beginning to churn. She continued. "I will never forget that evening; there had been a bad snowstorm that caused a terrible accident on the *autobahn*. Several cars spun out of control, which caused a backup for miles. Frau Dreschler's German hospital was further than ours. He chose to bring her to us, the Jewish medical facility. She was pregnant, in labor and bleeding very badly.

"This vile man demanded we look after her immediately and ordered the staff not to document their arrival or departure from the hospital. Regardless of the circumstances, an SS officer or a member of his family receiving health care at the Jewish infirmary would have been frowned upon by the Nazis. Out of fear, the visit was confidential and no record was kept," Ethel paused. Chayim and Reinhart listened intently.

"I was the nurse who worked with Dr. Edmund Fried; he delivered the child. As I said, your wife lost a lot of blood and was in a great deal of pain; the doctor administered an anesthetic before taking the baby by cesarean. He worked diligently to bring your boy into the world safely. Only it was too late — her excessive loss of blood caused the baby's suffocation and he was stillborn. That night, I assisted the same physician with another birth, and a male baby was born to a

Jewish woman. She labored for nearly two days. Dr. Fried was afraid to tell you what happened; he was scared of what you would do to him.

"In a split second he made a decision. He switched the two infants and gave you the Jewish baby. When he told the other mother her child died, she was hysterical. The doctor brought the broken-hearted woman *your* dead son to convince her. She looked at the newborn and said, 'That isn't my son, I don't believe you. I heard my baby cry.'"

Everyone remained silent. Gerhardt Dreschler stared at the woman. Suddenly he rose from his seat.

"It's a lie, you incompetent, filthy Jewish cunt. It isn't true, it can't be true, I would have known."

"Would you, could you have known? Each day I sat in the courtroom and watched what that innocent man underwent out of his love for you. The scrutiny he tolerated from the media due to the misfortune of being your child, and all the while I wanted to scream out, 'You are not part of him.' Not one ounce of the sinful man's blood flows through your veins. He should know the truth and be told that his body isn't poisoned with any part of you. The boy you raised represents everything you hate; what you despise most of all in this world. A German SS officer fostered and cultivated a Jew. Remember that when they hang you by the neck. Let it be your last thought in life before you enter an eternity of hell."

The sociopath was in disbelief of Ethel's words. He looked at his lawyer.

"I demand a DNA test, it will prove the lies this Jew bitch has spewed here today and show that Alexander Frece is one-hundred percent Aryan!"

Thirty-Six

Chayim Rabinowitz and Max Reinhart were stunned as they left the prison. They spoke no words while escorting Ethel Schultz from the penitentiary. The elderly woman felt resolve as she walked outside looking straight ahead without so much as a glance toward either man.

On his drive back into the city the defense attorney found her statements to be unreal. Max Reinhart saw the pleasure Ethel Schultz received while watching the Nazi squirm. She unburdened her mind after enduring years of torment, knowing the truth. How and what would he tell Alexander Frece?

Reinhart was almost at the hotel. He hadn't seen or been in contact with Alexander since that day in court. Max parked the car and entered through the back entrance. Outside there was a group of reporters waiting to see if Alexander would venture out in public. The desk clerk recognized the lawyer and allowed him elevator access to the 8th floor. He knocked on the door of room 813.

"Alexander, its Max Reinhart. May I come in please?"

Frece was disheveled when he entered the room.

"Hello Alexander, how are you?"

"How am I? You mean for a man whose father is a Nazi killer and felt gratified while slaughtering thousands of Jews?"

It was the first time he said aloud what lay so heavily in his heart. Reinhart glanced at him. "You might not be."

"I might not be what, the son of a psychopath? What do you mean? I saw the photos and heard everything that confirms Gerhardt Dreschler is a man who worked for the Reich with pleasure; he reveled in his position and went well beyond his call of duty to make sure blameless people suffered. Now you say I might not be?"

Reinhardt stood silently before answering. "What I mean is you might not be his son."

Alexander stared at him. "I don't understand, Max, what the hell are you talking about?"

"Some accusations have been made."

"What accusations?"

"The nurse that took care of Gerhardt's mother claims you are not his son."

"Why would she say that and how would she know?"

"You might want to sit down for this," Reinhart said. Slowly, he began to relay the story of what had occurred earlier that day. Alexander did not move or make a single sound.

"Max, you're talking crazy," he finally said.

"I know it sounds crazy, but it might be true. Dreschler asked for a DNA test."

Alexander was shocked to hear that the man who raised him would request proof. Reinhart thought it would be best to administer the test as soon as possible. When he left Alexander, he called Chayim to tell him he would take the test the next morning.

Chayim did not want to undertake any further action without consulting his lead counsel. Even though Rachel was still in the hospital, he needed to speak with her immediately. He arrived at Hadassah Medical Center that afternoon.

He greeted her warmly. "I'm happy to see you're coming around."

She saw her co-counsel seemed distressed as he stared at her. "We need to talk." He then glanced at Danni.

"Maybe I should leave," Danni said.

"No, Danni, please stay. I will need your help."

Rachel's expression turned serious, "What's wrong?"

Just as Reinhart had to relay the story to Alexander, Chayim was tasked with telling Rachel. She sat shaking in bed as she heard all the details. Rachel's head began to spin when she thought of her mother's words that were identical to Ethel Shultz's recollection of the past:

Not a day has gone by when I haven't thought of my firstborn. I remember it as if it were yesterday. Your brother, Benjamin, was born on January 25, 1942. It was a cold, snowy night in Berlin and the hospital was crowded because there had been an accident on the freeway. I labored for nearly thirty-six hours and the doctor said he was stillborn. I know it's not true. He cried. When I close my eyes, I can still hear him.

"Chayim, I need to know, did Ethel Schultz give you the name of the Jewish woman who gave birth?"

"No, why?" She became vividly uneasy and made it obvious. "I need to speak to her right away." He saw Rachel didn't want to give him any details, so he called Orley to set up a conference call with Ethel.

"Ethel, I really need to speak to you in person," Rachel said to her on the phone. "Please, I understand everything that you have endured today, but this is really, really important." Her voice started to quiver.

Ethel could hear the desperation in Rachel's voice.

"OK, tell Mr. Rabinowitz to come pick me up whenever he's ready."

"Thank you, Ethel. You don't know what this means to me."

Rachel hung up the phone and stared straight ahead without saying a word.

"Racheli, what's going on?" Danni asked. She demanded to know where David was, and Michael, who had just arrived at the hospital, explained that he was getting his phone fixed. She became frantic.

"Racheli, why are you acting like this?" Danni said, becoming more concerned by her behavior. She didn't answer Danni's question and looked toward her brother.

"It can't be true, Michael it can't be, oh God, it can't be."

"What can't be true? You aren't making any sense."

"The baby can't be alive; all those years we treated Mom as though it were a sad woman's distorted recollection, and she always swore hearing him cry." Her brother became very serious. Danni was confused. He tried to settle his sister.

"Shelly, go slow."

"There is a nurse who worked at the hospital where Mom gave birth to Benjamin."

Danni was still puzzled. "Benjamin?"

Rachel was sobbing as she looked at him. "Yes Benjamin; my mother gave birth during the war in Berlin before she was sent to Auschwitz. That was the reason why my father came to the states without her; she was eight months pregnant at the time and couldn't travel. My mother and her parents were going to join him in New York after the baby was born, but ..." Rachel was too emotional to finish the story.

Michael picked up where she left off. "As you know, my mother never made it to New York. She gave birth to a stillborn baby boy at the Jewish hospital in Berlin."

Danni was shocked and began to put together the pieces. "Oh, my God."

Michael stopped narrating. "Would someone please tell me what happened"?

Danni told him the whole story — everything Chayim relayed that Ethel Schultz said. Rachel listened and studied Michael; his expression showed his disbelief of the words being spoken. To think their mother's claim of hearing the cries of her child so long ago in a Berlin hospital might be true was an overwhelming prospect they had never expected. Continuing to observe one another, no words were spoken.

Danni thought to himself, *Could this be the reason why Rachel always felt empathy for Alexander Frece?* She had openly agonized over his cross-examination in court. It was hard to imagine the so-called son of a Nazi was possibly her very own flesh and blood. The thought was unfathomable.

After a long while Rachel regained her composure and broke the silence that lingered in the room. "All those years we heard Mom speak of Benjamin, and not one of us believed her." She was restless as she waited for Chayim and Ethel to arrive. Finally, there was a knock at the door and Chayim entered the room with Ethel.

"Hello, Mrs. Saunders. It's good to see you again."

"Hello, Mrs. Schultz, likewise. This is my brother, Michael Landau, and my fiance, Danni Hirsch." The two men shook her hand. "I appreciate your coming here on such short notice." Rachel sensed that she felt uncomfortable with Danni and Michael in the room. "Mrs. Schultz, please feel at ease, it's alright for all of us here to speak freely with one another. Mr. Rabinowitz told me about your earlier meeting with Gerhardt Dreschler." Rachel's eyes filled with tears. She eagerly tried to hold it together, but her whole mental and physical being began to fall apart.

"Mrs. Schultz, do you remember the name of the Jewish woman who gave birth to the baby boy?" Ethel looked at Rachel and thought the question was strange.

She nodded. "Her name was Dora Landau."

Rachel grabbed her brother and Ethel looked at them, confused, until suddenly her eyes went directly to Michael. She pointed at him and said, "Landau."

In a broken voice he said, "Are you sure?"

"Yes, Mr. Landau, very sure."

Michael told Ethel that Dora had always spoken about the baby she gave birth to in Berlin, always swearing he lived.

"Benjamin," Ethel said. "I remember her referring to the baby by that name."

Rachel became inconsolable. Chayim was shocked. Even though Danni had some idea, the confirmation that Alexander Frece was actually Benjamin Landau was shocking.

Michael continued to hold Rachel and whispered in her ear, "I don't' believe this is happening, after all this time he's alive."

Ethel looked at them. "Your mother was exhausted after a very hard labor. Finally, when your brother was born and he cried, she was barely conscious or coherent. I will never forget her smile when she heard the doctor say it was a boy. It was an expression filled with adulation and she said, 'My Benjamin.' Hours later, she became lucid and Dr. Fried showed her the stillborn Dreschler child. She told him it wasn't her baby; your mother wouldn't accept it."

Rachel freed herself from Michael's grasp and wiped her eyes. "Why didn't you tell us about this when we interviewed you?"

Mrs. Schultz was caught off-guard by the question before responding. "When you've lived with a secret that lays dormant for so long, you begin to believe it never existed. Like Dreschler, once those memories are rekindled, the fire ignites and burns; we can't conceal our feelings any longer, and we become consumed by them. Gerhardt Dreschler is living proof of this truth; his real inner self came to light when he was faced with the reality of the past. As the trial progressed, the heat of the hidden light became brighter and brighter," Ethel said, taking Rachel's hand. "Mrs. Saunders; I have wrestled with this demon every day in that courtroom. After what I saw the Nazi do to you, I knew I could no longer remain silent — that day, I watched Alexander Frece's face filled with terror and disgust. I'm very sorry for the shock and pain I caused here. That man needs to know he has no allegiance to a monster he thinks is his father."

"Mrs. Schultz, forgive my tone. Thank you again for coming here; I know this whole ordeal hasn't been easy. Once more you have shown yourself to be a very brave woman."

"Thank you, Mrs. Saunders. Would all of you please excuse me, I need to get some air."

Chayim assured her he would be downstairs in a few minutes to take her home. He turned to Danni and explained that Alexander Frece would take the DNA test the next morning.

When Chayim was gone, Rachel's thoughts ran rampant and she stared blankly.

"God, what have I done? I attempted to expose a criminal and publicly humiliated my own flesh and blood," she said. "Michael — he has to be told, our brother will never believe it, least of all from me.

Danni, when they run the DNA test, include two samples from us so we can show him proof."

Danni went to his car and called Mossad headquarters to speak to a forensic specialist. He instructed Jack, the specialist, to go to Rimonim Prison and collect the DNA sample from Gerhardt Dreschler. He also instructed him to collect one from Alexander Frece the next morning at the Dan Panorama. Danni urged him to use discretion and not to leak anything to anyone.

Rachel was released from the hospital that morning and was excited to be going home, hoping to find comfort in a familiar atmosphere. She was warmly greeted by her son and brother at the house. She was eager to take a shower. Rachel gingerly cleansed her sore scalp and felt a sting from the warm water. Twenty minutes later Danni came upstairs and found her sitting on the chaise lounge in their bedroom wearing a pair of yellow and lilac pajamas.

"Feeling better?"

The somber expression on her face answered his question. It was a look he became familiar with — one where her inner self was hidden and tucked away. She couldn't find the relief she sought. Wanting desperately to help and not knowing what to do made him feel powerless.

They heard someone pulling up in the driveway. Danni looked out the window and saw Jack. He let him in the house and the men walked upstairs with Michael.

As the group came through the bedroom door, Rachel stood instantly. Danni made the appropriate introductions and the samples were taken.

"The results will be ready on Monday," Jack said. "Yesterday when I went to Rimonim, before the guard took Gerhardt Dreschler back to his cell, he asked when Alexander Frece would be tested and I didn't answer him."

"Thanks for all your help, Jack. I'll walk you out."

After he left, David came upstairs with Danni.

"What's going on?" David asked. Rachel looked toward her brother for guidance. "Mom, come on; please tell me what is it? I could sense you weren't yourself when I came to the hospital last night."

"No sweetheart, I'm fine."

"Then what?"

Explaining was the hard part; it was still difficult for her to accept the veracity of the situation. Michael addressed his nephew.

"Did you ever hear your grandmother talk about someone named Benjamin?"

"Yeah, when I was little, Grandma told me many stories. I enjoyed listening to her make up the most incredible fables. Every night before I went to sleep she'd come in my room before Mom and tell me these amazing tales; we called it our special time together and often spoke about a baby boy named Benjamin," Michael said. "She said he was her firstborn child and I asked where he lived. Grandma always answered, 'I don't know, let's pray God is keeping him safe.'"

Rachel began to cry. "I didn't know that, sometimes I listened by the door while she told you stories, but I never heard her talk about Benjamin in your presence."

"Mom, there really is a Benjamin?"

In a broken voice Rachel answered her son's question. "Yes."

"Where is he?"

"We think Alexander Frece is Benjamin."

"I don't understand."

"It's true — your grandmother had another child in Germany during the war before being sent to Auschwitz. The doctor in the hospital told her the baby was stillborn, but she never believed it and always claimed to have heard him cry. A nurse who testified at the trial claims that Gerhardt Dreschler brought his wife to the Jewish hospital in Berlin where she gave birth to a child, and it was a male baby," Rachel explained. "This woman claims it was Dreschler's son who died and said the doctor switched Grandma's baby with theirs.

Alexander Frece has the same birth date as Benjamin and the nurse claims the Jewish woman who gave birth went by the name of Dora Landau."

David stood in silence and watched his mother. "You heard about this yesterday?"

"Yes."

"Are you telling me that Alexander Frece is my uncle and was raised by a Nazi?"

"We think so. The man who was here before took a DNA swab of Michael and me; this morning he went to get a sample from Alexander Frece, and yesterday from Dreschler. The results will be in on Monday, I didn't know how to tell you."

"Mom, I think you should lie down."

"Racheli, that's a good idea, while you relax; I will make you lunch," Danni said.

"I'm not hungry."

"Please, you have to try, for the baby." David looked at Danni then to his mother.

"Go on, Mom, take a nap, maybe when you wake up you'll feel like eating."

When she was alone with Danni, Rachel looked at him.

"Hold me, Hirsch, and make it stop." He was happy that she turned to him for comfort instead of withdrawing. He lay next to and held her in his arms.

"Make what stop?"

"All the pain. This hurts too much, it's unbearable. I feel like God has a grudge and is testing me, always testing me. I don't know what else he wants. When he took Alon, I was dead inside for over 20 years and didn't allow myself to love again for the longest time. Now this — he had me destroy a man who is part of myself. Do you suppose he wants my soul?"

"Racheli, stop this talk. God wants nothing from you."

He placed his hand on her stomach. "Look what he gave you, what he gave us. Never question his methods or reasons, only he knows his purpose and we must accept his will." Danni wasn't very religious; however he was raised in an atmosphere to believe in God and never second guess his wisdom.

David and Michael were out; Danni brought some lunch to their room after Rachel napped. While she ate her thoughts reflected on the family joke about "the Landau humor." Rachel wondered what kind of personality her eldest brother had under normal circumstances. Was he witty or serious?

"He has my mother's eyes; the first time we met him, there was something familiar about them. Think, Hirsch — his horse farm, my mother adored horses. I loved watching her ride when I was a little girl. Mom had a magnificent black stallion named Winston, sometimes she would let me sit on him with her, I use to enjoy being up there and gliding around the estate. Throughout the years every time we tried placating her, she became agitated, finally I truly understand."

The phone rang; it was Danni's parents. They didn't want to intrude on Rachel in the hospital, so they were anxious to see her now that she was feeling better. They made plans to have dinner that night.

He went back to their bedroom, turned on the T.V. and flipped through the channels. Suddenly he stopped. A newscaster was talking and the onscreen headline read: "Alexander Frece may not be the son of alleged Nazi Gehardt Dreschler." Danni listened.

"Oh, shit," he said. Rachel was visibly upset.

"How do you think they found out?"

"I'm not sure, my forensic guy deals with all kinds of confidential matters from my unit every day without any leaks to the media." Danni thought for a moment. "Crap. Remember what Jack said today?"

Rachel looked at Danni, confused. "I don't know what you're talking about."

"He said before the guard took Gerhardt Dreschler back to his cell he asked when Alexander Frece would be tested. That's it."

"What's it?"

"The guard must have put two and two together and leaked the story to the press for a handsome fee; I wouldn't put it past any of

Zvi's men. It's the only logical explanation. When Rabinowitz and Reinhart were at the prison with Ethel Schultz, they were behind a glass partition. Chayim said that Dreschler was on the other side of the divider alone while the guard waited outside. It had to be the man who brought Dreschler to Jack for the DNA test, that son of a bitch."

"Danni, you can't prove it."

"No, but I guarantee you that's what happened." Rachel remained quiet and didn't know what to say.

Little did they know, Alexander Frece sat in his room and watched the same coverage they were viewing. The hotel media frenzy intensified and he felt like a caged animal. The entire ordeal became mentally overwhelming, unbearable and depleted his inward strength. For the past several months he was living his life in a fishbowl and felt like he was drowning, but even as the water evaporated, he still couldn't breathe.

That evening Danni's parents arrived. Rachel was warm but her mind wandered. They were happy to see she was alright. Danni glanced at his bride-to-be, and she smiled while nodding her head in approval toward him.

"*Eema, aba*, we have some special news. In late September, you are going to have another granddaughter." His parents stared at one another before embracing. They were elated; Bella immediately went to Rachel and hugged her affectionately. Then she displayed the same sentiments to her son. Simon squeezed his future daughter-in-law gently, kissed her on the forehead and warmly hugged Danni. Their excitement was heartfelt.

Thirty-Seven

On Monday afternoon, Jack arrived at the house; Danni was home and opened the door. Rachel sat eagerly with her brother and son in the living room as the forensic specialist entered. She was anxiously waiting to hear about the DNA findings.

"Please tell us the results."

"Alexander Frece is not Gerhardt Dreschler's child; however, he is a perfect sibling match to you and Mr. Landau."

Prior to hearing the outcome read aloud, they knew in their hearts it was the truth. Ethel Schultz could not have made up the story. Receiving a legal documented confirmation proved to be a poignant moment. In that instant they acknowledged a member of the family who had never been forgotten by their mother. Rachel reached for her brother's hand and squeezed it. No tears were shed, the crying ended, her strength prevailed and reality set in. It was time to embrace the past and welcome the future.

Before Jack left the home he said, "Mrs. Saunders I did not say anything to the press." She stood and walked toward him placing her hand on his arm.

"Danni and I know you didn't, thank you for handling this delicate matter discreetly."

Rachel called Chayim and asked if he could contact Herr Reinhardt and requested they both come to the house. Upon their arrival, she appeared calm; her professional training took control. Danni opened the door, the defense attorney entered extending his hand and he returned the gesture. Max walked toward Rachel and did the same.

"Mrs. Saunders, I can't tell you how happy I am to see you up and about."

"Mr. Hirsch told me you came to the hospital to see how I was. You were very kind to do so, I appreciate your concern." She acted like a true lady; her recognition of his sincerity was well received. "Gentlemen, I would like you to meet my son, David. Herr Reinhart, this is my brother, Michael Landau."

She asked if anyone would like something to drink and they declined. All were assembled in the living room. When everyone was seated Rachel began the dialogue.

"Today the forensic expert came here to communicate the DNA results of Gerhardt Dreschler's and Alexander Frece's tests. The examination clearly proves that Gerhardt Dreschler is not Alexander Frece's father."

She turned her attention directly to Max Reinhart. "There's more — when Ethel Schultz told your client the information that you and Mr. Rabinowitz were witness to, she neglected to mention the Jewish baby's birth mother's name. It was Dora Landau, mine and Michael's mother."

Chayim listened and didn't appear shocked. Max was clearly taken aback when hearing the news and looked as though he would faint.

"Can I get you a glass of water?" In silence he nodded. When she returned and handed him the drink, Rachel saw his hand was unsteady.

"I know that we are on opposing sides."

Before replying he regained his composure. "Please, Mrs. Saunders; there is something I need to say to you," he said, looking around the room, "to all of you. We are having an off-the- record discussion? Rachel nodded in agreement.

"I was raised in a society where I was taught that those who participated in World War II were only upholding their responsibility and duty as citizens of the country from which they came. Perhaps I was reared this way because to actually face the realism of what happened may have been more than those responsible for it could bear. When I took this case, I thought I knew the facts," Reinhart said. "You all need to understand that during the years Gerhardt Dreschler spent in Austria under the assumed identity of Werner Frece; he was a pillar of the community. It was unfathomable that he tortured and committed treachery against so many." Reinhardt became focused on Danni. "Once you found everything hidden in his wine cellar, I knew I was brought up on a fallacy and was ashamed of my participation in the trial — humiliated that I was helping a mad dog justify his actions when they were inexcusable. After he attacked Mrs. Saunders I was overtaken with guilt."

Everyone listened and remained silent until Rachel interjected.

"I speak to you now as one attorney to another. Our jobs are not at all times cut and dry, as circumstances become evident during a trial we're not always exposed on the side of right. Once we become aware of this, it's often too late and we must overcome the animosity presented to us. As a lawyer, I believe you took this case in good faith based on what you thought was truth. What Gerhardt Dreschler did to me in the courtroom was not your fault," Rachel said. "But with that being said, I would like you to do me a favor."

"Yes of course, any way I can help."

"When you tell Dreschler and Alexander Frece the results, I would appreciate it if you don't mention having any knowledge of my mother, Michael or I as being part of the equation."

"Very well, I won't."

"Thank you." Rachel held two pieces of paper in her hand.

She extended her hand to Reinhardt and said, "Here is the proof Dreschler demanded."

Max walked inside Rimonim Prison and was brought to where the meeting took place between himself, Chayim Rabinowitz and Ethel Schultz. He wanted to make sure Gerhardt Dreschler was on the other side of the glass alone without any guard remaining in the room with him. Reinhardt waited for his client to enter the parameters of the space that separated the two of them. Finally he appeared and saw how eager Dreschler was to hear the news.

"Hello, Gerhardt."

"Max, do you have the results?"

"Yes."

"Are you ready to tell me that scum woman was lying?"

"I can't." His smug expression turned to one of fear and disbelief. The words he wanted to hear proving Alexander Frece belonged to him and was not the child of a Jew would never be said

"No, Gerhardt, it's a fact by all the Reich stood for — Alexander is not your son. Ethel Schultz was telling the truth. The man that stood by you and supported you can sigh with relief."

Dreschler was shocked at Reinhardt's bold interpretation and saw his attorney was taking pleasure in relaying the details to him. Max continued, "Just like the nurse said, not one ounce of your venomous blood flows through his veins. Today he is reborn again and will feel cleansed when hearing the news. I almost forgot to ask you, how is your wrist feeling after — what did you call it? Oh yes, your 'ordeal.'"

The Nazi felt sickened and was irate like his last day in court before he brutally assaulted Rachel. It looked as though he would ignite. Dreschler ran in shackles and handcuffs toward the glass wall and smashed it hard with his fists screaming.

"It can't be true! By all our Aryan domination stands for, you are lying just like that old Jew bitch."

The defense lawyer placed the piece of paper up against the glass. "Go on, read it. Look at each word carefully, memorize it." Suddenly the guard emerged from the hallway and entered the room. Dreschler was pulled back by the security officer. He tried to free himself from his hold.

The Nazi looked Reinhart directly in the eye. "You're fired, you Jew-loving bastard!"

Max tilted his head toward him. "Thank you." He walked out of the room.

He was not looking forward to confronting Alexander Frece; the pleasure he took in telling Gerhardt Dreschler was anything but a feeling of gratification for this innocent man who had been victimized by a false circumstance.

He knocked on the door of the hotel room and his heart began to race.

"Hello Alexander, it is Max Reinhart." Instantly he opened the door and motioned for him to enter the room. For a long moment they stared silently at one another.

Finally, Alexander said, "Please tell me the news."

"You are not Gerhardt Dreschler's son." Alexander began to shake uncontrollably.

Reinhart was standing alongside the crushed man; Frece grabbed onto him and continued his unsteady motion without saying anything.

"I know this is a lot to grasp, but if nothing else, you should feel relieved."

Immediately withdrawing from Max and walking toward a table, he responded with indignation. "Relieved?"

"Yes, relieved. You heard everything as I did — all the misery Gerhardt Dreschler was responsible for. You yourself referred to him as being a psychopath."

Alexander looked at a glass of water that stood on the desk next to him. He reached down and threw it at the wall near where Reinhart was standing. Max was startled as a piece of the cup hit his hand, blood appeared. He quickly walked to the sink and removed the small chip from his flesh. Alexander paced anxiously and walked to the bathroom. He observed the wound he inflicted. "I'm sorry."

Frece grabbed a small towel and pressed it against Reinhardt's hand. Max looked at him. "Don't worry I'm fine, it was an accident."

"Do you have the proof?"

"Yes I do."

"Can I see it, please?" He reached with his uninjured hand and pulled out the paper from his inner pocket which had the DNA results. Alexander studied the information carefully and asked Reinhart to drive him to the penitentiary.

"There are a lot of reporters outside," Max said.

"I don't care. If you won't take me, I will go myself." Reluctant to do so, he yielded to his request. Max waited in the lobby when they arrived at the prison.

Frece waited for almost an hour before Gerhardt Dreschler appeared in the room. He arrived in handcuffs and shackles just as he had earlier that day when meeting with Max Reinhart. This time, both parties were seated face-to-face in the same room and a guard stood close to them. Dreschler wouldn't make eye contact with Alexander or utter a word. It was as if he were someplace else; another dimension his mind drifted to.

Suddenly the stillness in the air was broken when Frece spoke, "Papa." No response was heard. Again he repeated, "Papa, please answer me. Say something."

Suddenly the Nazi raised his head and glared at the grieving shattered human being before him. "I am not your Papa, my son died in a Berlin hospital in 1942. You are not my son, Jew, go."

Alexander couldn't believe the words he heard and thought it was a dream. He sat and watched the man that reared and cared for him. The one he loved and supported through turmoil, the person he stayed loyal to.

"Didn't you hear me, Jew? I said go." Alexander rose from his chair with tears flowing down his face, turned, walked out of the room and ran down the hall to the elevator. Profusely pounding on the button until it arrived, wanting to leave the facility as soon as possible. When reaching the lobby, he made no eye contact with Reinhart.

"Let's get out of here," Alexander said. The car remained quiet and when it came to a final halt, no words were spoken. Alexander got out and slammed the door.

Thirty-Eight

The following morning, Reinhart paid Chayim Rabinowitz an unsched-
uled visit at the Knesset.

"Mr. Rabinowitz, pardon my intrusion."

"No, please do come in."

Reinhart told Chayim about his visits with Dreschler and
Alexander Frece the day before, as well as the meeting between the
supposed father and son.

"No words were spoken between us; he was clearly distraught,
lost and alone. I couldn't stop thinking about it all last night and
I'm worried about him, sir. Mrs. Saunders needs to be made aware
of this; the man is in an awful way. I don't know what he might do."
Chayim agreed, called Rachel immediately and put Reinhart on the
phone to explain.

After hanging up the phone, Rachel looked at Danni and called
for Michael. She told them they needed to go to their brother's hotel.
She referred to her other sibling by his true name; the words came
natural and felt right. Michael nodded. Danni knew they needed to
try to ease his pain. Rachel called ahead to the Dan Panorama and
alerted them of her and Michael's arrival. To avoid the media, they

entered through the back freight entranceway. A security guard took them upstairs on the cargo elevator.

When they arrived at his door her hands were shaking as she knocked. Rachel's neck was still visibly bruised and her voice was a bit weak.

"Hello, Mr. Frece, it's Rachel Saunders. I'm here with my brother Michael. We would like to speak to you, please open the door." Benjamin didn't answer.

She placed her ear to the door and heard him, gesturing to Michael that he was inside. Michael made the next attempt. "Mr. Frece, I know this isn't a good time, however if you would allow us a few minutes; it's urgent!"

Then they listened as the knob turned. Alexander looked at Rachel with contempt and noticed the discoloration on her neck and showed no reaction to it. Then his gaze was on Michael.

"Hello, thank you for opening the door. This is my brother Michael, can we come in please?" He stepped aside to allow them access into the room.

Rachel's body was trembling uncontrollably. Michael couldn't stop looking at him and kept studying his entire being. The eyes were uncanny; it was as though his mother were in the room with them.

He extended his hand to his brother. "It's very nice to meet you." Benjamin hesitated but returned the gesture and avoided making eye contact with Rachel. She felt his scorn.

Finally he did address her. "What do you want? I suppose you've heard?"

"Yes, we've heard." Her eyes filled with tears as she tried to control her emotions. He appeared unaffected by her display of emotion.

"I ask again, why have you come here?" She couldn't speak a word and stood silently.

"Mrs. Saunders, this is very out of character for you. Usually you ramble continually without taking a breath. Tell me why you're here or I ask that you both leave."

Michael interjected, "Please this is difficult for us."

"What is difficult?"

"I know who your birth mother was," Rachel said. Suddenly he became fixed on her.

"How do you know that?"

In an unsteady tone she continued and carefully examined both men standing before her. "We three share the same parents."

Benjamin's adrenaline began to soar. "What are you talking about?"

She pulled out and handed him the DNA test that proved her words to be true. He was stunned by the document and read it over and over. Rachel saw his hand become unsteady. Her eyes didn't leave his as she began to relay the story of what happened on January 25, 1942.

It was too much for him. Benjamin stood astonished and unable to immediately articulate a response to their words.

"I want you both to leave now," Benjamin said.

Michael sounded desperate, "I know this is hard."

Again the elder brother repeated, "I'm asking you to go."

The youngest sibling could not withstand his scrutiny as her tears rolled down her cheeks.

"What did you expect me to say? That this is great news? Are you any better than he is? After what you did to me in that courtroom, did you think your story would make me feel thankful that we share the same bloodline?" Benjamin began. "No, you are no different than him and you were blinded by your own ambition in this case. It consumed your soul; winning was your only objective, Mrs. Saunders. It did not matter who got hurt in the process, so long as you became the victor."

"Rachel had no idea who you were," Michael said, defending his sister.

"Well, sir, that doesn't matter. Her methods were despicable — your sister took me apart on that stand and I was publicly humiliated. Now I ask for the third time that you get out of this room."

Rachel quickly walked to the door and left. In her mind and heart she felt everything he just said was accurate; the attorney's actions toward him were callous. His verbalization of the past events reestablished the guilt she felt.

Michael followed behind her. "Shelly, wait."

"No Michael, let's go."

"Benjamin's angry; give him time to digest the news, you'll see, he'll come around."

"No he won't, I ruined it and everything he said is true. This is my own doing and I have to live with it."

Thirty-Nine

The next morning at Rimonim Prison, Gerhardt Dreschler followed his normal ten-minute shower routine. Each time a guard escorted him and waited in the usual outer parameters of the bath facility. Inmate Gabriel Fein arrived with them and began stacking the towels on the shelves near where the watchman stood. He was serving a life sentence for euthanizing his wife who had been terminally ill. Suddenly, another patroller appeared.

"We have a situation on Block Two!" he yelled to the other guard. Both sentinels scattered the area in a hurry, leaving Fein and Dreschler alone. On previous days, Gabriel observed the Nazi. This encounter with Dreschler was not the first for the convicted mercy killer.

Years ago at Treblinka, he recalled the humiliating abuse executed by the former SS officer. To amuse himself at the camp, the commandant asked prisoners to dance. His exact words were, *"Tanz, Juden!"* which meant "Dance, Jews!"

Trying to survive, in their shame, all did what they were told. Dreschler counted in German as each one moved, *"Ein, zwei, drei."* When he reached *drei*, three, his revolver was pointed, the trigger was pulled and innocent people fell to the ground. The beast repeated the pattern endlessly until all these emaciated human beings were dead. Gabriel was sixteen years old back then and recalled the awful episodes as though it were yesterday. By himself, without any guards on lookout, he opened the door to the shower where Gerhardt Dreschler was standing.

"*Tanz*, commandant. *Ein, zwei, drei.*" He was startled.

Gabriel Fein repeated, "*Tanz, commandant, ein, zwei, drei.*" The former SS officer looked at him defiantly and nodded his head no.

Gabriel walked slowly toward him and placed his hands around his throat. Unable to remove his grasp, Gerhardt began gasping for air as Fein repeated, "*Ein, zwei, drei.*"

That was it. After he said three, Gabriel rammed Dreschler's skull into the wall of the shower. He repeated the rhythm over and over upon reciting three; he shoved the Commandant's head into the tiles until the vile man was motionless. The pool of blood on the floor between Dreschler and Fein was massive.

The guard reappeared in the doorway and looked at Dreschler's lifeless body on the floor. He gaped at Gabriel in disbelief.

"I asked him to dance and he wouldn't. All those years ago at Treblinka he made the helpless ones in captivity dance. He embarrassed them day after day, each person did as they were told and commandant Dreschler shot them anyway," Gabriel said. "The bastard wouldn't do what he was told. Don't you understand? I was once his hostage and for a brief moment, I became his jailor. Seeing the pain in his eyes was exhilarating. For me there was nothing to lose, everything in my life that meant something to me is gone and I have no remorse for what I did here right now. In fact his death was not gruesome enough, he deserved a less sympathetic end then I gave him."

The news was announced around the globe; it was over. The Word War II criminal was dead. Gabriel Fein was sent to a psychiatric facility where he would spend the rest of his days. He would be remembered as a hero to those who perished at the hands of Gerhardt Dreschler instead of the inmate who helped end his wife's life.

Rachel and Danni were told about what happened to Dreschler. The memory of Agent Hirsch's words to Max Reinhart when he came to see Rachel in the hospital overpowered him: "Why don't you ask that animal you're representing, better yet, how about I go to

Rimonim Prison and smash his head into a table and keep doing it until the sick fuck stops moving." It was as if Gabriel Fein heard what he said and did the deed on his behalf.

Two weeks later when the notoriety died down, a call came to the Hirsch dwelling. The prime minister invited the couple to his home for lunch the following day. They obliged since Rachel had physically recovered from her injuries. Upon their arrival they were greeted warmly by the prime minister, Liam Vituri and Chayim Rabinowitz. It was the original clan plus one additional member that they met all those months ago to discuss the strategy of destroying a vicious creature.

"Rachel, it is good to see you looking so well."

"Thank you, Mr. Prime Minister Sir." Glancing at Danni, she smiled. "I've had a wonderful caretaker." Liam Vituri kissed her on the cheek.

"My most important man has done a splendid job in aiding your full recovery," he said.

Chayim came and hugged her. "Hello partner, it's good to see you."

She addressed everyone. "Thank you all for your kind words, gentlemen. We have traveled a very jagged road together and have achieved an extremely positive outcome from our journey. Justice has prevailed and we have become the champions."

The prime minister interjected, "Rachel, we owe you our gratitude; your handling of this trial can only be described as pure brilliance. People around the world have noticed and acknowledged your accomplishments with positive praise. You are truly a gifted attorney — one whose attributes will burn brightly in our hearts forever." He handed her a small box. "Please accept this gift from all of us, you may open it."

She obliged the request. Inside it sat a gold key on top of a note that read, "Let this key guide and unlock any mysterious passageway to reveal truth and sanctity."

After Rachel reviewed the salutation she looked to the prime minister. He recited the words from the paper aloud. "It means never be afraid of what lies ahead; always embrace life's challenges. God has chosen you as one of his special children, trust in his knowledge and welcome his direction, he will never forsake you."

After lunch Danni asked Liam if he could speak with him privately for a few minutes. The gentlemen excused themselves and went into a separate sitting room down the hall. Liam studied him. "Danni, is everything OK?"

"Yes Liam, for the first time in my life, everything is perfect. As you know, Rachel and I are getting married; we're expecting a child in late September."

His superior embraced him warmly upon hearing the news about the baby. "I wish you both a world of happiness."

"Thank you, but there's more. I'm retiring from the bureau; it's time. This is a new beginning for both of us. While my other children were growing up, I missed so much and don't want to make that mistake again."

"Danni, come on now, Mossad is who you are."

"No, Liam, it's who I was. The organization filled an emptiness that I no longer have. Rachel means the world to me. I won't put her through another situation like she had with Alon and I don't want this anymore, my life is complete with her."

Liam intensely studied his protégé. It was obvious; nothing he could say would change his mind. He shook Danni's hand. "You are the best man I ever had, never forget that."

"Thank you, it has been an honor serving with you."

Forty

Two months had passed; it was the day Rachel and Danni would be wed. They had a small ceremony at a synagogue in Jerusalem, only immediate family members were present. Michael came back to Israel with his children for the event. Danni's family was in attendance with David and Jacob. It was a happy time. Rachel was five months pregnant; she wore a lovely peach colored dress that visibly showed her belly and Danni was sporting a black suit. For today, no unpleasant memories existed for the two. Following the ceremony they hosted a little party at their Jerusalem house. After the celebration was over David, Michael, Lisa and Scott drove to the Landau home.

When everyone was gone and the newlyweds were alone, Danni took his bride upstairs and they made passionate love. Rachel rested in Danni's arms.

"I miss New York and I want to go back to have the baby there. It's late enough in my pregnancy where I can fly. Cheryl has a wonderful OB/GYN in Westchester; Dr. Kashan can forward him all my medical records," she said. "Hirsch, I love it here but I feel the need to be in the states right now."

Danni looked at her and saw the resolve in her eyes. He placed his hand on her cheek.

"Mrs. Hirsch, if you want to go to New York, then we shall." She smiled and kissed him.

"'Mrs. Hirsch,' go ahead, say it again."

It was the beginning of June when they arrived with David at the Scarsdale estate, and Lila was thrilled. The baby was active and constantly kicking her mother. Cheryl came to see them the following day and was delighted to witness how happy her friend was.

"Rache you look great, you're glowing."

"Thanks Cohen, it is funny — every day, like clockwork, I need a nap at 2; otherwise it's been a fairly easy pregnancy."

One week later Helena Krieger came with her aid to have dinner with them at the Westchester home. The elderly woman had made a miraculous recovery. She still needed the wheelchair, but her speech improved greatly. Rachel offered to meet Madam in the city for dinner if the ride was too strenuous. She was happy to make the trip to the suburbs and greeted the Hirsch and Landau clan warmly.

"My sweet girl, you look beautiful. Motherhood agrees with you."

It was a lovely evening, the weather was perfect and they dined outside. After the meal was over, Danni, David and Madam's aid excused themselves so the two women could talk alone together.

For the past several months Rachel had tried keeping her mind occupied. Yearning to forget the last days before Dreschler was killed, her thoughts always wandered to Benjamin Landau. The disdain he expressed to her upon their last meeting still haunted the corners of Rachel's conscience.

Helena still read her well. "Tell me, dear heart, what's troubling you?"

"It's about Gerhardt Dreschler's son, you are aware that Alexander Frece is no relation to him?"

"Yes, I heard about it, that poor man was hounded by reporters until he boarded the plane back to Austria. When he arrived there, it continued."

"Did I ever tell you that my mother gave birth to a child in Berlin during the war?"

"No, I don't recall you mentioning it." She relayed the whole story to Madam Krieger.

"Helena, you should have seen his face when my brother Michael and I went to tell him the truth, he hates me."

"Stop talking like that."

"No, it's true, my eldest brother loathes me. It was clear; he so much as said it in his words when lashing out at knowing who he really is. The animosity I've created isn't fixable and never will be."

"That isn't true; anything is possible, look at what happened to Dreschler. God saw that truthfulness and justice prevailed."

"Helena, I can't make it right; not this time, and I've tried to hide it from Danni. He never brings it up, every day I feel Benjamin's presence, just as my mother had."

"Listen to me, time is the greatest healer and God will show you the way."

Everyone kept telling Rachel about God. Trust in his knowledge, welcome his direction, don't question his methods and reasons, He will never forsake you. Now more than ever she relied on his guidance.

David resumed his medical classes during the summer months, which would allow him to catch up for the fall semester. Renovations were being made to the Scarsdale home in preparation for the arrival of baby girl Hirsch. Danni and Rachel moved into her parents' former bedroom. The space next door to it was her childhood place, which would now be their daughter's nursery and was decorated in soft pastel feminine colors accompanied by blonde wood furniture. It was the end of August when the redecorating process was completed.

She officially tied up all loose ends to her law practice and closed the office. Rachel was due in less than a month.

The next few weeks passed quickly. On September 23, 1998, after only three hours of labor, she gave birth to a little beauty weighing six pounds and eleven ounces. Dora and Nathan Landau lived on through their youngest grandchild — Dayna Naomi Hirsch was warmly received by her entire family. The little angel was dainty like her mother with black hair, fair skin and blue eyes. Danni and Rachel were overwhelmed with happiness. David came to see his new sister and was excited to be a big brother. All three were viewing the bundle of joy.

"Mom, she's gorgeous and so small."

"You were just as little and gorgeous, kiddo."

"This one has Grandma and my brother's eyes. Don't you think so?"

"Uncle Michael's eyes aren't blue; they're the same color as yours."

Staring at her son a long while before answering, "I didn't mean Uncle Michael; I was talking about your Uncle Benjamin."

The room became quiet. Danni broke the tension and walked to Rachel's bed and gently stroked her cheek with the back of his hand. He took Dayna from his wife's arms and cradled her in his.

"I think this cutie is going to be a piano player with such long, slender fingers." While studying the baby's hands, she grabbed her father's finger and clenched it tightly. Rachel smiled.

"I know one thing, Princess Hirsch sure loves her Daddy." Danni was a natural and in awe of their little girl.

The next morning, mother and daughter were released from the hospital. Lila greeted them warmly when they arrived home. Cheryl was their waiting with David. "Rache she's incredible, I think she looks like your mother."

"You're right, Cohen. She does; last night I spoke to Michael and told him that. I wanted to stop by and check on you and the baby, I will come again later in the week."

The infant took to her new surroundings and slept comfortably in the wicker cradle in her parents' bedroom. They wanted Dayna close to them right now. Rachel breastfed the newborn every two hours like clockwork and Danni remarked that she had her mother's appetite.

One afternoon when Dayna was sleeping, Rachel wandered to her father's study. Inside his book cabinet she came across several picture albums filled with photos dating back to her parents' days in Berlin before the war. Rachel began gazing through each one; they told a story of decades gone by. She came across other binders featuring her, Michael and their children.

Danni entered the room. "There you are, Mrs. Hirsch." Rachel gleamed at him when he entered. Her husband glanced at all the pictures on the desk. "What are you up to?"

"I'm going through some old family photo albums."

"Wow, is that your mother sitting on the horse?"

"Yes, it is."

"She looks so young."

"At the time Mom was only 17 years old and her one true passion was competing at the riding academy. My father used to tell Michael and me stories about going to watch her at the events and how the spectators cheered when she rode," Rachel smiled, flipping through the pages. "I haven't gone through these in years, come and sit with me. Look at Michael, this was taken—"

"I remember, your father took this picture when we were all at the beach and you wore a pink and gray bathing suit." Rachel turned the page, and there she was at six years old sitting on a bench with Danni, Michael and Alon. She wore a pink and gray bathing suit. She kissed him.

"You're unbelievable. How do you remember these thing? We were so small."

He took her hand and placed it on his temple. "Everything about you, Racheli, it's all here. From that day on the beach, Michael's vanilla fudge ice cream cone, to the time you gave me your handkerchief on the soccer field. I don't need to glance at pictures to remind me, it's locked inside my head."

"That's it."

"What's it?"

"I'm going to make an album with photos of my parents, us, Michael and the children."

"OK, that's nice."

"No, you don't understand, I'm going to compile a book and send it to Benjamin in Austria. This way he can look at his real family and see that he emanated from goodness." Rachel started to cry. "After what I did, he judges us all badly; let him truly envision who he came from. You don't need to look at these pictures because the memories of the past, as you just said, are locked inside your head. My brother doesn't have that luxury. I can supply him with the visual aspect he is missing and maybe, just maybe I can fix the wrong I've done and make it right. It's worth trying."

Danni saw the desperation in her eyes. "Yes, my love, it's worth trying. But even if nothing happens when you forward the photos, promise me you will stop punishing yourself. All of us have done things we're sorry for and tried making amends for them. You certainly have strived to do that, first when you went with Michael to Benjamin's hotel and now with the picture album. It kills me to see the pain on your face, after this it has to stop, enough, no more."

Rachel listened to his words but said nothing.

Each day she worked on the photograph journal, it told a story that began featuring pictures of her parents in their youth to the entire family in present time. It was masterful.

Upon the completion of the book she added one final vital touch — a well-thought out letter written in German. It was mid-November when the parcel was sent; each day she waited with baited breath and hoped to hear from her brother.

Dayna was two months old and growing rapidly; she was happy and beautiful. Rachel held her and looked into those big blue eyes.

"Hello my precious girl; do you know how much your mommy and daddy love you?" She always smiled when hearing her mother's voice. The baby was ready to sleep in her big crib in the nursery. It was the first time the couple were totally alone in their bedroom since Dayna's arrival.

As they lay in bed, Danni nestled his arms around her.

"A former colleague of mine contacted me and asked if I could assist with a prior case."

"What do you mean?"

"I was invited to lend a hand and provide some input on a past situation. Nothing dangerous, all that is required are some verbal thoughts on the matter, I promise."

"What did you say?"

"Nothing yet, I wanted to talk to you first."

"Where will you need to be?" He remained quiet and didn't answer her question. Rachel knew the drill, it was classified information. "How long would you be gone?"

"I'll be away about two or three days at the most."

"Do you want to go?"

"Only if I have your blessing. Trust me; I swear this is nothing that will risk my safety."

Rachel clung to him before replying, "Go, handsome, with my blessing."

Danni wasn't totally truthful with her, he was about to embark on a past crusade. His assistance was not called upon by an ex-comrade; the pursuit of these circumstances was of his own volition. All he kept thinking was, what if Benjamin Landau ignored Rachel's attempts at a family reconciliation? It had been two weeks since she sent her brother the package with no word. He knew the ache would be too great for her to bear, trying to shield his wife from any further grief, Danni decided to take matters into his own hands. He flew to Austria to meet face-to-face with the long lost family member.

Forty-One

As he pulled up in the driveway to the farm, everything looked as it had one year ago. Danni knocked on the door and when the front entrance opened he was eye-to-eye with Rachel's eldest brother, who seemed stunned to see him. He extended his hand and Benjamin would not reciprocate. Danni did not waver in appearance and showed himself to be unaffected by his brother-in-law's snub.

"Hello sir, do you remember me? My name is Danni Hirsch."

Benjamin nodded in acknowledgement of remembering the former Mossad agent. He looked outside. "Is she here too?"

"No, my wife isn't with me." The expression on his face read surprise when Danni referred to Rachel as his wife. "May I come in and speak to you? I've traveled a long way to say what needs to be said."

Reluctantly, he signaled Danni to come inside his home. Gretel was coming from the kitchen as Erik ran to his father.

Danni smiled at the boy. "Your son has grown; how old is he now, three?"

"Yes, he turned three last month," Gretel responded.

"Hello, Mrs. Frece. It's very nice to see you again, I don't know if you remember me."

She nodded her head. "I do."

Everyone conversed in English; unlike Rachel, Danni's German was poor. His spouse was very courteous. Her husband didn't look happy about the hospitable nature she displayed toward the Israeli. He kissed his son's head and handed Erik to Gretel. Once the two men were alone, Benjamin got to the point. "Why are you here?"

"I am here because I love my wife and see the pain in her eyes every day over what happened." Danni tried to keep his composure and didn't want to come across as being emotional. It was not his nature.

Where Rachel was concerned, his feelings took control of him, taking a moment before continuing to speak he noticed an unopened box with Rachel's handwriting lying on a small table near the entrance way. His sensitive state turned to one of annoyance. "I see you've received the box your sister has sent you." Danni looked him in the eye. "Why haven't you at least opened it?"

In a defiant tone he said, "I have no interest in anything your wife has sent me."

At that moment, Gretel and Erik reappeared and she handed a glass of water to Danni.

"Mr. Hirsch, please come into the sitting room with my husband and make yourself comfortable." Benjamin spoke to her sharply in German. Danni understood a little from his Yiddish interpretation and realized he wasn't pleased with the kind gesture.

"Thank you, Mrs. Frece, I appreciate that, my schedule is off track with the time difference, sitting would be nice." She looked to her husband with a forlorn expression and it was obvious that he felt badly for the outburst. Placing his hand gently on her chin he said in a more compassionate tone, "Mr. Hirsch, come this way."

Again the two men were by themselves. Danni sat and studied Benjamin for a long moment before speaking. Rachel was right — his eyes were a replica of her mother's.

"I see that you love your wife very much, Mr. Frece. It looks like we both have something in common."

"You and I, sir have nothing in common."

Danni was unrelenting. "I beg to differ; we both love the women we're married to. If you saw Mrs. Frece being tormented by something, I have no doubt that you would try and do everything in your power to end her anguish. When Rachel had to cross-examine you on the stand, it tore her up inside. She didn't want to."

"Then why did she do it?"

"You know as well as I that her back was up against the wall. Max Reinhart orchestrated what happened, and she was in a no-win situation when he called you to the stand," Danni paused. "To be perfectly honest, I couldn't understand the empathy my wife felt for you from the time Gerhardt Dreschler was arrested. I found it to be unsettling; Rachel realized you were a decent, untainted man. That day at the prison when your car was vandalized, she made sure the guilty person involved had been punished. The Nazi who committed inhumane actions was cold; Rachel saw that he was given a blanket, shoes and socks. Then he tried to kill her in open court. And all you're thinking about is the cross examination which took place. Look at the broad picture and do yourself a favor; open the package your sister sent. Aren't you at all curious about what's inside it?"

The room became silent; Danni had nothing else to say. What ever happened now was in God's hands. He stood and walked out of the room, Benjamin followed. They were met at the front door by Gretel and her son. Danni smiled and thanked them for their hospitality. She replied, "You are very welcome, Mr. Hirsch."

"My wife is right; our daughter does have your eyes. Good day to you both."

Once he was gone, Benjamin kissed Gretel, reached for Erik and held him close. He walked with the toddler to his bedroom and put him down for a nap. When returning to the inner front portion of the house he found Mrs. Frece standing by the table which housed the package from New York. Gretel admitted she had been listening to their conversation and she handed him the box, encouraging him to open it. He hesitated before slowly unwrapping the brown paper covering. On top of the album lay an envelope reading, *To My Brother.* Inside it was the letter Rachel composed in perfect German. Benjamin was too nervous and couldn't view the note. He handed it to his wife and she read it aloud.

My Dearest Brother,

I have often wondered how much of people's lives are predestined before they are born and what percentage is based on their own successes or failures.

When I was a child, our father taught me to always remember whom I came from. He said these special individuals would guide me to my future achievements and triumphs throughout life. Those words have remained with me always. There have been times where I've lost sight of his sound judgment and I hold regret in my heart.

This remorse rings true of the personal grief I caused you in a Jerusalem courtroom. After all these months, your sharp words still sting the essence of my being. It is your belief that I'm just like Gerhardt Dreschler. Ambition consumed my soul at the trial, and I wanted to win no matter what because I believed that a treacherous man needed to pay for the atrocities he committed against the innocent. It was my goal to be victorious on this mission. In having done so, I harmed my own flesh and blood, and that was never my intention. Knowing I am the cause of your pain is an unbearable weight to carry, which I want to be lifted and taken away from both of us. Guilt is an emotion demanding our atonement, and I long to feel forgiveness and hope you can find it in your heart to do so.

Mother named you Benjamin. In Hebrew it means, "Son of my right hand." It represents God's strengths, and you are a stolen compromise in the sense that you were taken from her grasp and the almighty ensured your survival with an unspoken bargain that was given. My husband once told me never to question God's methods and reasons, only he knows his purpose and we must accept it.

If any decency existed in Gerhardt Dreschler, it emanated through you. Dora Landau gave birth and life to a son and God made sure your existence was perpetuated. I now understand that the man who raised you was God's instrument to shield and safeguard her child. Perhaps all those years after the war you were this guardian's salvation and represented his hope. The first time we met, I knew you were raised in a loving environment. I heard your words about how nurturing Werner Frece was. The former SS officer kept his life from the war locked away in a sacred vault where his hatred laid dormant.

Never feel lost or alone because this is not the reality. In the most orthodox sector of our religion, a terminology is used known as bal-chuva, *which means "the one who has returned to the faith." Should you choose to embrace your heritage, Michael and I will welcome you, Gretel and Erik with open arms. If you find the expedition home too difficult to make alone, I, your sister, will be happy to meet you in any part of your journey and guide you the rest of the way.*

It is my hope that this photo album may help define who you are. Remember, my oldest brother; you come from a family filled with love.

Yours,
Rachel

Alexander became overwhelmed and began to cry. Gretel sat in his lap and hugged him.

"Don't you see, my darling? Like your sister said, you come from love. I've always known that, I'm a very lucky woman to have such a wonderful man in my life."

He gazed at her. "I'm not who you thought I was."

"Alexander, please listen to me, you will always be the same caring and loving man I fell in love with, no matter who your parents are. Remember how much you always wanted to have siblings? God has given that to you.

"Gretel, you read the letter, I said awful things to Rachel the last time I saw her. Even toward Michael I behaved badly."

"You were upset, I'm sure they realized that."

"It doesn't justify my actions, Mr. Hirsch was right; I saw how uncomfortable she was that day in the courtroom while questioning me, I was blinded by anger and took it out on her."

"Your sister understands or she wouldn't have sent you this book or the letter." He stared at the photo album and opened its cover. The first picture he saw was of Dora as a teenager mounted on top of a horse. The caption read, "You get your love of horses from Mother." Dora looked young, beautiful and full of hope.

The next page showed a photo of their parents posing for a wedding picture. Its title read, "Mother and Father on their wedding day." Page after page displayed photographs accompanied by subtitles. There were pictures of the whole family from childhood to present time, the final one featuring Dayna wearing a flower-printed pastel lace dress. Along with the album and letter, Rachel enclosed a phone number with her address.

When Danni returned to his hotel he called Rachel. He told her he was coming home, and she was glad to hear that he was safe and that everything went well. She told him Dayna missed him and they were both eager for him to return.

The following evening, the Hirsch women greeted their weary traveler at the door affectionately. Dayna gave her father the biggest smile and Danni reveled in it as he took her from Rachel's arms and kissed her silky sweet-smelling black hair. He kissed Rachel and she told him Lila had prepared all of his favorites. Danni was happy to be home, but he wondered, was his trip in vain or did he actually get through to Benjamin Landau?

The next morning, Rachel was downstairs in the living room putting the baby in her swing. The phone rang.

"Hello." The other party was silent. "Hello?"

Then suddenly a deep voice was heard, "*Guten tag*, Rachel?"

Her heart began to race.

She could see Danni coming down the stairs as she replied in German, "Yes this is Rachel."

"This is your eldest brother calling from Austria." As she heard the words her eyes filled with tears. Not knowing how to address him, Rachel responded, "It's so good to hear your voice."

"It's good to hear yours too." It was an awkward moment for both of them.

She continued, "I trust you and your family are well?"

"We are all fine, thank you. Mr. Hirsch mentioned your daughter when he was here; she's a beautiful little girl." Rachel was confused. "My husband mentioned our daughter to you?" she said, looking at Danni.

"Yes the other day when he was here. Are both of your children in good health?"

"Yes they are, thank you for asking."

"How are Michael and his family?"

"Everyone is doing well."

Then Danni read it on her face, she knew where he went.

"Your letter and photo album were—" the man became choked up and she sensed it when he was unable to complete his thought.

"I hoped they would help you understand a bit about who we are."

"Yes, my sister, they did." It was the first time he verbally acknowledged her as such. "Gretel and I would like to come with Erik to visit all of you. Would that be alright?"

"Yes, that would be wonderful, Alexander, just wonderful."

"You can call me Benjamin if you like."

"We all are looking forward to your trip here, Michael and his children will be arriving to our home for Chanukah in less than two weeks."

"Isn't it the holiday for the festival of lights?"

"Yes Benjamin, a very happy family celebration we will have."

"It sounds marvelous; I will call and let you know when we have made all the arrangements."

"Very good, I look forward to hearing from you."

"Keep well."

"I wish the same to you and yours, goodbye."

"Not goodbye, Rachel, I'll see you soon."

With tears in her eyes she hung up the phone and looked at Danni.

"You never told me how your consultation went this week."

He returned Rachel's stare. "It appears to have gone very well, and it looks like I achieved the outcome I hoped for."

She ran and threw herself in his arms. "I have never loved you more than at this moment, Hirsch. Benjamin is coming with his family for Chanukah and he called me his sister. What did you do?"

"I just told him the truth. Every day I saw how this situation ate you up inside and I couldn't bear watching you suffer anymore."

Rachel called Michael and told him the news. He was shocked but elated to hear what had happened. Rachel thought about the prime minister's words: "Trust in God's knowledge and welcome his direction. He will never forsake you."

The phrase held true and at that moment, this truth embraced her.

Forty-Two

It was hard to believe that a year passed since the last Chanukah celebration that took place in Israel. So much had happened and changed in all their lives. Danni and Rachel's relatives were together again. The Scarsdale estate was large enough to house the entire lot. Benjamin and his family would arrive the next day and reside in the guest house. Jacobs's health had been weaning, making it too difficult for him to join the others.

David became a pro at holding his baby sister. Ariella and Ronni were there with Erez and Gila. Danni's mother and father stood arguing with their grandchildren about who would hold Dayna first while Michael grabbed his niece from his nephew as the Hirsch's fought for their turn. Lisa and Scott were amused by it all. Helena Krieger was in attendance for the occasion. Unfortunately Cheryl, Stephen and their children were spending the holiday in Paris. Lila was busy in the kitchen and happy to have the house filled with people.

The bell rang; Rachel went and opened the door. She was stunned to see her eldest brother standing in the entryway with Gretel and Erik. His arrival a day early was unexpected, yet very well received. He smiled at his sister then handed her a bouquet of beautiful yellow tea roses.

"Hello, Rachel." Instinct guided her arms around him as the flowers fell to the floor.

"Welcome home, Benjamin, welcome home." He held her tightly and they both wept. Rachel embraced her sister-in-law warmly and kissed Erik. She reached down and picked up the flowers.

"I'm sorry; they're lovely and they happen to be my favorite, thank you."

"In one of the photos you sent me, I noticed you wearing a corsage with them. I wanted to surprise you and Michael."

"Well, it is a wonderful surprise."

Danni came to the door and was astonished to see them. Immediately, Benjamin smiled and extended his hand to Rachel's husband. Instead Danni clutched him and Erik.

"It's good to see you again, please make yourselves at home." He also kissed Gretel. The host and hostess took their coats and asked if anyone would like to freshen up. They were pleased by the gesture. Danni took them upstairs, Rachel went near the living room and tried to get Michael's attention. He handed Dayna to her grandmother and went to his sister.

"Shelly, you're flushed and you look anxious, what's going on?"

"They're here, Michael!"

"Who?"

"Benjamin and his family, they are here?"

"Where? I thought they weren't getting here until tomorrow."

"They came a day early to surprise us; Danni just took them upstairs for a few minutes."

"Shelly, calm down."

"He's really here, I can't believe it. I wish Mom could see him, he reminds me so much of her."

Danni was coming downstairs with them. Michael walked toward the staircase and eagerly waited to greet his brother. Benjamin reached the bottom of the landing. They were eye to eye in height and squeezed each other firmly; neither wanted to let go. The elder said in English

"Hello, little brother," the elder said in English. Michael laughed with tears.

"No one has ever called me that before. Welcome, big brother, Rachel and I are so happy you and your family are here."

"Excuse my manners; this is my wife Gretel and son Erik." Michael greeted them fondly. Rachel walked to them and extended her hand to Benjamin. "Are you ready to brave the crowd inside?" He looked at her and nodded yes to the question.

When they entered the living room Rachel remained holding his hand. The area became still and all eyes were on them. With her other hand, she reached for Michael who was standing next to her. Everyone was staring at Benjamin and his family. Wanting to lighten the moment, little sister Landau came across in her usual charismatic way.

"You can see by the time my mother had me, all the Landau height was taken." They all laughed. Rachel became emotional and her voice quivered as she spoke. "Michael and I have been given a very special Chanukah gift; I would like you all to meet the one who has returned to us, our brother Benjamin."

It was a harmonious culmination of the past, present and future to come.

Still the crowd stood quietly until David walked up to him to introduce himself. Then, the rest of the family followed suit, and it was as though it were a receiving line at a wedding reception. Benjamin and his family were happily welcomed into the Landau home and the extended family was thrilled to meet him. As the introductions were made, Rachel walked to where Helena was sitting and placed Dayna in her lap. She was no longer using a wheelchair; her mobility improved tremendously. Smiling the elderly woman gleamed at Rachel.

"You see, my child; I told you nothing is impossible." Benjamin and Gretel walked to where the two women were seated. Gretel recognized Helena from her notoriety in Vienna and Benjamin recalled the elderly woman's presence in the courtroom.

"I would like you both to meet a very dear friend of mine, Madam Helena Krieger," Rachel said in German. Mrs. Frece was noticeably excited.

"Madam, it is an honor to be here with you."

"It's a pleasure to see you on this lovely occasion too, dear," Madam replied.

Erik said he was thirsty, so Rachel led him and Gretel to the kitchen. Benjamin and Helena remained together in the living room.

"Madam Krieger, it is very nice to personally meet you," Benjamin said.

"Likewise, I am also pleased to make your acquaintance."

Having been raised by the man that took Ana Krieger's life, he was overtaken with shame and guilt. "I would like to tell you how sorry I am about what happened to your sister."

She interpreted the remorseful look on his face. "Thank you, I appreciate your sentiment." Helena saw he felt the need to elaborate, but didn't know what to say. She reached for his hand. "Sir, please understand you are not responsible for anything that happened."

He felt a sense of comfort and relief when she spoke the words.

Gretel was in awe of the Landau home; it reminded her of a movie, as she grew up with humble means. Rachel walked them to the guest house. Michael helped Benjamin carry the luggage.

"Gretel, you brought too many things," Benjamin said. As Rachel opened the door to the house she giggled, "A woman after my own heart."

The dwelling within was lovely and decorated in very good taste. It consisted of an eat-in kitchen, formal living room, dining room, two bedrooms and two bathrooms.

"Everyone has been so kind to us," Gretel said.

Rachel embraced her. "You are family and we are elated to have all of you here."

The Austrian woman felt comfortable in her presence and began to speak. "Alex returned from Israel a broken man, and I didn't know what to do or say. It was as if his inner self washed away and only an empty shell remained. Mr. Hirsch was able to reach him the day he came to see us; your husband is a good man and loves you very much."

"It's easy to see that my brother loves you very much, his face lights up in your presence, I saw that the first time we met. And please refer to my husband as 'Danni,' we're all family."

Benjamin, Gretel and Erik felt comfortable in the guest house and slept soundly.

Snow had fallen overnight and stopped by morning. The property appeared calm; it was picturesque and looked like a winter wonderland. Danni decided to brave the weather and take his family, David, Lisa and Scott to New York City. He wanted to give the siblings some private time without all the others under foot. Later that morning, Benjamin and his family came to the main house. The blueberry waffles Lila made earlier resonated throughout the home. Erik sat in Rachel's lap and said he was hungry.

As Benjamin watched his son's ease around his sister, the words he spoke in an Israeli courtroom came to mind.

"I'm sure you have heard the expression, 'children are the greatest judges of a person's character. They have an innate sense of their nature. If a child gravitates toward someone it shows the individual to have a strong moral fiber.'"

His sentiments never proved to be truer than at that moment. She walked with her nephew to the window.

"Do you see what's outside, Erik?"

"Yes, it's snow."

"Do you like the snow?"

"No, it makes me wet and cold." Benjamin, Gretel and Rachel began to laugh. Poor Michael had a hard time with German. His Yiddish was limited. He didn't understand what was so funny until his brother explained, and then he joined the chuckles.

Gretel commented on how well Rachel spoke German. Michael interjected with a boastful thought: "Our sister speaks six languages and was a translator at the American Embassy in Israel when she graduated college."

Benjamin looked at him. "And you are a world-renowned architect, I've seen pictures of some of the structures you've designed, and they are brilliant."

"Michael, you should see Benjamin's stud farm, he owns the most gorgeous Lipizzan stallions. Mom would have loved your place."

Erik reached for Dayna's hand and kissed it. Seeing the two joined together showed a renewed family continuity of the youngest generation. As Lila placed a new batch of waffles on the table, she noticed the strong resemblance Benjamin had to Dora.

"Sir, looking at you is like looking right at your mother."

Later that day, Rachel suggested taking a driven tour around the property. Gretel volunteered to watch the kids so the three siblings could have some time together. First thing in the morning the driveway and roadway was cleared by the home caretakers. The Landau estate sat on three acres of land which included the guest house, a swimming pool, tennis court and stables that could accommodate ten horses. Benjamin experienced life's benefits as well, raised in a large modern villa; he attended the University of Vienna and studied philosophy. Werner Frece was a man of vast means after his extortion of money from the Jewish demise. Gretel, however, came from a family of factory workers and her overall reaction to the Landau home the prior evening made the woman's earlier station in life obvious.

When they reached the stables everyone left the car and walked outside into the brisk air. Benjamin seemed surprised.

"There aren't any horses."

"Once Mom stopped riding we sold the horses. She gave vitality to this place."

Rachel interjected, "When I was a little girl, I had a pony named Allegra. She was untamable to say the least, and I was afraid of her. But not Mom — only she knew how to handle that small colt." She bragged her eldest brother's hand. "Our mother lives through you."

Benjamin stared silently at them for a long moment. "I would like to see where our parents are buried."

"We can go tomorrow if you like," Michael said.

Later that evening when the other family members returned, the Chanukah celebration continued. Lila made an elaborate dinner spread with traditional holiday favorites. Benjamin and his group seemed less overwhelmed and more relaxed with the crowd.

Rachel joined her husband in bed after Dayna's midnight feeding and enjoyed the quiet of the moment. Danni saw the happy expression on her face.

"Hirsch, it was a wonderful day, better than I could have imagined, all because of you."

"No Racheli, I just gave your brother a nudge in the right direction."

"Once he realized how special you and Michael are, everything else fell into place as it should."

"We're going to the cemetery tomorrow; Benjamin asked to see where our parents are buried."

The following afternoon, they arrived at Mount Eden Cemetery located in Central Westchester County. They approached an elegant grey granite mausoleum. Above it the inscription read *Landau*. Michael unlocked the door and accompanied his brother and sister inside. The enclosure offered a tranquil, serene and inviting setting to the world beyond. There were nine compartments, bt only two were marked. The first read: *Nathan Landau – Beloved husband and father who will remain in our hearts forever.* The inscription written on the other said: *Dora Landau – Beloved wife, mother and courageous brave woman who will remain in our hearts forever. A true survivor!*

There was a small shelf above each drawer where remembrance stones were placed to mark someone paying respects to a loved one. The three children stood in front of their parents' resting locales.

Rachel and Michael each put a rock on the ledges of their parent's sanctuaries. Then they walked away and stood toward the back of the inner portion of the mausoleum and gave their eldest brother time alone with their parents. Benjamin searched inside both outer coat pockets. He removed two items wrapped in tissue paper. They were custom-made black slate stones. The first he placed on top of the shelf where Nathan was laid to rest. The second rock sat where his mother was, this gemstone had a unique design. Chiseled into the boulder was a picture of a woman mounted on a horse, he had it modeled from the photo Rachel sent of Dora at age seventeen sitting on a mare. Reaching into his inner breast coat pocket, Benjamin pulled out two Yarmulkes and a piece of paper. He placed one on his head and handed the other one to Michael, and asked the others to stand with him. The prayer for *Mourner's Kaddish*, the Jewish prayer for the dead, was written on the paper he held. They stood together and the eldest Landau child read aloud in English.

"Glorified and sanctified be God's great name throughout the world which He has created according to His will. May He establish His kingdom in your lifetime and during your days, and within the life of the entire House of Israel, speedily and soon; and say, Amen. May His great name be blessed forever and to all eternity. Blessed and praised, glorified and exalted, extolled and honored, adored and lauded be the name of the Holy One, blessed be He, beyond all the blessings and hymns, praises and consolations that are ever spoken in the world; and say, Amen. May there be abundant peace from heaven, and life, for us and for all Israel; and say, Amen. He who creates peace in His celestial heights, may He create peace for us and for all Israel; and say, Amen."

A period in time came full circle. Nathan and Dora were united with all three children. Their legacy would continue to thrive through them, despite the efforts of an evil past to extinguish its flame. God's unspoken bargain to a mother ensured the well-being of prevailing life, and finally, the courageous, brave woman was whole and at peace.

Acknowledgements

This novel would not have been possible without the help and support of my sister, Laurie Goldman, who worked endlessly with me to perfect all aspects of this story. She never wavered with her encouragement and assurance that this project would be a success. Laurie, I owe you my gratitude and love for helping me make this dream become a reality.

To Howard Benick, who helped me perfect the details of the trial. Your legal expertise was instrumental in making sure every part of my story was precise.

To my daughter, Nicole, who always looks for the good in everyone and whose linguistics skills inspired me to incorporate various languages into the story.

A special thanks to my editor, Emily Kaufman, who worked closely with me by executing her attention to detail, and with due diligence ensured that every aspect of this book was reviewed with the highest integrity any writer could ask for.

CPSIA information can be obtained
at www.ICGtesting.com
Printed in the USA
BVHW071043100419
545158BV00002B/172/P

9 781480 875302